Praise for Julianna Scott

"(*The Holders* is) an engaging, well-paced story. Julianna Scott is a fresh new voice in the paranormal romance genre"
Juliet Marillier, author of the Sevenwaters *series*

"A fierce and intelligent heroine, a sibling with a challenging destiny to discover, a heart-warming romance, and an X-Men type school for special powers in the Emerald Isle, all add up to a superbly gripping tale. I loved Becca and can't wait to read more of her world. A fantastic read!"
Suzanne McLeod, author of the Spellcrackers.com *urban fantasy series*

JULIANNA SCOTT

The Holders

STRANGE CHEMISTRY

An Angry Robot imprint
and a member of the Osprey Group

Lace Market House
54-56 High Pavement
Nottingham NG1 1HW
UK

43-01 21st Street, Suite 220B,
Long Island City,
NY 11101
USA

www.strangechemistrybooks.com
Strange Chemistry #8

A Strange Chemistry paperback original 2013
1

Cover art by Lee Gibbons

Distributed in the United States by Random House, Inc., New York.

ISBN: 978 1 90884 443 9
eBook ISBN: 978 1 90884 444 6

Printed in the United States of America

9 8 7 6 5 4 3 2 1

For Scott, mo anam

1

The moment I saw Ryland's silhouette in the window of our old tree house, I knew something was wrong.

Ry was – as he liked to put it – the world's best hider. This was due mostly to the fact that he was a skinny kid and could fold himself down to practically nothing. A talent he exploited when it came time to do chores, or when anything green appeared on Mom's dinner menu. The tree house had at one time been his favorite place to hide, but he never went up there anymore, or at least not since a family of raccoons had gotten in two summers ago. Mom had chased them out, but he still refused to go in, citing the possibility that they might come back and could jump out and get him at any moment. He had a dozen or so hiding places that were safely located inside the house, so I knew that whatever it was that had chased him up into the tree, it had to be bad. Bad enough – in the mind of a ten year-old anyway – to risk a possible raccoon attack.

I made my way across the yard, glad that I'd decided to cut through the cemetery on my walk home that day.

If I had stuck to the sidewalk, I would have ended up at the front of the house, and never would have seen him.

"Ry?"

I heard shuffling on the wood floor of the tree house followed by a sniffle and a squeaky, "Becca?"

"What's wrong, Ry?" I asked, starting the precarious climb up the thin wooden planks. Reaching the top, I poked my head through the square opening in the floor and found Ry sitting in the corner hugging his knees to his chest, his eyes as red as his hair.

"Where is your coat? It's cold out here," I said, as I hoisted myself up into the cramped space. The long Pittsburgh winters hadn't exactly been kind to the little shack, and I found myself hoping for both our sakes that the rotted structure and rusty nails could support my extra one hundred and twenty pounds.

"I'm not cold," he said, sniffling. "I thought you were at work."

"Just got home. I saw you hiding up here when I walked by." I slid my jacket off and wrapped it around his shoulders, ignoring the nip of the early October air. "What's the matter, buddy?" I asked, as I reached over to rub his back and he shrank into my side, hiding his face.

"They're going to take me away," he mumbled into my shirt.

I grabbed his shoulders, holding him away from me so I could see his face. "Who is?"

"The men in the house. They're talking to Mom. They're going to take me away."

"We're not going to let that happen, you know that," I assured him, though I could already feel my neck getting hot as I prepared for battle.

Who was it this time? Representatives from another institution? Another doctor with his magical prescription pad? Or was it that nosey bitch Ms Paust, the elementary school's guidance counselor, back for another round of "In my professional opinion…"

"Mom says I'm gonna go this time," he choked. "She says it's OK."

His bottom lip shook as a new batch of tears spilled over onto his already shiny cheeks.

"OK, listen to me." I held his chin, forcing him to look me in the eye. "You stay in here until I get back, do you hear me? You don't come out for anyone but me, understand?" He nodded. "I'm not going to let anyone take you, OK? Just stay up here and try not to worry."

I climbed down the tree as quickly as I could without breaking my neck and ran toward the house. Who could it possibly be? Ever since I'd convinced Ryland to stop telling people about the voices things had been OK. No trips to the counselor, no calls from teachers or concerned parents. Sure, they all still watched him out of the corner of their eyes like he might spontaneously burst into flame, and his classmates still avoided him, but no one had actually approached Mom or come to the house in weeks. I thought we had finally gotten past all this.

"Mom!" I was yelling before I had made it all the way inside the door, "Mom, where are you?"

I found her in the kitchen taking a full pot of coffee out of the machine. As soon as she turned toward me and I saw her face, I could see that something was different. Something that made my throat close and my nails dig deeper into my palms.

Ryland was right: they had gotten to her.

Damn it, I knew I shouldn't have taken that stupid waitressing job! If I'd been home, these people – whoever the hell they were – wouldn't have made it past the front door! How long had they been here? What could they possibly have said to get her on their side?

In these situations, Mom and I had always been a team. In the beginning, we had tried to reason with the people who came to "discuss Ryland's condition", but they were never the sort of people you could talk to. They made it clear that they would do the talking and our job was to listen and agree. Finally, during the third "house call" with a therapist from some children's hospital, I got so mad at the woman's snotty tone and total disregard for anything Mom or I had to say that I lost it. I started screaming and shouting, and threw her out. Since then, that was the system Mom and I adopted.

OK, the system *I* adopted, and Mom tolerated. She didn't want to see Ryland locked up any more than I did, but she was far too soft-spoken and even-tempered to do what needed to be done. But that was fine, as I was more than happy to do the dirty work. This time would be no different. I took a deep breath and braced myself, ready to do whatever I had to. And if I was going to be on my own this time, so be it.

"Who are they?" I asked. "What are they doing here?"

"Becca, please." Mom forgot the coffee and was in front of me almost instantly, her hands firmly on my shoulders. "It's not what you think – no, honey, listen to me – it's not the same this time. They just want to help."

"Help? You can't be serious, Mom!"

"There is a school that–"

"A school, of course, that's what they all say. 'Nut house' isn't PC anymore, remember?"

"Becca, please, I think these people may be able to..."

I was out of the room before she could finish her thought. Help him? *Help him?* Why on earth was she buying this crap all of a sudden? Oh well, it didn't matter; I would take care of it myself. They'd obviously gotten to her somehow, but they weren't going to get to me.

Following the sound of male voices, I headed to the front room, ready to evict our uninvited guests. "Get out," I clipped, finger pointed at the front door.

The two men slowly stood – though from courtesy or shock, I couldn't tell. The man on the right took a cautious step forward. "You must be Miss Ingle–"

"I said out. Now. Both of you."

"Becca!" Mom snapped, rushing past me with the tray of coffee and mugs. "Gentlemen, this is my daughter Becca, please excuse her. Becca," she turned to me, "calm down."

"They're not taking him." My comment was directed less at my mother, and more at the two men I was glaring at over her shoulder.

I took a second to actually look at them, and was a bit taken aback by what I saw. The first guy looked to be in his late forties with a long crooked nose, and dark flashing eyes that were surrounded by deep-set wrinkles – more than likely the result of a life spent scowling. The way this guy looked alone would have been enough to make Ryland run and hide.

The other man, sitting next to him – the one who had tried to speak earlier – was almost a shock to my system after studying his partner. He was young, twenty maybe, with fair hair and light eyes. His jeans and button down shirt were neat, and his hair was cut short and styled. Sitting next to each other, they looked like some sort of "before and after" anti-drug poster you'd see in a high school nurse's office. I might have been amused, if they weren't currently here to lock up my brother.

"Listen honey, please," my Mom pleaded quietly. "They are from a private school in Ireland. It's the school that…" she hesitated, and in that split second I could see the words in her eyes before she could bring herself to say them "your father runs."

Of course. Jocelyn. Also known as my father. The man my mother had been madly in love with. The man who swept her off her feet, only to walk out on all of us less than a month after Ryland was born. The man we hadn't seen or heard from in ten years. If anything could have convinced my mother to side with them, it was throwing Jocelyn into the mix.

If I was angry before, now I was livid.

She must have seen the rage fly across my face, because

she was quick to continue, "They say that they know what's wrong with him and that they can help."

"There is nothing wrong with him," I growled between clenched teeth, never taking my eyes off the intruders.

The older scary-looking guy leisurely folded his hands in front of him and raised his chin. "Ryland is in need of care that only we can provide," he said, with a cocky air that made me want to kick him in the shins. "He should be honored to be admitted to such a fine institution."

"Institution. Exactly." I snapped.

"St Brigid's *Academy*," he corrected with a glare, "will give him th–"

"It's just a school," the younger man interrupted, in what I can only imagine was his best peacekeeper voice. "I promise."

"You promise? What are we, twelve? Next I suppose you're going to pinky swear me that this will all be for his own good, and expect me to let you take him?"

Ignoring my snide commentary, the younger man continued, "St Brigid's attracts some of the finest students from across the UK and Europe."

"Then maybe you should stay over there."

"Becca!" Mom snapped. "Please, just listen," she begged, but now with real irritation in her tone.

I closed my mouth and crossed my arms, as the younger man continued to plug his hopeless cause. "We host some of the finest instructors from all over the world. Our graduation rate is nearly 100%, after which, the majority of our graduates continue on to some of the most prestigious universities in the world. The diversity of our curriculum rivals most–"

"Yeah," I interrupted, no longer interested, "it's a hell of a school. Got it. Let's just say for one second that I am buying this private school crap. Why on earth would one of the top academies in Europe come to personally recruit a kid who hasn't gotten above 80% on a spelling test since the first grade?"

The younger man opened his mouth to reply, but unfortunately the older man beat him to it. "Jocelyn feels it is time for the boy to join him."

The younger man shot a look at his companion that made it clear that even he – who had known me less than ten minutes – knew that was absolutely the wrong thing to say.

"The boy?" I growled. "You know what, that is probably exactly what Jocelyn said, because odds are he doesn't remember *the boy's* name!"

The older man brought himself up to his full height and had the audacity to shake his finger at me like he was scolding a dog, "Young lady, this situation does not concern you. Ryland needs to be among people who understand his condition and can help him control it."

"You bas–" but before I could even get the "tard" out, the younger man stood up, stretching one hand toward me, palm out, while placing the other hand on his partner's shoulder in a gesture that would hopefully keep him from talking.

"We don't want to hurt him," the younger man said, but I was done caring.

"You listen to me," I snarled at both of them. "I don't care who you are, where you're from, or who sent you, but believe me when I tell you that I will lay down in front of any car that tries to take Ryland from this house!" With that, I stormed out of the door, and up the stairs to my room, cursing under my breath.

2

The bedroom door banged as I shut it behind me, and I headed straight for the window against the back wall. One look outside told me that Ryland was still hiding in the tree house, and from here I could watch to see he stayed there. This spot was also perfect as it was right next to the heating vent in the floor which, when opened, allowed me to hear any conversations going on in the living room below.

All right, so I'd camp here until they left. No problem.

Except it was a problem. As much as I wanted to sit still and keep an eye and ear on things, I couldn't; I was too riled up. In an effort to calm down, I changed out of my work clothes and pulled my long hair out of my "work appropriate" bun. I grabbed my brush, pulled my desk chair up to the spot by the window, and started brushing out my mess of hair, not taking my eyes off the back yard.

I'd really started to think that this was all over. I thought life could finally be normal.

When Ry was younger and the voices started he would panic every time he heard them and tell anyone nearby – me, Mom, his teachers at school, his friends, their parents – anyone. We thought it was just a normal childhood "imaginary friend" sort of thing, but it wasn't long before everyone realized it was more than that. These voices he heard came at random times and usually said really weird things. Like once, Ryland had an all-out panic attack at a baseball game because there was a voice screaming that if the Pirates didn't win someone was going to die. Another time he was at school and had to be pulled out of class because he started crying hysterically when his teacher returned their most recent math test. Everyone assumed that it was because he'd gotten a bad grade, but he insisted that it was due to the voices that had suddenly come, yelling and crying in this head.

It wasn't long before he stopped receiving invites to friends' houses, started sitting alone at lunch, and began making regular trips to the counselor's office. Everyone thought he was crazy.

Finally the guidance counselor, with the help of the school psychologist, started sending people to talk to Mom about getting "help" for Ry. The problem was when they said "help" what they really meant was locking him up to be observed and medicated, and I couldn't let that happen. He was my brother, and I had to take care of him.

But more than that, I knew he wasn't crazy. Deep down, I knew it. Yes, he heard voices, and yes it was strange, but why was everyone so convinced that Ryland was imagining the voices he heard? What if they were real? No one had ever even tried to figure out what was going on or if there was a way to help him – actually help him, not simply slapping a "crazy" sticker on his forehead so they could hide the problem behind an institution and drugs. I seemed to be the only person who wanted an actual explanation for the problem, not just a by-any-means solution.

A knock at my door made me jump. I reached for the handle, thinking it was Mom, but the voice on the other side wasn't hers.

"Rebecca?" It was the younger of the two men.

"What?" I snipped.

"Do you mind if... Can I speak with you for a moment?"

I was about to tell him to go to hell, but something in the tone of his voice stopped me. Maybe I should talk to him. The fact that they hadn't left yet meant they were going to be persistent, so I might as well get ready for the long haul. Anyway, better him than the crooked-nosed creature he had brought with him. "It's not locked," I said, though I still put as much venom in the words as I could.

He slowly opened the door, stepping in so cautiously it looked like he was trying to avoid landmines. He stopped five or so feet from where I stood with my arms crossed, ready for battle.

"So, talk," I said, after a few moments of silence.

"We really do want to help your brother."

Really? More of this? What, so cute guy thinks he can just waltz up here and win me over with some alone time.

I snapped. "Oh, sure, you want to 'help' him 'control' his 'condition'," I said, making sarcastic air quotes. "Do you really think you are the first people to come and try to take him away 'for his own good'? Do you think I don't know what that means? I don't care what you've been told, he's *not* crazy. If you think that I am just going to stand by and let you lock him up in some institution somewhere, so you can–"

"I would never do that," he interrupted quietly. His tone hadn't been more than a whisper, but it was so earnest and solemn and, honestly, a little scary, that I couldn't help but believe him. And just like that, it was gone; all my rage and aggression flew out of me like air out of a popped balloon. I sank down onto the edge of my bed, too tired to yell anymore. Besides, something inside was telling me that this man didn't deserve a beating from me. I had no idea where that hunch was coming from, and I didn't like it. He was the enemy, and I had to be strong. Yet unnatural as it felt to show weakness, I also couldn't fight it. I sat hunched over on the edge of my bed, staring up at the stranger in my room, hoping I didn't look as lost and helpless as I suddenly felt.

He glanced toward the window and saw my chair. "May I?"

I nodded. He sat down and swiveled the seat so that he was facing me. He leaned forward resting his elbows on his knees, looking calmly at me.

"So?" he said with a small smile.

"So."

"There are things I'd like to explain to you, as well as I can anyway."

I made a small sweeping motion with my hand, letting him know he was welcome to begin. However, he shook his head. "I think we might make more progress with a question and answer session."

"A what?"

"You ask me questions, and I'll answer them. I'll be honest, I prom–" he hesitated with a smile, "I pinky swear." I huffed a laugh in spite of myself. "I just don't want you to think that we mean Ryland any harm, because that couldn't be further from the truth."

"What I'm worried about is the difference in our definitions of the word 'harm'. The people that want to lock him up and medicate him into a stupor don't consider that to be 'harming' him either, but I certainly do."

He nodded, but didn't comment. His eyes never left mine, and I got the strange impression that he was really listening to me. Most people don't listen. When you listen you hear the sounds and the silences. You hear the words people say, and the words they don't say. Real listening takes more effort than most people are willing to give.

With a sigh, I decided to play his game. What could it hurt? Hell, maybe I'd even get a few answers along the way. "Who are you?" I asked after a moment, as that seemed the best place to start.

"My name is Alex Bray. The man with me is Taron Calgot. We both live at St Brigid's Academy in County Clare, Ireland."

"Wait, you live there? Like, all the time?"

"Yes. Taron works as one of the lecturers, and I work in... recruitment." His pause seemed odd, but I let it go. "I have also taken many of the upper level classes that St Brigid's offers, and would like to one day be brought on as a teacher."

"And what do you want with my brother?"

"We want to help him. We really do understand. Ryland has... abilities. Abilities he can't control yet. He can do things that the average person can't. That's why we want to take him to St Brigid's, so he can be with others who are like him, and learn to control his abilities in a safe environment."

He finished and was silent, waiting for my next question, but I was at a loss for words. This was definitely a new one. He hadn't said anything about "fixing" Ryland; he'd simply said "control". I could admit it sounded promising, but I knew better than to get my hopes up.

"How do you know all this?" I asked.

"Because," he paused and looked at me as if to gauge my reaction, "I have abilities too. I'm like Ryland, and so is Taron, and your father." He must have seen my eyes flash at the term "father" as he quickly continued. "And there are others. We all have abilities that the normal person doesn't have."

"And, exactly what do you mean by 'abilities'?" I asked, growing more skeptical by the minute. "Please don't tell me you're talking about comic book-style stuff, like x-ray vision, or flying."

"Well..." Alex paused, as though he were afraid to continue. "No one can fly, at least not that I'm aware of."

I stared at him, waiting for him to smile, as obviously this was a joke. But he just sat there, looking back at me without so much as a smirk. "You're serious with this?" I asked, after I was sure there was no punchline coming.

"Yes," he nodded.

Oh. My. God. And people thought Ryland was crazy? "Yeah," I said, not sure whether I should be laughing or offended that this guy actually thought I was that stupid. "Thanks for the talk, but you and your buddy can go sell psycho somewhere else."

"Please, I know how it sounds, but–"

"Out," I clipped, standing, ready to physically remove him if necessary.

"I'll show you."

"Show me?" He really wasn't going to give up.

"Yes. I can show you what I do, if you'll let me."

"OK, fine," I challenged, almost amused. I sat back down on the bed and crossed my arms, waiting for the show I was more than sure wouldn't come.

"Thank you," he said, apparently happy with his tiny victory. "It will only take a moment, and then you can decide if you'd like to talk further. I will warn you though, it's, well, strange, so just try not to freak out or anything, OK?"

"I'll do my best," I said flatly.

He walked over to my bedroom door and shut it softly, immediately sending alarm bells ringing in my head. Strange guy... in my room... shutting us in...

"Just so you know, I scream really loud," I informed him, eyeing the closed door.

"Don't worry," he said, undeterred by my announcement, "I will stay over here."

"Do I need to say the magic words?" I asked, hoping my sarcasm would help me ignore the fact that I was actually getting nervous. Of course nothing was going to happen, but he was also taking this way too seriously for a stupid joke.

"No magic words, though it will be easier if you stand," he said, gesturing to the middle of the floor. I got up and moved to the spot he had indicated in front of him, while he stayed where he was, hands behind his back. "You ready?" he asked after a moment.

I nodded.

I waited quietly for a second or two, thinking maybe he would do or say something, but he didn't. Nothing happened at all. It was just me and Alex, standing a few feet apart from each other in the middle of my room.

But then, suddenly, my vision went blurry. Everything in my room seemed to shift out of focus, like there was something in my eye that I needed to blink away. All the colors and shapes began to melt into each other until I couldn't tell where one thing left off and another began. My eyes flew to Alex, thinking that he too would be an edgeless fuzzy blot of color, but he was still there, standing exactly where he was, the only thing in the room, other than me, that was still crisp and clear.

His eyes met mine, and when he saw that they held only wonder and confusion but no fear, he smiled and the fuzzy blobs of color began to move. The greens sank down to the floor and grew, spreading out under our feet, reaching far beyond the boundaries of my small bedroom. The blues and whites soared upwards, expanding as they went, creating a clear sky high over our heads. Lines, edges, textures, and dimension returned, but in the forms of grass under our feet, clouds in the sky, and water – an entire ocean of it – stretching out over the horizon. Suddenly all the lines were clear again, only now Alex and I were standing on the edge of an enormous cliff. To my left, an ocean swelling and falling with white foam caps on each of its rolling waves; to my right a seemingly endless field of gently sloping hills covered in lush green grass. It was the most beautiful place I had ever seen.

I looked over at Alex, who was still standing a few steps away from me, watching me calmly. "Where are we?" I breathed.

"In your bedroom," he answered quietly. "What you are seeing are the Cliffs of Moher in Ireland. They're near St Brigid's."

"*You're* doing this?"

"Yes."

I turned towards the edge of the cliff trying to make sense of it all. This couldn't possibly be an illusion, it was all so real. I could hear the waves pounding into the bedrock of the cliffs below us. I could feel the wind pouring up over the edge of the cliff.

And then it hit me; I could feel the wind. Feel it blowing past my face and onto the fields. Yet my hair, which was hanging free and should have been whipping like mad around my face, lay perfectly still against my back. I took a step towards the edge of the cliff when suddenly my leg hit something. I looked down but there was nothing there. I could feel the object pressing against my shin, but the only thing in front of me was open air.

"What is that?" I asked Alex, swinging my leg again, kicking it.

He smiled, obviously happy I wasn't having some sort of mental breakdown. "Your bed. We're still in your room. Here..." He reached down and patted what looked to be empty air, though it made a sound. "Feel." I reached down towards the invisible obstruction, to find that it was indeed my bed. I couldn't see it, but it was there – the sheets, the pillow, and the quilt with the little embroidered rosettes – all of it.

My vision began to blur again, the sounds of the sea tapered off until they were only an echo, and a few moments later I was back in my room looking down at my quilt. I twisted around and plopped down onto the edge of my bed, disillusioned, yet somehow exhilarated. Alex pulled the desk chair up next to me and sat. I glanced up at him to find him studying me.

"Are you all right?"

"I think so," I said, though my voice shook more than I would have liked. Dear God, had that really just happened? Was it even possible? I blinked a few times and shook my head, hoping I wasn't losing my mind. "What was that?" I finally asked.

"It's called Casting, it's what I do; my ability. I can project images on reality, making people see whatever I want them to."

"Is that what Ryland is doing?"

"No, Ryland's ability is different. He can..." he paused, looking again to read my reaction. "The things he hears, the voices, they are people's thoughts."

"You're telling me my brother can read minds?"

"Well no, not yet. Right now, he is just overhearing things once in a while by chance, but he'll learn to control it as he gets older."

"And that's what you're going to teach him at this school?"

"Not me specifically, but yes. That, among other things."

"And the other kids there, they are like him?"

"Some of the children have abilities, but not all of them."

He was looking at me with unveiled worry in his eyes. Poor guy must have thought I was about to implode, and honestly I probably should have been crying or screaming, or something else a normal person would have been doing, but I was strangely calm. For some inexplicable reason, this all seemed to make perfect sense to me. People had been trying to convince me for years that Ryland was crazy. Crazy because he needed more attention, crazy because our father left us, crazy because some people are just crazy, but they had all been assumptions based on nothing, and I hadn't believed a word of it. Go figure that the story about magic visions and mind readers would be the one I would actually buy.

Maybe I was the one who needed medication?

I looked down at the floor, realizing that for the first time I was torn. I knew I had to do what was best for Ryland, but now I wasn't sure what that was. What if these people really could help him? What if, for the first time in his life, he could finally be somewhere where he fit in? Where he could have friends and a normal life? Sure it seemed unlikely, but clearly there was something going on here that was beyond my understanding. I mean this guy had just sent me to Ireland without ever leaving my room. There was also the fact that they had been sent by the one known as my father, who – according to Alex – also had some magic ability. Much as I hated to admit it, if that were truly the case, then he might actually be able to help. Maybe...

I sat quietly for a few minutes trying to organize my thoughts, while Alex waited patiently. After a long moment I came to a decision. "Can I ask you something?" I asked, looking up at Alex.

"Of course."

"And you'll be honest?"

"I promise," he stated with a grin. He'd said that a few times now, and though I'd mocked him for it, even I had to admit that he was the first person I'd ever met who could say that without sounding like a four year-old.

"Is going with you to this school truly the best thing for Ryland?"

He didn't answer right away, as though he were taking my question very seriously, his eyes never leaving mine. "Yes."

I nodded to show him that I did believe him before continuing with a small grin. "Can I ask you another question?"

"Sure," he said, smiling suspiciously at my tone.

"Why do I get the feeling there is a lot more to this than you're telling me?"

"Because you are very perceptive," he chuckled. "It's not that I'm not telling you. I'm *not* hiding anything; it's just that the story – the whole story – will take much longer than we have time for tonight. But I'll make you a deal. I'll tell you everything – anything you want to know – before we take Ryland. That is of course, if you give us permission to take him."

"Pretty sure my Mom has already given you that."

"But you haven't."

"Does that matter?"

"I'm sure it matters to your brother. And it matters to me."

In that moment I knew, deep down, that this was right. This was what Ryland needed. I might not have known what was going on, or even who these people were, but something inside me knew they could help my brother. And knowing that, there was only one thing I could do.

"When are you supposed to leave?"

"Don't worry about that, I can take care of it. You can take your time; no one is going to pressure you."

"When?" I asked again.

"We have flights scheduled for Friday, but that's not import–"

"How about I make *you* a deal?" I said, cutting him off. Alex raised his eyebrows, interested. "He can go with you on Friday."

"Really? Are you sure?"

"Yes... as long as I can go too." It was already clear that Mom was going to let them take Ryland with or without my approval, but no way in hell was I going to let him go alone.

"You mean transfer to St Brigid's?"

"What? Oh, no, I graduated high school two years ago."

"I thought you were only seventeen?"

"I am. I graduated just after I turned fifteen, but Mom didn't want me going off to college so young."

"So, you're advanced," he said thoughtfully, "that's... interesting."

"Why?"

"No reason," he said, though I didn't believe him. "So you will just be coming to observe?"

"That, and for Ryland. He is way too young and scared to make a trip like that alone, and there's no way my Mom can go." Or, that is to say, no way was I letting my mother anywhere near Jocelyn, but I kept that part to myself. "And anyway," I continued, "I'd like to see this school with my own eyes. It's not that I don't trust you, I just think it will make everyone feel better if I can see this place first hand. If we get there, and I am OK with what I see, and I'm positive Ryland is happy, then I'll come home. Deal?" I asked, holding out my hand for him to shake.

"And your Mom will be OK with this?"

"You leave that to me."

"That sounds like a plan," he said with a smile and reached for my hand. But right before he grabbed it, I pulled it back. "One more thing," I added, "I don't want Jocelyn to know I'm coming."

"What?"

"I don't want him to know I'll be there."

"That... may be difficult," he said, confused. "Is there any particular reason?"

Because if he knows I'm there I'll have to see him. "Does it matter?" I asked more defensively than I'd meant to.

Alex thought for a moment before nodding. "I can make sure he doesn't find out you are with us, but so you know, once we are there it might be hard. He lives in the same building on campus as the rest of us – the same building you'll have to stay in."

"That's fine. I can handle it from there." I knew how to keep a low profile, that wasn't a problem. All that mattered was that I would have the advantage. It's much easier to avoid someone who isn't looking for you.

"All right, then," Alex said with a smile.

"And I'm still holding you to your end of the deal, you have to tell me everything."

"OK..." He hesitated, looking pensive. "But now it's my turn to ask for a favor."

"Which is?"

"I promised to tell you everything, and I will, but I am going to have to ask that you keep what I tell you to yourself."

"What, like not tell my Mom?"

"Or Ryland." He must have seen the suspicion enter my eyes, because he quickly explained, "Jocelyn was adamant that your mother not find out about all this. One day, when Ryland's older and understands everything for himself, he can make the decision as to whether or not to tell her, but for now, it's better if she continues to believe that St Brigid's is nothing more than a typical school – which honestly it is in most respects."

I didn't like it, but he might have had a point. All of this was going to be hard enough on Mom, without knowing her son may or may not be some sort of mind-reading carnival act. "And Ryland? Doesn't he deserve to know what's happening to him?"

"Of course. But trust me when I say that it will be better for him to find out slowly, with other kids who are in the same situation. He will handle it better if he knows he's not alone."

There was a sad note in his voice that made me think that he knew all too well how alone Ryland sometimes felt. I still wasn't sure about all the secrecy, but I decided to give Alex the benefit of the doubt, for now.

"All right. Mum's the word. But you have to tell me everything."

"OK," he laughed.

"All of it?"

"All of it. But maybe not all at once."

"OK," I said with a satisfied smile, and lowered my hand for him to shake. "When do we start?"

"Well, I think we've covered enough for today," he said, taking my hand in his, "but it–"

He stopped suddenly and froze, staring over my shoulder.

"Alex?"

Coming back to himself he brought his eyes down to meet mine. "Sorry," he said, squeezing his eyes shut for a moment, still looking a bit uneasy. "It's a… a seventeen hour trip to St Brigid's… so…" he released my hand and smiled, though not as easily as he had done a moment ago. "So we'll have plenty of time."

3

"And Becca gets to come with me?"

"Yes."

"And I don't have to stay if I don't like it?"

"No, of course not, but you do have to at least try to like it."

I was cross-legged on my floor listening to Mom's futile attempts to put Ryland to bed. Ry's questions were slower in coming now and were broken up by the occasional yawn, but he was still doing his best to throw a few more in – though it seemed that most of them were repeats – before he fell asleep.

After Alex and I had struck our bargain that afternoon, we went downstairs and told the plan to Mom and Grumpy – I mean, Taron. Mom was relieved that I was tentatively OK with all this, but more so that Ryland didn't have to go all that way on his own. Taron however, was anything but thrilled. He wasn't happy at all about the idea of me accompanying them back to Ireland, but Alex had gotten him out of the house before he could give me a reason to backhand him.

Once they were gone, Mom and I went to get Ryland out of the tree house, which was no easy feat. We had to assure him that the men were gone, assure him that no one was going to take him anywhere tonight, and assure him again that the scary guys were definitely gone. Finally, Mom started to threaten that if he didn't come down he wouldn't get any dinner. When that didn't work, I told him that if he stayed up there much longer the raccoon would get him. That earned me a smack on the arm from Mom, but it did the job as Ry was down less than a minute later.

And then the questions began.

Who were those men? Why didn't you send them away? Becca's coming too? Where are we going? Where is Ireland? Are there other kids there? Will it be like school here? What if I don't like it? What if they try to hurt me? Becca, are you really coming? How long will we stay there? And on and on. All through dinner and well into the evening, Mom and I sat, answering all his questions to the best of our knowledge and trying to reassure him that everything was going to be fine.

It wasn't until he found out that his father would not only be there, but was actually the one who had sent the men to get him in the first place, that his face changed from squinty curiosity into doe-eyed wonder.

Ugh.

As furious as it made me I ignored it, as my brother's misguided admiration for the father he'd never met wasn't something I was in the mood to deal with.

We'd finally got him to go up to bed, and even then

with Mom trying to tuck him in the questions continued to roll on.

"Just go to sleep Ry, we'll talk more about it in the morning, OK?"

"I'm not tired," he said while yawning.

"Go to sleep." I heard Mom walk towards the door and flip the light off. "Good night, buddy."

With a soft click she closed the door and walked across the hall to lean on my open door frame. "You going to bed?"

"I don't know. I guess." I was tired, but didn't really think I'd be able to sleep.

"Want some ice cream?" Mom asked with a smile. "We've got Magic Shell."

Needing no further persuasion, I followed her down to the kitchen, and from my usual seat at the table, watched her scoop Oreo ice cream into two bowls. I tried to make it seem like I wasn't examining her every move, but I was. She seemed far too calm. As though this had just been a normal day.

"So," I asked, trying my best to sound nonchalant, "You OK with all of this?"

"Well, that's a bit of a loaded question," she answered, placing a bowl of ice cream and a bottle of Magic Shell on the table in front of me. "Am I happy that by the end of the week both my kids will be on a different continent?" She sat down across from me, and began absent-mindedly stabbing at her own bowl of ice cream with her spoon. "No, not at all. I am, however, overjoyed that Ryland might finally be getting the help he needs.

And I am relieved that you are going with him. You'll need to make sure you can get the time off work."

"I'll only be gone for a week or two, it's no big deal. I'm a waitress at Eat'n Park, Mom, not a brain surgeon. They're not going to have any trouble filling my shifts."

"It's still a job, which means you need to make sure it's OK. If they say no, I'll take Ryland myself."

"Um, yeah, that is so not going to happen. I'm not letting you anywhere near him." She knew I didn't mean Ryland.

"I'll do what I have to. I can't let Ry go all that way by himself. He's still so little…" She left her sentence hanging as she stared off into her bowl.

"I'll call my boss tomorrow, get the time off, and I'll go with Ryland. No problem. I'll take care of him, Mom."

She smiled up at me, and I could see the tears shining in her eyes. "I know you will, baby," she said, squeezing my arm. "And what about school?" she asked, clearing her voice, and wiping under her eyes with her thumb. "Are you still going to try and go this spring?"

I had been thinking about it, and while I really did want to go thus far I hadn't been in any particular rush. Graduating high school at the top of my class at fifteen years old didn't come without its perks. I'd been offered full scholarships to over a dozen universities, most with what they called standing acceptances, inviting me to enrol with them whenever I was ready.

Mom hadn't wanted me to go off at fifteen because she had worried I was too young. I agreed with her, not because I truly felt unready, but honestly, because I didn't want to leave Ryland alone. I was terrified I'd come home for a visit one day, and he'd be gone because Mom had finally broken and let one of them get to her. Of course, I trusted Mom to take care of Ry, but I couldn't trust the shrinks and specialists not to use her underlying guilt to break her. I had always been there to help her, and, with me gone to college, I wasn't sure how long she would be able to last.

Not that I could tell her that.

When she asked me about it a few months ago I had momentarily considered starting in the fall, but had let the enrolment deadline pass accidentally-on-purpose, telling Mom I would look into starting in the spring. I'd planned on putting it off another semester, but now, if there was a chance Ryland might finally be happy – and more importantly, safe – I might actually be able to bring myself to go.

"Yeah, but I'll be home before then. Spring enrolment for most schools doesn't even start until next month."

"All right, well stay on it this time."

"Mmhmm," I said, pretending to concentrate on breaking my Magic Shell.

"There is one more thing we need to discuss, you know."

I felt my stomach muscles clench as I realized where this conversation was headed. "Oh?" I said, taking a bite of ice cream, playing it cool.

"First of all, you were completely out of line today."

"I know, I'm sorry." I wasn't, but I really didn't feel like fighting about it.

"Secondly, you have to realize that going over there means that you will most likely run into your father." I tensed at the word, but said nothing, as my mother was the only person I allowed to use that term in reference to him. "And I want you to promise me you will behave yourself."

"What fun is that?" I mumbled over a mouthful of ice cream, deciding it was better not to inform her of the deal I'd made with Alex and my intentions to avoid him entirely.

"Becca, you really have to stop that. Just give him a chance. This could be an opportunity to get to know him."

"Please tell me that's not why you are OK with all this. Because you think we'll 'bond with Daddy', and all will be right with the world."

"No, of course not," she sighed. "I'm OK with it because..." She paused, shaking her head. "I have to do *something*. We can't pretend his problem is going to magically fix itself, and this is the first option that actually seems like it may truly be good for him. At least they don't sound like they want to lock him away. It may not work, but at least we have to try." She looked down into her bowl before continuing. "And yes, like it or not, your father does have a lot to do with it. I just want you to keep an open mind that's all, for Ryland's sake if for nothing else. He will be meeting his father for the first time, and I don't want you painting him as a horrible monster."

"When have I ever done that?" I asked, more than a little offended. If there was one thing I was proud of in terms of my feelings toward Jocelyn, it was the fact that Ryland had no idea what they were. For all he knew, I was as excited as he was to be meeting our long lost Poppa.

"You haven't, I know, but this will be different. You have never had to keep yourself in check with Jocelyn in the same room, and you know how you can get."

I snorted a laugh, almost choking on my ice cream. "No throwing punches, got it."

"I'm serious, Becca."

"OK, fine, and what am I supposed to tell Ry, when his Super Dad illusions come crashing down all over the place?"

"Maybe they won't." I noticed she couldn't actually meet my eyes as she said it.

"Of course they will! God, what is *with* you two! This man is not perfect! He's not someone you should constantly be defending, and he's certainly not someone Ryland should be looking up to!"

As soon as I'd finished, I saw my Mom's face sink and immediately regretted my rant. She didn't need this from me, not tonight.

"Anyway," Mom said after a moment, taking advantage of my deliberate silence, "I just want you to think before you speak, OK? That's not too much to ask, is it?"

"No," I mumbled not looking at her, last spoonful of ice cream still in my mouth.

"I'm sorry, what was that?" She put her hand up to her ear dramatically.

"No."

"Thank you. Now, I think it's time for bed. We can talk more in the morning, but I think we could all use some sleep."

"Night, Mom." I stood and started shuffling around the table towards the stairs.

"Good night, baby," she said, grabbing the back of my head as I passed, kissing my forehead.

I went upstairs, brushed my teeth, changed into my sleep-shirt and shorts, and fell over onto my bed, staring up at the ceiling.

Ireland. I was going to Ireland. Had the situation been different, I would have been totally excited, but as it was, I wasn't sure how I felt.

First off there was Ryland, who might finally be getting the help he needed, but who also might actually be, well, a freak. Yeah, people had been calling him that for years, but I never considered it could be true. I was also suddenly – and stupidly – afraid to *think* things around him, as it turned out he might just overhear me. Pretty sure that's not something the normal sister has to worry about. Diary reading, sure, but mind reading? That had to be new.

Then there was Jocelyn. Normally, just thinking about him was enough to make my blood pressure go up, and now I actually had to meet with him? Maybe Mom was right to worry: I might end up decking him.

I rolled over with a huff and yanked the covers up over my shoulder. I took a few deep breaths, trying to hone in and make use of any techniques I may have picked up from the two yoga classes I attended before quitting out of sheer boredom. I was more of a kickboxing girl. Though, as there were no punching bags handy, I would have to rely on breathing and mellow thoughts to calm me down.

I hated him. He'd abandoned us, plain and simple, and I hated him for it. Not so much for what it had done to me personally, though that did hurt – or it used to hurt, I'd since moved past it – but more for what he'd done to Mom. She tried to hide how much it tore her up inside, but I knew. Even as a kid I could see how much it hurt her to hear his name or have him mentioned, so I stopped talking about him altogether. At night I would lie in bed and hear her crying in her room when she thought I was asleep. And even after ten years, sometimes I would still catch her looking too long at a picture, or wiping her eyes when she was sitting alone.

It made me furious that someone could have hurt her so badly. That someone as kind, and compassionate, and amazing as my mom, had been fated to fall in love with someone as self-centered and unworthy as Jocelyn. Though I knew that none of this was her fault, which is why I usually tolerated her constant defense of him. She had always – and it seemed would always – hold him up on a pedestal, and while I didn't like it, at least I could understand it.

It was Ryland's admiration of the man that made no sense to me. They had never even met. Well, I guess that's not technically true as Jocelyn had been there when Ryland was born and spent a grand total of two weeks with him before disappearing, but as far as I was concerned, that didn't count. Other than those two weeks, Ryland had had no contact with him whatsoever. He wouldn't have known his own father from a stranger on the street, yet anytime Jocelyn was mentioned Ryland was enraptured. I guess I could understand a little. He was almost like the mystical Dad, out there somewhere, maybe doing astonishing deeds: fighting dragons, killing Martians, swinging over large gorges on vines – you know, Indiana Jones stuff. Ryland could still have a dream, because he didn't know any better. He had no memories of a man who said he loved you one minute then was gone the next. He didn't have to remember a father who used to call me *mo ghile beag* or "my little darling", which was the only Gaelic I knew, only to miss ten of the seventeen birthdays I'd had so far. He didn't know how much Mom had suffered, and still suffered, because of the man he idolized so much.

Ryland didn't understand. And that was why I never dispelled his Dad delusion by telling him the truth. Why do that to him? He'd figure it out on his own one day when he was older and knew a little more of the world, but until then I let him think what he wanted because it made him – and Mom – happy.

With a sigh, I rolled into a more comfortable – and less tense – position. After all, there was no need to induce an aneurism when for all I knew I wouldn't even have to see the man. If he really was one of the head masters, then he would probably always be busy. All I would have to do was stay out of his way. That should be easy enough.

I closed my eyes and took another deep breath, determined to find something else to think about, preferably something that would encourage sleep, not keep me from it. I pictured the magnificent vision I'd seen in this very room earlier today: the lush green grass, the clear open sky, the rolling ocean and pounding waves… and a pair of light blue-gray eyes and blonde hair. Alex. That was a nice name… Alex.

4

At 8 o'clock Friday evening, Ryland and I kissed Mom goodbye for about the thirtieth time, assured her once again that we'd call every day, and that we'd be good, and countless other things we'd been assuring her for the last three days, grabbed our carry-ons, and boarded our flight to Ireland. Or, more specifically, boarded our flight to Paris, France, at which point we would board a second plane to Dublin, Ireland, after which it was a two and a half hour drive to St Brigid's. Grand total travel time: only seventeen and a half hours.

Yeah... *only*.

Though I can admit, the first few hours of the flight went by quickly enough. I read the book and two magazines I'd brought, ate dinner, and played a few rounds of travel Scrabble with Ryland. It wasn't until about five hours in – what would have been midnight in Pittsburgh – and barely over halfway to Paris, that I realized just how long a trip this was going to be.

I tried to sleep, but it was no use. I was the sort of person who had to be comfortable to fall asleep, and comfort just wasn't happening. Not that I could complain about our seats. We had actually been very lucky as the flight wasn't anywhere near full, which meant that after takeoff we were all able to spread out. I had a two-seat row to myself, Ry had the row behind me, and Alex and Taron had the five-seat row next to us to share between them. Despite the space however, I couldn't settle. I tried lying down, reclining my chair, leaning against the wall of the plane, crossing my arms on the tray table, and countless other configurations; nothing was comfortable for longer than a few minutes at a time. The tiny airplane pillow that was lumpy on one side and totally flat on the other wasn't helping things either. Too bad I wasn't more like Ryland who was sprawled out on his back, covering both seats in his row, one leg up in the air resting on the wall of the plane while his head hung off the base of the seat, dangling in what would normally be leg space. Honestly, a little turbulence and he'd be on the floor, but at least he was sleeping, which was more than I could say of myself.

I stared absent-mindedly at the map of the Atlantic Ocean and the little cartoon plane that was supposed to represent us on the TV screen in front of me. There was a red line trailing behind the little plane showing the route and distance we'd traveled so far, and a green line in front of the plane showing the route and distance yet to go. Ryland had gotten a kick out of this and kept measuring the lengths of the two lines with his fingers as if to prove to himself that the plane was in fact moving.

Too bad I wasn't so easily amused. I didn't want to read anymore, wasn't interested in any of the movies that were playing, and couldn't very well play travel games by myself, which meant there was nothing but five hours and thirty two minutes of long, empty space in front of me. All day I'd had activities and people to occupy my mind, but now, with everyone sleeping and nothing else going on, my thoughts kept drifting to the one subject I'd been consciously trying to avoid all day.

Alex.

After two days of sideways glances and daydreaming, I finally had to admit that I had a fairly substantial crush on this guy, and I was not about to become one of those girls who got all goofy and obsessive about a guy they barely knew. I was terrified that if I didn't get this under control I'd end up like a character on one of those terrible reality shows that basically have no plot at all besides who's crushing on who, who's sleeping with who, who's cheating on who, and so on. The day that became me, would be the day I checked into a nunnery.

Yet, diligent as I tried to be, there wasn't an hour that had gone by since leaving the house this morning that I hadn't caught myself staring at him, or thinking about him, or wondering what his middle name was.

I sat up with a groan, turned on my reading light, and took the copy of SkyMall out of the seatback pocket in front of me. If anything could distract me for a while, it was SkyMall, where you could find just about anything you could possibly want, from the perfectly practical to the unbelievably ridiculous. I was reading the description of the Portable Boot and Shoe Dryer, when someone walked up to the end of my row.

"Can't sleep?"

I looked to my right and saw a man with slightly rumpled honey-blond hair, wearing jeans and a gray T-shirt grinning down at me. It was Alex. I smiled, suddenly feeling warm and jittery inside. "No, my pillow sucks. You?" I asked, keeping my voice down so as not to disturb the rest of the passengers whose pillows seemed to work better than mine. I closed the SkyMall, and shifted in my seat to face him.

"I was, I just woke up," he said, sitting down in the empty seat next to me. "Trick is to bring your own pillow."

"Woke up? Isn't it a little early for that?"

"Maybe for you, but for those of us who run on Ireland time, it's about six in the morning."

"Oh, right. Still, too early for me."

We sat in a comfortable silence for a few moments, which was odd considering how much time I'd spent thinking about him since we had last spoken. Moreover, it made me realize how stupid I was being, letting this "crush" thing go to my head.

I decided I needed to change my game plan. I couldn't just decide not to have a crush on him, as I didn't really decide *to* have a crush on him in the first place. However, what I could do was treat him just like I would any other guy. I would be his friend, figuring that the sooner I had friendly feelings for him, the sooner the other feelings – whatever they were – would go away.

Armed with this new attitude, I looked up at him and smiled. “I’m glad you came over. I was starting to think you were going to bail on your end of the deal.”

“Sorry,” he said as his eyebrows furrowed a bit, “I’ve just been… it’s not that I didn’t want…” He paused and rubbed his hands over his face.

“If you’re tired we don’t have to do this now,” I offered.

“No, no, I’m fine. I’m not tired, it’s just been… a weird few days,” he finished with a smile that was somewhere between wry and sad.

He didn’t explain, and I didn’t ask, assuming if he wanted me to know he would have said. Besides, that wasn’t what I was most interested in knowing right now anyway.

“So,” I said.

“So?”

I turned and crossed my legs on top of the seat, propped my right elbow on my knee, rested my chin in my hand, stared directly at him and smiled, in a somewhat blatant ’I’m listening, so start talking‘ gesture. He chuckled – which was good, as that was the point – and turned in his seat, bringing one knee up under himself so he could fully face me.

“All right,” he said, looking thoughtful, “where to start?”

“The beginning is usually best.”

“Yes, but somehow I get the feeling that if I started by saying ‘In the beginning’, you’d laugh at me.”

He was teasing me. I liked it. “Yeah, probably,” I said smiling.

"So what then?" he asked with a smirk. "Once upon a time?"

"Mmm..." I pretended to ponder. "What else you got?"

"A long time ago, in a galaxy–"

"Yeah, OK," I giggled, rolling my eyes, trying to remember to keep my voice down, "how about we stick to 'A long time ago'."

"All right then," he said clearing his throat, "a long time ago, thousands of years ago actually, there was a race of people living in Ireland called *Cumhacht Coinnigh* or Power Holders. They were like regular humans in every way except that they each had what they called a *beannú an bandia*, a 'blessing of the Goddess'. This 'blessing' was actually a special power or ability. Some Holders could read and control the thoughts of others, some could heal the injured or sick, some," he gestured to himself, "could conjure false images, while others could change their appearance right before your eyes. There were people who could make charms and spells, some who could read and measure the powers of others, and a few who could actually walk in the future. There were all sorts of powers that people had back in those days, some that we aren't even aware of as their lines have died out completely."

"Lines?"

"Abilities are, well, for lack of a better word, genetic. Holders have the same ability that their ancestors had. Ryland will read minds because that is what Jocelyn does, just like I can cast because that's the power someone had back down the line in my family."

"What about me? Jocelyn's my father, why don't I do anything?"

"Well, first off you're a girl. Abilities in women have always been few and far between. Even in the ancient times Holders were almost always men."

"Why?" I know it was stupid to be offended by something no one had any control over, but I kind of was.

He smiled at my tone. "We don't know; that's just the way it's always been. Now that's not to say it never happens, but even when it does, the women are never as powerful as the men. Sorry, wasn't my call," he said, with a grin. "But it's not just gender; inheriting an ability is never a sure thing. Just because a man is a Holder, that doesn't mean that all his kids will inherit the trait, just like all his kids may not inherit his hair color."

He paused, giving me a minute to collect my thoughts before going on, though oddly enough I didn't really need to. Just like during our first conversation in my room I was amazed at how normal all this sounded. I wasn't weirded out, or scared, or... anything. Ironically enough, my lack of fear was actually starting to scare me a little bit. But before I could think too much about that, something else crossed my mind. "Wait, you said that someone else had been a Holder 'back down the line' in your family. Wouldn't it have been your father?"

"Well, no, not necessarily. It doesn't always work that way anymore. In the beginning, all the Holders were in Ireland, kept contained by the limits of the island itself. However, over time, they began to slowly spread out, traveling to new lands and settling all over the world. As they started to build lives elsewhere and have families with people of other nations, the race began to slowly die out. Nowadays, most of the people who are 'Holders'," he made air quotes, "have an ability that is so washed out and diluted that they aren't even aware they have it. Someone who long ago would have had the ability to control minds is now no more than a person who seems to always be able to talk their way out of trouble. Someone who should have the ability to heal is now only a particularly gifted doctor. But every now and again the Holder trait will flare for some reason, and someone will end up with a power as strong as his ancestors would have had."

"Like you?"

"Like me," he said. "And Ryland, and Taron, as well as others you'll meet at St Brigid's."

I opened my mouth to speak but closed it again, lost in thought.

"Are you all right?" Alex asked after a minute or two of silence, a worried look in his eyes. "Because we can stop for now if you want."

"No, I'm fine... actually that's what's weird. I shouldn't be fine. Why am I fine?" I asked foolishly, as if he should have an answer.

"Actually I've been trying to figure that one out myself. But I suppose if I had to guess, I'd say it's because it's in your blood. You did graduate two years early."

"What's that got to do with anything?"

"Those in a Holder line are usually advanced or gifted in one aspect or another. Maybe your intelligence and ability to learn quickly is due to a little bit of Holder in your blood."

"Wait, seriously?"

"Makes sense, and I've seen it before."

"So, that's why you said my graduating early was interesting?"

He nodded.

"Well that's just… lame! Ryland gets to read minds, and that's all I get?"

"Better than nothing," he said, trying not to laugh. "And who knows, maybe somewhere deep down you've always known that Ryland was different in some special way. That you both were."

I *had* always known, about Ryland anyway. People had been trying for years to convince me that Ryland was crazy but somehow I've always known that couldn't be true. Maybe Alex was right. Maybe it was in my blood.

"So how about Captain Fun-Times over there? What's he do?" I asked, scowling across the aisle at the sleeping figure of Taron.

Alex laughed quietly. "The thing you have to understand about Taron is that he is very passionate about our cause and about Holderkind in general. It can sometimes make him seem…"

"Like an ass?" I suggested.

"Something like that," he chuckled, "but don't worry, it's not you."

"Sure seems like it is."

"I know, but he means well. He has been with Jocelyn longer than any of us, and his ability has been very helpful over the years. It's called Discerning, meaning he is basically a human lie detector. He can tell instinctively if someone is telling the truth, or lying, or if their words or actions have been compelled by mind control."

"Yeah, well helpful or not, I don't trust him."

"Give it time," Alex smiled.

Happy to change the subject I asked, "So, are you all are born with this? Does that mean there are super babies running around?"

"Yes and no. Yes, we are born this way, but no," he smiles as though he is genuinely amused by my stupid comments, "there are no super babies. Once a Holder reaches adulthood, which is usually somewhere between fourteen and sixteen, they have what we call an Awakening, at which point their ability becomes active. Before that, they are almost entirely normal, except for the occasional glimpse of the ability they will one day have. For instance, when I was younger I would sometimes see things that weren't really there."

"And Ryland hears voices," I said, talking more to myself than to him. "Voices that are actually thoughts."

He smiled, seeming happy that I understood. "Exactly. Though, I will tell you that his case is somewhat extreme. Normally we wouldn't expect someone so young to hear any more than the occasional whisper or impression. The fact that he is hearing full sentences is sort of a big deal."

"Like, 'big deal' as in bad?"

"No, he's fine; it's nothing to worry about. This is a part of the story that we're not going to get into tonight, but just suffice it to say that Ryland is very special."

Something in his tone seemed a little off and instantly piqued my interest. "Meaning...?"

"We'll get to that soon, but not tonight," he chuckled. "We have to get to St Brigid's first. There are a few things there you need to see before that part of the story will make any sense."

"But there's nothing wrong with him, right?"

"No," he said looking me in the eyes with so much warmth and honesty that for a second I forgot what I'd asked him, "I promise."

"OK," I whispered, with an entirely uncalled for sigh.

God, I really was becoming one of *those* girls...

"Maybe you should get some sleep," he said, looking down suddenly.

"I know I should," I said, looking away, pretending to readjust the blanket on my lap, "but I don't think it's on the cards tonight."

"Try," he said, looking up with another smile that was not fake, but not quite happy. "Tomorrow's going to be a long day."

"Right," I nodded, sad that he was leaving. As he stood to go, I remembered something. "Alex?" He turned back to me with a small smile that seemed... tired? I wasn't sure. "I've been meaning to apologize for how horrible I was to you that day at the house."

He had his hand in the air to stop me before I'd even finished. "Don't," he said, very seriously. "Don't ever apologize for that." He paused for a moment, his eyes, though still serious, grew soft. "I think it's amazing that you are willing to do anything to protect your brother.

With the way we are, being different, people, even family members, don't usually understand. He's lucky to have you. I wish..." he looked away for a moment, then steadily back at me, and once again I was pulled into his stormy colored eyes. "I wish I'd had someone like you."

Before I could respond he was gone, and I was left to try and sleep over the roar of my own thoughts.

5

Before I even realized I'd fallen asleep, I felt a hand shaking my arm. "Wake up! We're almost there!" I cracked one eye open to see a freckle-faced little carrot top with about the worst bed-head I'd ever seen.

"Go away," I mumbled, hugging my pillow closer and snuggling in.

"Look!" he said, climbing on top of me to lift up my window shade.

"You stink, get off me!" I moaned, pushing him onto the floor and sitting up.

"I don't stink, you stink," he mumbled, straightening himself up and moving over to look out the window.

"What time is it?"

"I don't know. My watch says 5.00, but the clock on the screen says 10.00," he said, not taking his eyes from the window.

Suddenly I realized something: a pillow. I had been sleeping on a real pillow. I reached over and smoothed my hand over the soft worn cotton, totally at a loss.

"Where did this come from?"

"Where did what come from?" Ryland asked, not bothering to look.

"This pillow."

"How am I supposed to know where your pillow came from?"

It was a full-sized bed pillow, with a pillowcase and everything. A far cry from the lumpy postage stamp pillow the flight attendant had given me. Suddenly, something Alex said the night before came to my mind: 'The trick is to bring your own pillow.' My eyes popped open and I inhaled sharply –Alex? Was this his pillow?

"What's wrong with you?" Ryland had turned from the window and was looking at me.

"Nothing," I said, as casually as I could, then, knowing that little boys can ask far more questions than is good for anyone involved, quickly changed the subject. "You're a mess, go to the bathroom and clean up."

"I'm fine."

"You're not fine, and if I have to be seen with you, you're going to go clean up."

I started pushing him towards the aisle while he continued to whine, "I already washed my face with the wet towel they gave me with breakfast…"

"Then at least fix your hair, you look like a serial killer." He snickered and slumped off towards the lavatories. "Use water," I called after him, to which he answered with a "yeah, yeah" wave behind his back.

I rummaged through my carry-on and pulled out my brush and a hair tie. I combed out my mane, and braided it into one long plait. I hadn't thought to bring my toothbrush on the plane with me, so I grabbed some gum out of my jacket pocket to get the sleep funk out of my mouth. I stood and stepped out into the aisle relishing how good it felt to be able to stretch. I headed for the lavatories figuring I should check on Ryland's progress, and sure enough when I got there I saw him stepping out of one of the tiny doors, hair still sticking out all over.

"Nope, get back in there," I said, pointing behind him.

"But I used water..." he whined as I spun him around by the shoulders and followed him in, closing the door behind us.

After another five minutes in the matchbox bathroom, in which Ryland had to kneel on the closed lid of the toilet in order for both of us to fit, we emerged two respectable-looking human beings.

As we turned the corner heading back to our seats, the first thing I saw was Alex, leaning casually on the headrest of the aisle seat of my row.

"Good morning," he said, as we approached.

"Morning," Ryland said with a wave, before dropping into his row and resuming his perch by the window.

Alex stepped aside so that I could re-enter my row, and I slid over to my seat, lifting his pillow into my lap as I went. He sat down next to me tentatively, as though he thought the action might somehow offend me.

"This is yours I assume," I said, handing him the pillow. He simply smiled and took it. "Thank you." To that, he gave a funny laugh and wouldn't meet my eyes. "What?"

"You..." he chuckled again. "You thanked me last night, actually."

"I did?" I didn't remember seeing him at all after our conversation, much less speaking to him.

"Yeah, when I gave it to you."

"Was I awake?"

"Um, no, I don't think so." His ears grew red, and I was immediately wondering what I'd said, worried it was something really dumb.

Luckily, before I could find out what it was, the seatbelt sign lit up and the flight attendant announced our descent into Charles De Gaulle Airport.

"Does that mean we're there?" Ryland was practically bouncing on his seat, shaking my headrest to get my attention.

"No, this is Paris. And sit down and buckle up, what's wrong with you?" I scolded, shoving his hands off my seat.

Ignoring me, he hopped down and ran out around us, climbing into the row in front of Alex and me. He turned to face us and got up on his knees so he could see over the headrest. "How can we land, we are still really high up."

"We're descending, not landing. It means going down."

"When will we land?"

"I don't know, half hour or so?"

"A half hour?" Ryland groaned, melodramatically dropping his head down on the top of the seat. "Then we have *another* plane ride?"

"Yep."

"But that will be a short one," Alex added.

"How short?" Ry asked.

"Only about two hours," Alex assured him.

"*Then* we'll be there?"

"Yes," I said with a sneaky grin, "after the car ride."

"*Car ride!*"

"Oh, it won't be that bad, we'll be there before you know it," I said, picking up my discarded SkyMall from last night and thumbing through it.

"Yeah right, you said that yesterday, and we're *still* not there!"

"Well, whining about it isn't going to get us there any faster," I said, not looking up from my magazine.

"Only Mom can say that!"

"OK, let me put it this way," I looked up at him, "stop whining, or I'll call the flight attendant over here and make him yell at you for not sitting right in the chair."

He crossed his arms over the top of the seat and rested his chin on them. "Fine," he mumbled against his arm. I glanced over at Alex, who was trying very hard not to seem amused by our bickering, before turning my attention back to SkyMall.

"I like your necklace," Ryland said suddenly.

"I'm not wearing a necklace," I said.

"Not you," he said, with a little too much attitude.

I glanced up to see he was looking at Alex.

"Do you?" Alex smiled, pulling the necklace he was wearing all the way out of his shirt. "Well, I'm glad to hear it, because you are going to have one just like it."

I turned to take a closer look. It was a small circle pendant on a thin black woven leather cord. The pendant was silver in color and had a deep blue gem set in the center of what looked to be interwoven Celtic knots.

"Cool," Ryland said, leaning over the back of the seat to get a better look.

Movement down the aisle caught my attention. "Ry, turn around and sit down, the flight attendant is coming and you're going to get in trouble."

"Can I stay up here?" he asked.

"Yes, just sit."

"OK," he said, flopping right way round.

With something between a grin and a grimace, I turned to Alex, "Sorry about tha–"

"Can I sit by the window?" Ry asked, smushing his face in the small gap between the seats in order to see me without standing up.

"Yes," I growled. "Sit wherever you want, just sit!"

"OK, OK, geez," he grumbled as he slid over to the window seat.

"And buckle your seatbelt!" I whispered just as the flight attendant walked by. Once he'd passed, I turned back to Alex, who was still looking bemused by our banter. "Sorry," I whispered.

"Don't be," he said, his smile making my heart beat just a little faster. "He's a good kid."

"Yeah, so I'm told." I couldn't help but grin. "So, what is that?" I asked nodding towards his necklace. "I assume it has something to do with…"

He nodded, knowing what I meant. "It's called a Sciath, it means shield. Every Holder has one."

"What's it do?" I asked, keeping my voice low enough to avoid the miniature set of ears in the next row.

"It helps us to use our abilities – to control them.

For instance, if I didn't have mine, I would still be able to cast, but I wouldn't be able to control who saw my projections, or how long they lasted. It would also be possible for me to start projecting things against my will, though now I'm old enough for that not to be too big a problem. That's more a issue with newly awakened Holders."

"So, do you wear it all the time? It seems like you really only need it when you use your ability."

"Well… there's one more thing. It protects our weakness."

"Your what?"

"Every ability comes with its own weakness. We're not sure why, best we can figure is that nature likes balance. Our Sciaths hide our weaknesses."

"Weakness like what? Like Ryland hearing random voices?"

"Sort of." He nodded. "Ryland hasn't had his Awakening yet, and so doesn't have his weakness. Actually, what I told him is only partially true. When he gets to St Brigid's he will get a charm that will control his ability, but it won't be his Sciath. He won't get that until after his Awakening. We give charmed necklaces to all the un-awakened users so that they have an easier time before the change. In Ryland's case, it will stop him from hearing thoughts randomly or as you have been calling them, the voices."

I felt a rush of relief. "Stop them? You can really do that?"

"Of course," he said, smiling.

"But after he has his Awakening, he will have a weakness? What will that be?"

"Well, in normal instances, he would have the same abilities and weakness as Jocelyn. I don't know if you would remember, but Jocelyn's Sciath is actually a ring."

"Oh my God," I whispered. "That huge red one?" I did remember. It was an enormous – or at least seemed enormous to a little kid – gold and red gemstone ring that I could never remember seeing him without.

Alex nodded, "That's it. It's actually a ruby, and that's his Sciath. Without it, he can still read minds, but he has no choice but to hear everyone's thoughts all at once, like a never-ending flow of noise in his mind. But with his Sciath, he hears nothing at all unless he wants to and even then he can choose whose mind he wants to read and hear only their thoughts. He can also sift through past thoughts and memories, and even control the mind – making people believe things that aren't real, or creating or erasing memories. Though he never does that, as he is strongly against having any sort of control over a person."

As I listened to him talk I could hear the underlying respect and admiration for the man he spoke of. The man whom I could barely stand the thought of without grinding my teeth. Alex seemed like such a good man. I wondered what Jocelyn could possibly have done to earn his respect, though this obviously wasn't the time for such a question, so I let it go. Then I realized something. "Wait, you said 'in normal instances'. Will Ryland be different?"

"Remember I told you Ryland was special? Well, it plays into that."

"And when do we get to that part of the story?" I asked with a grin.

"Soon," he said, smiling.

"So what about you? What's your weakness?"

He looked away and cleared his throat, looking suddenly uneasy. Almost as if… Oh God, I'd embarrassed him! I felt so comfortable around him that I never stopped to think that he wasn't sharing in my crush-driven delusion. "I-I'm sorry," I stammered. "I didn't… it's no big deal. I'm-I'm sorry."

"No," he said, glancing at me, then down again to his hands, "it's fine. It really is no big deal. I project emotion."

"Emotion? Like feelings?"

He nodded with a shy wince. "When I'm not wearing my Sciath, anyone who can see me can also see everything I am feeling at that moment."

"Oh," I said, "and you can't control it?"

"I can't even see it. If I think about it, I can hold it in, but it's hard; like tensing a muscle. I can't keep it up for long."

"Casting emotions doesn't seem so bad."

"No?" he challenged, raising his eyebrows. "Would you want the whole world to know exactly how you are feeling, all the time? Every single little emotion, not only the most present ones. You wouldn't mind it if everyone that you came across knew exactly how you felt about them, with nothing more than a glance?"

"Oh... no." I hadn't considered that. "No, that would be bad."

"Yeah."

I started to think about what everyone would see right now if they could read my emotions, and of course my mind immediately went to the ridiculous crush I had on the man sitting right next to me, and I realized that he would be able to see it plain as day. Suddenly I felt my cheeks grow warm and I quickly looked down, pretending to adjust my shoe, praying he didn't notice the blush.

"I should probably get back to my seat and start packing up, looks like we are going to land soon."

"Sure," I said, only allowing myself a short glance at him, not yet ready to trust the color of my face.

"There is one more thing I wanted to tell you," he said as he stood.

"What's that?"

"It's about our ageing."

Curiosity trumped my embarrassment and I looked up. "Your *ageing*?"

"After a Holder is awakened, the ageing process slows considerably."

"OK..." I said, not sure where he was going with this.

"At some point I'm sure you'll meet with Jocelyn, and I wanted to prepare you."

"My Mom already tried," I said, with an eye roll. "She's convinced I'm going to freak out and put him in the hospital or something."

"No, no," he said with a smile, "I meant prepare you for physically seeing him. I know it's been over ten years, and I just wanted to let you know that he will more than likely look exactly the way you remember him."

"Oh." I hadn't really thought about what Jocelyn would look like, though now that Alex mentioned it I suppose I would have expected to see a few wrinkles or some gray hair. I could have told Alex not to worry, as I had no intention of seeing Jocelyn at all, but with Ryland in the next row now wasn't the time to reveal that little tidbit of info. "Good to know," I said. "Thanks."

He nodded and turned to go, but I stopped him, "Wait, so... how old is he?"

"Are you sure you want to know?"

"Go for it." How bad could it be?

"I don't know his exact age, but I do know that he was born in England somewhere around 1800."

"1800!" I squeaked, remembering at the last second to keep my voice down. "You're telling me that my father could be over two hundred years old?"

"Didn't you ever wonder why he has a name like Jocelyn?"

"So, that used to actually be a guy's name?"

"Oh, yeah. In fact, it wasn't adopted commonly for women until the last fifty years or so."

"Two hundred! Eww! How long do you all live?"

"Depends on the person. Full Holders are the only ones who have any alteration in their lifespan, and the more powerful ones can live anywhere from five to eight hundred years. Most of us only go to about three hundred or so."

"Three hundred?! How can you say that like it is no big deal?"

He shrugged with a smile. "I'm used to the idea, I guess."

"Wait, OK, so now I have to know, how old are you?" I asked, bracing for the answer.

"How old do you think I am?" he countered, his smile turning wry.

"I don't know, one hundred and four?"

"One hundred and four! What about me screams 'old man', may I ask?"

"I don't know, so younger?"

"Yes, younger!"

"I probably shouldn't guess again…" I said, trying not to giggle.

"Good lord, I'm twenty two!"

"So no old folk's home then?" I was laughing outright, and even Alex was smiling in spite of himself.

"Excuse me sir, but you are going to need to take your seat," said a slightly annoyed flight attendant who seemed to come out of nowhere.

"Sorry." Alex turned to leave as the attendant walked back to the service bay. "One hundred and four, really?" he whispered, glancing at me before stepping out into the aisle and returning to his seat.

I pressed my lips together and laughed under my breath, before turning to the window to join Ryland in watching our final descent.

6

I'm not going to throw up, I'm not going to throw up, I'm not going to throw up…

My newfound mantra was endlessly circling in my mind as we bumped down the road towards St Brigid's Academy. Two plane rides and a two and a half hour van ride were apparently all my motion sickness-prone stomach could handle, and all I could do was pray that we arrived at the school before I made an ass of myself by getting sick all over everyone's luggage. If I'd thought that asking Taron to drive a little smoother would actually accomplish anything, I might have tried it. However, considering that Taron and I hadn't gotten off to the friendliest start, nor had he spoken even a word to me since leaving my house that first day, I didn't figure he'd be in the mood to help me. Actually, I was afraid that he'd get a kick out of my discomfort and would do anything he could to make it worse – which as the driver, he could easily have done. So, I simply sat as still as I could, forehead pressed against the cool glass of the window, praying to the stomach gods.

"We're here," Alex called back to us from the front passenger seat.

"Whoa, cool! Check it out, Becca!" Ryland gushed over something I dared not open my eyes to see. I rejoiced inwardly at our arrival, but refused to move a muscle until we had come to a full and complete stop.

"OK," Alex said happily, as the van finally came to a halt, "everybody out!"

Ryland hopped out as soon as the door slid open, but I hung back a moment, taking a few deep breaths of the cool misty air pouring in the open door.

"Welcome home, lads!" a strange male voice greeted Taron and Alex. A decidedly Scottish voice. I looked out the open door to see a heavyset man with dark hair and a long black coat clapping Alex on the shoulder.

"And who have we here, now?" the man said, stooping down to eye level with Ryland. "Master Ingle, is it? Pleasure to meet you, sir." He smiled warmly and extended his hand, which Ryland hesitantly shook.

Feeling a bit better – and not wanting to seem like the carsick wussy – I climbed out of the van and took a deep breath of the cool October air. The first thing I noticed however was that while the temperature was close to what it had been in Pittsburgh, the air here smelled different. Fall at home had always smelled like drying leaves and burnt wood, making me think of football and pumpkins and apple pie. But this air was different. It was damp, though not unpleasant, and smelled like sea foam, rain clouds, and musk. The whole atmosphere filled me up, from my hair to my toes, and sparked something deep in my chest that I couldn't quite put a name to.

"Ah, we have a second?" the stranger asked, pulling me out of my trance. I looked over to greet him, but hesitated when I saw the way he was gawking at me. "Lord have mercy..." he said under his breath. "Alex, is this...?"

Alex stepped forward and placed a hand on the man's shoulder. "Um, yes. Mr Anderson, this is Ryland and Rebecca Ingle." He motioned to us each in turn. "Becca, Ryland, this is Mr Christopher Anderson, one of the teachers here at St Brigid's."

"Pleasure to meet you, lass, a pleasure indeed. I dare say I think I'd have known her anywhere," Mr Anderson said with a wink, offering me his hand. "She's the very image of her father."

Knowing that he meant that as a compliment, I forced myself to smile – though I couldn't quite manage a thank you – and shook his outstretched hand.

"Why didn't you say she would be joining us as well?" Mr Anderson asked Alex.

"Sorry," Alex said, glancing at me. "I didn't have a chance. Actually, can I speak with you a moment?" Alex led Mr Anderson off to the side, and I smiled slightly, relief calming my nerves. Alex kept his word.

As the two of them talked out of earshot, Ryland pulled on my sleeve. "Can I look around?"

"Yes, but stay where I can see you."

As he went running to the other side of the van, Mr Anderson and Alex finished their conversation and parted, Mr Anderson joining Taron to assist with the luggage, while Alex came over to stand beside me.

"I asked Anderson not to say anything," he said quietly. He didn't explain, but I knew what he meant.

"Thanks. He doesn't mind?"

"No, not at all. I just told him you didn't want him to know until you had a chance to talk to him yourself. Sorry, I know that isn't the plan, but I was worried anything else would seem odd or raise questions. But he said he understands, and promised to keep quiet. He's a good man, you don't need to worry."

"Thank you," I said again, truly grateful that he was willing to do this for me.

"No problem," he said. "Though I should warn you, there is one person that I had to tell so that you would have a room ready for you while you're here. I gave her the same explanation that I gave Anderson, so there won't be an issue, I promise."

"It's fine, don't worry," I assured him with a smile, hating that he actually looked guilty. "I understand."

"And sorry," he added, giving me a sympathetic smile, "about what he said."

"You don't have to apologize, its fine." I shrugged. "He meant well."

"He did, but just to warn you, you'll probably get that quite a bit at first. You do... well, you do look a lot like him."

"Really?" I asked, a bit taken aback. "That's weird, I didn't used to." But then, I guess a lot can change in ten years.

"But anyway," he said in less hushed tone, "this is it."

As he gestured I took my first real look at our surroundings. We had pulled up in front of a large gray stone building that looked to be as ancient as the ground it was built on, while still being in remarkable condition. There were several other similar looking buildings scattered nearby, all with the same stately elegance. I turned to look down the road we had arrived on, and saw a large gate that appeared to be wrought iron, about a quarter mile back. It was connected to a high wall on either side of it that ran off in opposite directions, probably encompassing the entire campus. Everything, from the stone battlements of the buildings to the beautiful landscaping, had a strange look of nobility and grace to it. It was as if the campus itself was aware of some proud, ancient secret that we mere mortals were not privy to. Even the gray evening sky hung above us like a misty canopy, casting a shadow over the grounds that was haunting yet lovely at the same time.

"What do you think?" Alex asked, as I was taking it all in.

"It's beautiful."

As I turned back to examine the main building we had parked in front of, something yellow caught my eye. A young woman with bright blond hair was bounding down the large front steps with a huge smile on her face.

"You're here, you're here, you're here!" she squealed, as she came barreling towards us.

"That's Chloe," Alex informed me, "the one I had to tell about you. She is one of our graduates. She's been...

ooff!" He was cut off as Chloe slammed into him, throwing her arms around his waist in the process. Why I suddenly had the urge to throw her off of him, I had no idea.

OK, maybe I had *some* idea...

She released Alex and began chattering a mile a minute, in a thick Irish accent, "I'm so glad you're back! I've been waiting all day! Is this her? It has to be her! Hi." She skipped over to me and grabbed both my hands. "I'm Chloe Quinn, it's so nice to meet you!"

"Chloe," Alex said rolling his eyes, embarrassed, "take a breath."

"Sorry," she mouthed, sliding away from me, and trying to look casual.

She was a good six inches shorter than me, and had a fuller figure while not being overly large, with more freckles spread over her nose and cheeks than I'd ever seen on any one person. In any event, she seemed sweet as could be and totally harmless. Though why she was so excited to see me, I couldn't figure.

"No, it's fine," I assured them both with a laugh. "It's nice to meet you too, Chloe. I'm Becca." I offered her my hand and she took it with both of hers, glowing with delight like a kid at Christmas.

"All right, let's go," came Taron's gruff bark from the other side of the van. The bags had been moved from the van to a car that Ryland was already sat in.

"Where are we going?"

"To take Ryland to his dorm so he can get some sleep. After that, we'll go to the hall where you'll be staying."

"He won't be with us?"

"No, students don't live in Lorcan, not even the Holder kids. It's only for the professors who are Holders, me and Chloe. Ryland will be housed with kids his own age."

"Oh, sure", I said, with what I hoped was a nonchalant smile. No need to let the world know I was having a minor case of separation anxiety.

With a smile, Alex turned toward the car, clearly expecting me to follow. However when I looked over at the waiting vehicle, my stomach turned.

"Um Alex," I discreetly touched his arm as he walked by, "is there, umm... any chance I could walk?" I ask, somewhat sheepishly.

He noticed me eyeing the car and smiled. "Carsick?"

I tried to smile, but I'm pretty sure it looked more like a wince.

"I thought you looked a bit green," he chuckled.

"I'm fine now, as long as I don't have to get in another–"

"I'll walk with her!" Chloe interjected, hopping to my side and hugging my arm.

"Is that OK?" Alex asked, making it clear that I could say no. I considered it for a minute, thinking that if I did say no, Alex would be the one to walk with me, but then I realized that, one, that was pathetic, and, two, that'd leave only Taron to take Ryland to his room, and I couldn't do that to Ry.

"Sure, that would be great," I agreed. "Just give me one sec," I said to Chloe, patting her arm. Stepping over to the car I avoided Taron's glare and called through the window, "Ry, come here." He lumbered out of the car, his initial awe with the school having been replaced by jetlag. "Listen buddy, Alex is going to take you to your room so you can get some sleep."

"I'll give you the number to Becca's room, so you can call her if you need anything, OK?" Alex said, having come up behind me.

"OK," Ryland said around a yawn.

"I'll come to see you in the morning," I assured him, tousling his hair. "Good night buddy."

Alex put a hand on his shoulder and led him back to the car. "I'll meet you at Lorcan," he said to Chloe, before climbing in the car and driving off.

I watched until the car was out of sight, trying to force myself not to worry about Ry. After all, if this went well I'd be leaving soon, and he would have to get used to doing things on his own.

I took a deep breath and turned to Chloe, who was waiting silently, with her hands clasped together, practically bouncing on the soles of her feet. "So, which way?" I asked, unable to keep from smiling at her barely contained excitement. She gestured to the sidewalk, and we started to make our way down the road into campus.

"I like your outfit," I said, partially as a conversation starter and partially because it actually was pretty cool. It looked like a school uniform – the St Brigid's uniform I assumed – that had been modified to add personal flare. Her white button down shirt was open down to the bust, showing a white camisole fringed with black lace. The sleeves of the shirt had been cut short and had cuffs made of lace about halfway between her elbow and shoulder. Her dark green knee length wool skirt had a large three dimensional origami flower sewn onto it, with a matching one pinned in her hair. "Were those neckties?" I asked, pointing to the flowers.

"Yes, aren't they great? I hated wearing those stupid ties. That was the first thing to get a makeover when I graduated!"

"That's really cool, you'll have to show me how to do that." She didn't answer, but from the look on her face I was pretty sure I'd just made her day. "When did you graduate?"

"End of last semester. I was brought here when I was six, and have never left. That's probably why I decided to stay instead of going right to college. I'm so used to it here, and Alex and Min and the rest of the Holders are like family, and-"

"Wait, other Holders? You're a Holder?"

"Hmm?" she asked, her train of thought having been derailed. "Oh, yes."

"But Alex said that women don't usually have abilities?"

"Nope, just me and Min. That's why I'm so excited! Didn't Alex tell you? You are the first lady to be in on our little secret in years! I haven't had another woman to talk with since I was a girl!"

"So there are no other women here? It seems like a big school."

"Oh sure, there are lasses in with the regular students in the school proper, but no Holders. Lorcan has been a men's club for as long as I can remember," she giggled.

"What about... was it Min?"

"Oh Min's great, but she's well over three hundred years old. Not the sort you have over for girly chats."

"Right," I chuckled under my breath. I had the feeling that Chloe wouldn't have cared if I was a two-headed murderer straight out of prison, as long as I was under thirty and had boobs.

"So, what do you do? Your ability, I mean."

I noticed her shoulders sink just a bit. "Oh, nothing much. I'm a Walker is all, and not a good one."

"What's a Walker?"

"Time Walker. We can walk in different times."

"Like time travel? That sounds awesome!"

"Not exactly, no. A full Walker can go to any time or place he wished at a single thought, although he wouldn't be able to interact with anyone."

"Because he would mess up history?"

"No," she laughed. "You watch too much telly! No, I mean literally, he couldn't, because he isn't really there. He is only able to see the world at the time he chooses, and no one from that time has any idea he's looking on. Like a spirit or ghost."

"So, someone could be here with us right now listening if they wanted to?"

"Sure, I suppose so," she smiled.

"But why did you say it was nothing? It sounds pretty cool to me."

"Well," she sighed, "I'm a female. Like Alex told you, my gifts aren't half of what they could be. All I can do is move in time, not space. And only forward, no past."

"Is that bad?"

"Well, it's not bad, but it's not exactly useful. Here," she said, stopping and taking a few steps back, "I'll show you. Give me a date."

"Any date?"

"Anything, as long as it's the future."

"OK," I said, getting excited, "how about November 26, 2015."

Chloe took a slow breath through her nose and closed her eyes. "All right, I'm there. I am still standing in this spot, at the same time of day, only what I see is this spot and time on November 26, 2015."

"What do you see?" I whispered, as though talking too loud might break her trance – or whatever it was.

"Not much. All the buildings are the same. That tree needs a trim," she said raising her arm and pointing to the tall willow on the other side of the footpath. "A full Walker would be able to walk around to other parts of campus, or the world for that matter, with no problem. But as soon as I try to move..." She took a step forward, hesitating for a moment, her eyelids tensing up like she was trying to hold onto something. After a long moment she sighed and opened her eyes, deflated. "I lose it."

Well, that was... anticlimactic, I thought to myself. Not at all like Alex's Casting demonstration.

"See, like I said, no big deal." She sounded so sad.

"Hey, it's more than I've got," I said, as we began walking again. "Alex said that the fact that I graduated two years early from school is my 'ability', how lame is that?"

She smiled, perking up a bit. "Yeah, I suppose it's all right. I just wish I were more useful. What I really want is to be in the Order, but Jocelyn says I'm not strong enough and that it'd be too dangerous."

"The Order? What's that? Help with what?"

"Oh," Chloe bit her lip, looking apologetic, "I should probably let Alex tell you about all that. He knows more about it than I do."

A particularly cold breeze caught us and we both gave a shiver. "Come on then, let's get on to Lorcan and get warmed up. And on the way, I can give you a tour!"

"OK," I said, smiling at her sudden enthusiasm, glad that she was back to being bubbly.

We walked along for about ten minutes, Chloe naming all the buildings we passed, and giving me any pertinent history she knew about each one. Most of the halls were named after Irish saints – Cian, Niall, Aidan, Martin, Cillian – the majority of whom I'd never heard of. She talked about the history of the grounds, and the names of the trees and plants, and said hi to the occasional passerby, though they were few and far between as it was getting dark, and most people were in for the night.

Try as I might to pay attention, my mind began to wander off on its own tangent, namely Jocelyn. I was suddenly acutely aware of the fact that for the first time in ten years we were in vicinity of one another. Every time Chloe pointed out a new building or hall, I realized that he could actually be in there. My heart started to beat faster and I had the urge to duck into a doorway and hide, as if I were actually afraid that he was going to pop out from behind a bush or jump out of a tree at any moment.

Yeah, right.

It was long past time to get a grip. With a huff, I stuffed my hands in my pockets and forced myself to listen to Chloe's never-ending river of dialogue. She pointed out the cafeteria, and the library. Showed me the dorm where Ryland was housed, and all the different academic buildings that Ryland would have his classes in. We turned onto a smaller footpath that seemed to be leading us away from the campus proper. As we passed through a line of trees, I wondered aloud, "Seems like everything is back over there."

"Don't worry, nearly there," Chloe told me, pointing down the path, and sure enough, there was one building left. In fact, one of the largest buildings we had seen so far.

"Here we are," Chloe said as we arrived, resting her hand on the banister of the large stone steps leading up to the entrance, "Lorcan Hall."

It was one of the coolest buildings I had ever seen. It was as though someone from the eighteenth century couldn't decide whether they wanted to build a church or a castle, so they combined the two. Huge columns framed the giant oak doors, each with two ornate iron hinges and a knocker that looked too heavy to lift. The windows were all stained glass, and had pictures of saints and angels on them, surrounded by intricate Celtic knots.

"It's amazing," I said, still in awe.

"I knew you'd like it! Come on, I'll take you to your room."

The inside of Lorcan Hall was just as grand as the outside – stone corridors, tapestries, leather furniture, and more stained glass than a Catholic church. After climbing way too many stairs, we finally stopped in front of one of the ornate doors on the third level.

"Here you are. I'm so happy you're here!" she said, pulling me into a tight hug. "My rooms are right down the way if you need anything," she added, pointing along the corridor. "There's a pink flower on the door, you won't miss it."

"Great, thanks."

"Well," she stepped back reluctantly, "I guess I'll see you in the morn!" She waved one more time before continuing down the hall. "Fine sleep!"

"Um, yeah, you too," I said, watching her turn the corner before stepping into my room.

Fine sleep? Must be an Irish thing.

I felt around on the wall for the light switch and flipped it on, in no way prepared for what I was about to see. I had expected a small, dorm-style room – you know, cinder block, one window, prison bed – typical college fare. However, what lay before me could barely be considered a room, much less a dorm. It would better be defined as an apartment! Or at the very least, a studio. I stepped into a small living space complete with couch and TV. To the right of that, through a large open archway was a bedroom with double bed and linens. Connected to that was a bathroom with a toilet, sink, and bathtub with a shower. Best of all, one look inside the bedroom revealed my luggage already there waiting for me on the bed.

Mmm… bed…

Looking at the large mattress with soft white sheets immediately took its toll on my jetlag, and all I could think about was undressing and climbing in. But of course, as soon as I moved to take off my shirt, there was a knock at the door.

It was Alex.

"Hi, sorry, I heard you come up," he said, seeming a bit on edge, or at least less casual and at ease than he had earlier.

"No, it's fine," I said, trying to keep the shake out of my voice. "I'm glad you stopped by. Is Ryland OK?"

"He's fine. Passed out as soon as we got to his room." He handed me a card. "This is his building and room. That's the phone number."

"Good, thanks." Why was he nervous? Why was I nervous? Why was I all of a sudden acutely aware that we were mere steps away from my bedroom?

"Is…" He cleared his throat awkwardly. "Is your room OK?"

"Oh gosh, it's awesome! I was expecting a one-room cell." I laughed, hoping to ease the tension.

"The rooms in Lorcan are nicer because we live here, but there aren't many. This room was the only one not in use. My room is," he cleared his throat again, "right above yours, if you need anything. And Chloe is just down the hall," he added quickly.

"Yes, she told me, thank you."

"So... good night then," he said, with a strange almost sad look in his eyes. He was probably tired.

"Good night."

Once he was out of sight, I closed the door and shuffled back over to the bed, kicked off my shoes and climbed in, not even bothering to take my clothes off. As I snuggled down into the pillow, I heard footsteps on the floor of the room above me.

Alex's footsteps.

He was pacing back and forth on what I could only assume was the floor of his bedroom. Normally something like that would keep me awake, but tonight oddly enough it was soothing, and I drifted off to sleep to the soft, rhythmic beat.

7

52… 53… 54. That should be the one.

"Ry," I called through the door, knocking three times, "you in there?"

A few seconds later the door flew open, and I was greeted by a smiling little boy – who looked like he'd been dragged face-first through someone's flowerbed.

"Ryland! What in God's name happened to you?"

"What?" he asked, totally clueless, stepping to the side so I could come in.

"'What'? Look at you, you're filthy! And is that grass in your hair?" I tried to pick a piece out only to have my hand swatted away.

"Oh yeah, probably. After breakfast some of the guys wanted to play football, but actually they meant soccer!"

"Really, wow, weird," I said, knowing full well that soccer was known as football to the majority of the world. "What's that?" I asked, squinting down at the small charm hanging from his grimy neck.

"Oh, yeah! Alex brought it for me last night, it's

awesome! He said it would make the voices go away, and it did!"

"Really? You can tell already?"

"Yeah, because it's not just the voices, all the noise is gone too!"

"Wait, noise? What noise? You've never said anything about noise."

"Because I didn't know. It was just noise. Not loud, like it was far away, you know? But it was all the time and I thought everyone heard it. But now it's gone and it's so quiet!"

"Wow, that's great, Ry," I said, trying to sound like I wasn't choked up.

My God, this may actually work...

I casually turned away looking for a distraction and found a large black folder with the school's green emblem on it sitting on the bedside table. "What's this?" I asked, picking it up and taking a seat on the edge of the bed.

"A folder with some stuff about the school in it. It was sitting there when I got here last night."

Flipping through it I found a pamphlet with a list of courses, a guide to building hours, a student policies handbook, and random other informational items. Thankfully, one of these items was a campus map, which I folded up and stuck in my pocket, having already gotten lost twice trying to re-find Ryland's dorm, which Chloe had pointed out to me.

"Why weren't you at breakfast?" Ry asked me, as I sat down on the edge of his bed.

"I slept in."

"Too bad, it was great! Except for the porridge. Have you ever had porridge? It's really gross!"

"So... you like it here?"

"Yeah, it's great! Did you know they have a rock climbing class? How awesome is that?"

"Yeah, that sounds cool." This was definitely not the Ryland I'd expected to find this morning. Where was the shy introvert, who was afraid to talk to other kids? Was this all a show? That seemed unlikely. He'd barely even looked at me since I walked in; too busy changing his shirt, digging through his suitcase, and arranging his collection of action figures on the shelf below the window. But come on, I told myself, there was no way he could have changed that much overnight. "Ry, are you sure you're not just–?" but I was cut off by a knock at the door.

"Ryland? You ready?" a boy's voice called.

"Yeah, come in!"

The door opened and two boys walked through. "We gotta hurry or Clancey's team will get the best spot!" the taller of the two said.

"Who's that?" the shorter boy asked, pointing at me.

"I'm–"

"That's just my sister," Ryland informed them. Then, turning to me, added, "We've got to go, but I'll see you later, OK?"

Well. I see how it is...

"OK, sure." I stood and walked out into the hall, knowing a get out when I heard one. I turned back to say goodbye, only to see the door was already being shut behind me.

Just my sister? *Just* my sister? Oh yeah, I was *just* the sister who flew to the other side of the world, *just* to make sure he wasn't locked away in some nut house!

...little punk.

I knew I shouldn't be irritated, but I couldn't help it. OK, maybe it wasn't irritation per se, but that seemed like the best word for it. Calling it "hurt" seemed way too sentimental and clingy. And honestly, I had no business feeling that way, in any event. Wasn't this what we wanted; for Ryland to finally have a normal life with friends? Exactly. So, it was stupid for me to be bummed that he might suddenly not need me so much anymore. Stupid – and counterproductive I might add – as the main idea of all this was for me to leave him here and go home. He was supposed to stop needing me. He was supposed to be learning to do things on his own. Ergo, the lump in my throat was entirely uncalled for.

Entirely.

Not wanting to go sit alone in my room, I decided to make use of my new map and take an impromptu tour of the campus. I had hoped to spend the morning exploring with Ryland, but it was still nice to have a chance to walk the grounds and get to know the place that he might soon call home.

It really was a gorgeous school, I had to admit. The grand architecture and ancient style of the buildings were nothing short of magnificent, and it made the whole place feel more like a university than a school. It was also busier that morning than it had been the previous evening, all the activity filling the campus with a lively buzz. There were students of all ages coming and going, some carrying large bags of new textbooks all ready for the start of classes, while others played games of soccer on the central quad or sat in groups on the steps of the buildings talking casually, all of them trying to make the most of their last day of freedom.

So many students – were any of them Holders? Alex had said there were others with abilities attending St Brigid's, but I had no idea how many. Could the boy who'd just scored a goal for his team down on the quad also know how to read minds or instantly heal the sick? Could the girl flipping through her new notebook and chatting with her friends also be able to flip through time or make images appear and disappear on a whim? There were dozens of kids out that morning and any one of them could have been harboring an ability that the rest of the world knew nothing about, and the idea was as amazing as it was intimidating.

I continued my explorations around the property, becoming increasingly impressed with what I found. The dorms were segregated by gender and very well-maintained for as old as they clearly were, the grounds were immaculate with not a bit of trash or stray weed to be found, and the walkways, while winding, were well-marked and easy to navigate.

One of my favorite discoveries was the massive library, which had to be more than three times larger than any I'd ever seen. I spent quite a while perusing the shelves of books, happy to find that even though I was in a completely different part of the world, the whole building had the same wonderfully comforting smell of the libraries I'd grown up with back in the States. It was an aroma as nondescript as it was specific, and as it filled my nose, I couldn't help but smile. Apparently books smell like books no matter where you are.

The classrooms and lecture halls were equally impressive, most with wooden desks that weren't anywhere near new, but had been very well-cared for – not covered in crude carvings and ink stains like the wooden desks I had known – and all the rooms had the refreshingly classic black chalkboards – not the ugly green ones my school had been filled with.

It was past one by the time I got back to Lorcan Hall, and my mood was decidedly better. I wasn't sure what to do with myself, and briefly considered going up to my room and calling my mom, but with the time difference I knew she'd already be on her way to work, so that would have to wait a while. With nothing else to do, I figured I might as well poke around Lorcan for a bit, and maybe find something to eat while I was at it. Who knew, I thought to myself, maybe I'd run into Alex along the way...

No! I really had to stop that. I would be going home soon – sooner than I thought, given the way Ryland was taking to things – and Alex would be staying here. As my Mom would say, no use barking at a squirrel you can't catch.

I wandered the halls aimlessly for a while, not finding much. It was obvious that Lorcan wasn't used for regular classes as the few classrooms I found were either almost entirely empty or being used for storage. There was a lounge area in the front with a small library in it, an alcove in the east hall with a piano, a few restrooms here and there, and so on, but nothing all that exciting. Though happily I did come across a vending machine, providing me with a much needed lunch.

It wasn't until I passed by a large pair of carved doors, and heard voices coming from the other side, that my interest was piqued.

"I say we have him try it right away. How else are we to know if any of this is real? It could simply be a waste of time," a male voice said.

"No matter what happens, it wasn't a waste of time, you know that. He's better off here than he was in the States no matter what happens."

I recognized the second voice as Alex, but who was he with?

"He's just a boy." A female voice with a Russian accent interjected. "He isn't ready to take on such a large burden."

Just a boy…? Better off here than in the States…?

Ryland! They were talking about Ryland! I crept up to the door and carefully pressed my ear against the polished wood.

"It needs to be done slowly and carefully," the female voice continued. "If everything isn't handled perfectly, someone could find out that we've brought him here."

"Exactly! Which is why we need to make sure–"

"Reid," Alex cut him off, "it's almost two, don't you have a meeting?"

"Damn," the same male voice said under his breath, "all right, well, see to it that he decides soon. We no longer have the luxury of time."

Suddenly there was the sound of motion – of feet walking towards the door. My throat began to spasm as I tried to decide what to do, fast realizing that I had no options. If I ran they would hear me, if I did nothing they would catch me, and in either event they would know I'd been eavesdropping.

I froze. The footsteps had reached the door. I was out of time.

I held my breath as the door opened, and a moment later I was standing face to face with... Taron. I waited for the scolding, the yelling, the haughty derision... but none came. He just stood there looking at me. Thinking offense might be the best defense, I opened my mouth, planning to offer some excuse or maybe even a denial. However, before I could get a word out, he yawned – yes, yawned – right in my face, and walked off down the hall without a word to me at all. He was soon followed by Mr Anderson, a short older woman in a knit shawl and frizzy hair, and a middle-aged bald man with a long nose and wire-rimmed glasses, none of whom so much as glanced in my direction. I was standing right there, in the middle of an otherwise empty hall, obviously eavesdropping on their conversation, and no one cared?

The last person out of the room was Alex, who hung back, leaning casually against the doorframe, watching the backs of the others as they walked up the hall, also not so much as glancing in my direction.

"You should try holding up a glass next time," he said, after the last of the figures had turned the corner.

"What?"

"You'll hear better," he said, turning to face me.

"What was that? Why...?" I stopped, shaking my head, trying to piece together what had just happened.

"Why didn't they say anything to you? Because they couldn't see you."

"Wait, you did that? But... how? You can't make people disappear... can you?"

"No," he said, shaking his head and grinning, "but I can cast an image of the hallway without you in it."

"How did you know I was out here?"

"I felt – er, heard you," he corrected quickly, looking away. "I was standing right by the door."

"So your skills not only allow you to impress unsuspecting women by taking them to far off lands from the comfort of their bedrooms, but can also help you aid-and-abet snoops?" I asked, hoping a joke would cover the fact that I was mortified to have been caught spying on them. "You should work with Peeping Toms; they'd probably pay good money."

I looked up to find his eyes on me. "I impress you?"

Oh God, had I said that? My neck grew hot as his eyes held mine, waiting for an answer. "Yes, of course," I said, figuring there was no harm in being honest. "Anyway," I added quickly, pretending I didn't notice his ears turn red at my compliment, "thank you."

"No problem." He closed the door and put his hands in his jeans pockets. "So I imagine, considering you overheard, that you have some questions."

"I had some anyway, but yeah."

He nodded. "I think you're ready for the rest of the story. Any chance you could give me about twenty minutes before we get into it though? I promised Mr Anderson I'd help bring over a few things for his next class."

"Twenty minutes?"

"Twenty minutes." We began to walk side by side up the hall. When we reached the main corridor, he pointed, "If you take this all the way to the end and turn right, there is a small rotunda. I'll meet you there." With that, he smiled and left.

It took me a grand total of forty-two seconds to make it to the rotunda, which was small and contained nothing besides yet another pair of large oak doors. As there was nowhere to sit and wait, I figured I would waste the rest of my twenty minutes continuing the tour I'd started before I'd gotten sidetracked. This proved to be a lousy idea however, as it took me a grand total of twenty four seconds to get lost. After I passed the same hallway with the same leather couch for a third time, I collapsed down on it, totally annoyed with myself. Maybe Alex would come looking for me when I didn't show up to meet him. Or maybe I could get upstairs and find my room, then come down using the main stairway and–

"You seem to be lost."

As soon as the voice hit my ears, the back of my neck started to prickle and every hair I had stood on end. I knew that voice. I hadn't realized it until that very moment, but

I'd have known that voice anywhere. Time itself seemed to hang in the air as I slowly turned my head to face the speaker. A man I'd not seen in over ten years.

Jocelyn Ingle. My father.

It was him. It was really him. The same hair, the same eyes, even his stance was just as I remembered it. He began walking towards me slowly, the look on his face somewhere between curiosity and fear, as if he wasn't sure what to say.

I knew the feeling.

When he was only a few steps from the couch, I stood, honestly having no idea what would come next.

"Can I help you get somewhere?" he asked.

"I was..." I cleared my throat, suddenly finding it hard to speak. "Th-the main staircase," I stammered, not sure what to call the little rotunda and knowing I could find it on my own from the stairs. "I was supposed to meet Alex... I was there, but then I kept walking... and now I'm here..." I trailed off, wondering what the hell had come over me. I was stuttering like an idiot! Where was all my rage? My anger? Not only wasn't I doing what I'd always promised myself to do when I met Jocelyn again, but now I couldn't even bring myself to speak in full sentences!

"Oh, so you've met Alex?"

"Yes, he brought me... us. He brought us here."

"Was there a tour for you today?" he asked, smiling warmly and motioning for me to walk with him.

"No, not that I know of. I haven't had one, probably why I got lost." I was rambling again, but at least this time I was making sense.

"Do you like it here?" he asked me after a few silent moments.

"Yes," I said glancing over at him, "it's really nice."

"Good, I'm glad."

"Though this is the second time today I've been lost." For God's sake, why did I keep saying that? He *knew* I was lost!

"Yes, that happens," he chuckled. "It takes some getting used to, but you'll get the hang of it."

Never in my wildest dreams did I think this would happen. We were talking. Talking just like regular people. Sure, there was weirdness that obviously neither one of us wanted to address, but after ten years that was understandable. What was shocking to me was how good it felt to talk to him again. To see him again. Why on earth had I wanted to hide?

"Here we are," he said as we reached the main staircase.

"Oh, wow. That wasn't hard at all."

"I've got to go, I'm expected," he said, gesturing over his shoulder.

"Oh, yeah sure. No problem."

"Well," he held out his hand, "it was nice meeting you Miss..." He'd left the sentence unfinished, the way someone would do when they were waiting for the other person to fill in their name.

Nice meeting you.

"Right," I breathed, staring blankly at his hand. "Of course that's what we're doing here. What was I thinking?"

He pulled his eyebrows together, confused. "I'm sorry?"

"No, I'm pretty sure you're not," I said, a bitter edge in my voice. Ignoring his still outstretched hand, I turned and headed towards the stairs.

"It was nice to meet you," he said again, his tone making it clear that he was completely baffled by what had just happened.

I couldn't take it. With my hands balled into fists at my sides, I turned to look at his retreating figure and said, with as much sarcasm and venom as I possessed, "Nice to meet you too... *Dad*."

I saw him freeze dead in his tracks. Saw him turn back and look at me, understanding finally in his face. I met his eyes for a split second before turning and walking past the stairs and out the front door, without looking back.

8

I ran out of Lorcan and down the steps, barely seeing where I was going. Rounding the corner, I huffed off into the wooded park area alongside the building, muttering and cursing under my breath.

How could I have been so stupid?! Why the hell did I let myself think… *Ugh!*

Suppressing the urge to jump up and down screaming, I pushed on faster through the trees, not caring that I had no idea where I was going. However, with the dry fall branches ripping at my arms and face, and the hard, rocky ground grinding at my feet, it didn't take long for my fuming stampede to dwindle to a frustrated stagger. Pushing my way through a particularly thick line of brush, I came out to find a sloping hill leading down to a small lake. I jogged down the hill to the water's edge, loving the rush of the effortless speed provided by nothing more than gravity. Stopping at the bottom, I bent over and rested my hands on my knees to catch my breath. After a few minutes I'd succeeded in getting my lungs to stop burning, but I'd had no luck in bringing my blood pressure down. I ran my hands through my hair – dislodging some twigs and leaves in the process – and began pacing up and down the bank of the lake, biting my tongue in a last ditch effort not to cry.

I hadn't cried over my father in almost a decade, and I damned well wasn't about to start again now.

"Becca?"

I whirled around with a gasp to find Alex standing a few feet away.

"Sorry," he said quickly, as I let out a shaky breath, "I didn't mean to scare you, I saw you come out..." He hesitated a moment looking pensive.

You..." I breathed, still panting a bit. "You followed me?" I wasn't sure whether to be flattered or annoyed.

"No, it was just that you looked upset, and I..." He stammered, his ears turning red.

"Wait, how did you get through...?" I looked him up and down then turned to look back up the hill at the line of brush I'd fought through, wondering how he still looked so put together while I looked like a survivalist.

"There's a path," he said, pointing up behind him.

"Of course there is," I mumbled. That would figure.

"Are you all right?" he asked tentatively, as though he was afraid I might spring up and bite him.

Well let's see, my brother wants nothing to do with me, and my father wouldn't know me from a stranger in the street. "Yes," I lied, "I'm fine."

"Are you sure?"

"Yeah, I..." I looked up into his eyes and saw such honest concern, that it somehow made my mouth begin to work independently from my brain. "I just never thought..." I began pacing again as I rambled, digging my hands angrily through my mess of hair. "I'm over it! I've *been* over it! I've known for years how it was! And yet I still let myself get caught up... I was an idiot! If I had stuck to my guns like I always said I would, none of this would have happened! *Mo ghile beag*, you know that's what he used to call me? My Little Darling! And now he doesn't even..." I died off then tried again: "I mean I don't care, I just didn't expect..." I gave up with a sigh, blinking and biting my tongue again.

"What didn't you expect?" he asked softly.

I stopped pacing and stood with my arms crossed in front of me facing the lake. "For him not to recognize me." I said, resenting the crack in my voice.

"Jocelyn?" he asked, walking up behind me. "You saw him?"

I nodded. "I saw him, and he saw some random girl who had lost her tour group."

I saw him wince out of the corner of my eye. "I'm sorry," he said gently.

I waited for the defense. The, "well, you knew he wasn't expecting to see you", or "it has been ten years", or even, "oh, I'm sure he did", but nothing came. I turned to try and read him, but saw only sad concern in his eyes.

"Sorry," I mumbled, looking down again. I shouldn't have laid all my father issues on someone who was inexplicably one of the guy's biggest fans.

"No, please," he said shaking his head. After a few silent moments he asked, "Do you want to go back up? I can tell you about Ryla–"

"No," I snapped, turning away, "I don't want to talk about Ryland, or… any of it." I could tell he was just trying to find me a distraction, but much as I didn't want to talk about Jocelyn, hearing about Mr I'm-suddenly-too-cool-for-my-sister, wasn't going to help my mood either.

"Right," Alex said quietly, "I'm sorry, I'll…"

When he didn't finish his thought I turned around, only to find him walking away.

"No," I called, jogging after him and catching his arm, "I'm sorry, I didn't mean…" I looked up at him imploringly – and probably a bit desperately. "Please don't go."

Only when he went to leave did I realize how much I wanted him with me. I couldn't explain it, but for some reason I felt better with him nearby. As much as I didn't want to talk about Ryland right now, the thought of him leaving me alone was worse.

He slowly smiled, his eyes lighting up a bit before he turned and looked over his shoulder. "Here," he said, "come."

I followed him about a hundred yards or so around the perimeter of the lake until we reached a large willow tree, the branches of which were so long that most of them brushed the ground. As we got closer, I could see a circular stone bench wrapping all the way around the base of the trunk. There were wide steps leading from the foot of the bench down to the lake, though parts were overgrown with grass and moss and obviously hadn't been used in a while.

"What is all this?" I asked.

"They used to hold biology classes out here before they moved the science building across campus," he told me, holding aside a few of the low hanging branches so I could walk through. "I come down here a lot."

We sat together on the bench and looked out over the lake. The steel-gray afternoon sky was reflected on the surface, turning the entire lake to liquid silver. I closed my eyes and took a long breath of the cool, misty air.

"It's so beautiful here," I sighed, leaning back against the trunk of the tree.

"Really?" he asked, sounding something between surprised and hopeful. "You think so?"

"Sure, don't you?"

"I do." He nodded. "I love it here. More than anywhere else I've ever been. But a lot of people think it's gloomy."

"No," I said, looking out over the water. "It's not gloomy. They just don't get it."

I glanced back over to find him looking at me with a goosebump-inducing look on his face. When I smiled, he looked away quickly and cleared his throat. "No," he said, as if it were no big deal. "They don't."

We sat pleasantly for several minutes, not saying anything, each of us lost in our own thoughts. I was perfectly happy with this until my thoughts started to turn back to Jocelyn, at which point I decided conversation would probably be the best way to go.

Better yet, this might also give me a chance to learn a little more about Alex.

I rested my head against the tree, turning to face him. "So, Alexander."

"Yes, Rebecca?" he asked, mimicking my tone with a suspicious grin.

"What about you?"

"What about me?"

"I want to hear about you," I said matter-of-factly, pulling my feet up onto the bench and lacing my hands together over my knees.

"What would you like to know?" he asked with a smile.

I shrugged. "I don't know… Where were you born? How did you get here? What's your middle name? Favorite movies, food, books – whatever. Take your pick."

He hesitated as though what I'd asked him was far more important than a simple conversation starter. "Well," he said, resting his head back against the trunk of the tree, "I didn't grow up with many movies, but I have seen almost every animated Disney film that's come out, so if I had to pick one of those I'd have to go with the Emperor's New Groove."

"That is a good one," I laughed.

"My favorite food is macaroni and cheese, which, by the way, you will not find a good version anywhere in this country," he said, glancing at me with amused irritation. "Let's see, what else… I never learned how to swim, I love Sherlock Holmes novels, and I speak fluent

Gaelic. Oh, and my middle name is Michael. Was that everything?" he asked, grinning at me.

"That about covers it, I guess. You're a pasta-eating, Sherlock-loving, Irish wannabe, who would drown if I pushed you in the lake," I giggled.

"Exactly," he said.

"Or at least I'm assuming you're only a wannabe. You weren't actually born here were you?"

"No, though wannabe is a little harsh," he said, feigning offence. "I'm not sure where I was born, but I grew up in Texas."

"So, I should add 'cowboy' to the list?"

"No, definitely not," he laughed.

This was so nice. Once again, Alex and I were totally alone, and yet, I couldn't have felt more comfortable. There was no awkwardness, or tension, just an ease and companionship I would never have expected to feel with a person I'd met only a few days ago. Maybe our strange connection was due to the fact that we'd done so much together in such a short amount of time, though I couldn't help wondering if it was more than that.

Just as I was about to ask another question, something he'd said a moment ago stuck out in my mind. "You don't know where you were born? How is that possible?"

"I was adopted."

"Oh," I said, hoping I hadn't hurt his feelings.

He must have heard the reluctance in my tone because he smiled. "Don't worry, it's fine."

"How did you end up here? Did your parents send you?"

"Not so much, no," he said, shifting in his seat. "When I was about six, I started to see things. Things that weren't there. Of course, now I know that my ability was starting to develop, and I was beginning to cast, but at the time I was only a boy who would randomly see monkeys running around the house or a large hole in the wall that no one else could see. My parents were convinced there was something wrong with me, while I couldn't understand why no one else could see the things I did. I was taken to doctors, and specialists – anyone my parents could find – but no one had any answers. Finally, one of the doctors referred us to a special facility that was said to offer unique programs and state of the art treatments for difficult cases."

"Like a research facility?"

"No, a… mental facility," he said, glancing down.

My eyes widened, but I didn't comment.

"They took me there one morning for a series of tests that would last overnight. They checked me in, wished me luck, and told me they'd see me in the morning. That was the last time I saw them."

I stared at him, not comprehending. "Did… did something happen to them?"

He smiled, though there was no humor in it. "That's what we thought at first. The doctors and nurses tried to contact them, but they had filled out all my admission forms with false information. By the time they found our real address, my parents had moved. They had never intended to come back for me."

"They just left you there?" I was outraged. "But there was nothing wrong with you!"

"They didn't know that. Even I'd started to think I was crazy." He paused for a moment while I sat there silently dumfounded. "As it turns out, it was a lucky break that I was considered mentally insane, as that meant I couldn't be put into the foster system where I probably never would have been found. I lived there in the facility for seven years, until..." He hesitated, glancing up at me. "Until Jocelyn found me and got me out when I was fourteen. He brought me here, and I've been here ever since."

"What do you mean, 'found you'?"

"He was on a scouting trip and came across my file." He saw the question in my eyes before I had a chance to voice it. "Scouting is what we call it when we go out and look for people who might be Holders and don't realize it. For the past few years, Taron and I have done the scouting together. Most of the time we are looking for kids. Every so often we find an adult, but it's rare. Rarer still for us to bring an adult back with us. If a Holder reaches adulthood with no pronounced issues, it's usually because his ability is too diluted to be noticed. In those cases, it's best to leave well enough alone. Anonymity is very important to us, and the fewer people who know about us the better."

"But you told me?"

"Yes, but your situation was different. I knew you weren't going to do anything to endanger us, particularly when it would also have put Ryland at risk."

"But what about parents? You didn't want my mom to know, but don't they eventually have to find out?"

"Eventually yes, but we never tell them unless it can't be avoided. We've always believed that it is each Holder's right to be the one who tells their loved ones, and only when they're ready. Some do, but a lot of others don't. They come in, learn about their ability, how to control it, then leave, happy to live the rest of their lives as if there is nothing different about them at all. Whether they realize it or not, most people don't want to be different. Telling loved ones about something like this should be a choice, not a requirement. Besides," he paused with a sad smile, "it's only the lucky ones who have to make that choice at all. When we came to your house to get Ryland, and had the chance to meet with your mother... well, it's not usually like that. More often the kids we find are from hospitals, mental institutions, or sometimes prisons."

"They put kids in jail for being different? Aren't there laws against that?" I asked, my anger growing by the minute.

"In some countries, yes, but we find kids all over the world, and some cultures aren't so understanding," he answered sadly.

"But hospitals and institutions must have tons of sick kids. How can you tell which ones are actually Holders?"

"Usually we can do it with their records alone. After a while you start to notice the typical red flags. But if there is still any doubt all it takes is a conversation with the child to know for sure."

For several minutes I sat silently, going over it all in my mind. Everything he'd told me was so heartbreaking and at the same time so inspiring that I was at a loss for words. The one thing I was sure of, however, was that my respect for the man sitting next to me had grown tenfold over the last five minutes.

I looked back up at him, almost awestruck, "You really do that? Go to hospitals and prisons looking for kids?"

"We usually go out twice a year. We'll make a special trip if we happen to get a tip, though they are rare these days."

"Do you find a lot? How many are here now?"

"On scouting trips we average five or so in any given year. And even then, most of them aren't full Holders. Right now, we have twenty-two Holder students enrolled, so with Ryland, twenty-three. There are about five others around Ryland's age who are not yet awakened, and the rest are spread out in age with four about to graduate. Though out of all twenty-three, Ryland is the only one who will grow to be a full Holder. The others' abilities are too diluted and weak to be of any real use or trouble to them. Before Ryland, our last full Holder was Chloe, and even she is severely limited."

"What do the Holder kids do after graduation? Do they stay like Chloe has?"

"No. Usually they go off to a college or University and start their lives just like anyone else would, or sometimes the ones with families will go home. Occasionally Jocelyn will hear from a graduate, but not often. When we teach the Holder student about their abilities we make sure to give them all the information they need, but we never tell them about the Order or any of the specifics that could prove... damaging. The only students we tell are the ones who will become full Holders, and even then, it's done cautiously."

"That's why Chloe knows?"

He nodded.

I shook my head slowly, bewildered. I had so many more questions about the school and the other Holder students, but I couldn't find the words. The only thing I could think about were all the terrified kids out there who were being locked away and abandoned, all for something they had no control over. "How..." I asked in amazement, "How do you do it? How do you keep going? It seems so sad."

Something like joy lit behind his eyes and he smiled. "No. No, not at all." He turned in his seat to face me fully. "I can't tell you how I felt when Jocelyn came to me and told me that I wasn't crazy and that there were others like me. It was like a dream come true. And now to have the chance to save other kids who are alone and scared like I was... it's incredible."

"Still, I'm sorry for what happened to you." I looked away, feeling the anger bubble up in me again. "I never would have let them..." I trailed off, not knowing if I was talking more to him or myself. What I did know was if I had anything to say about it, no one would ever hurt Alex like that again.

"I know." There was so much tenderness in his voice that I had to look up, only to be met by the most wonderfully soft expression in his eyes. "The day we came to get Ryland – the way you fought for him – it was the most amazing thing I'd ever seen. When I told you that I wish I'd had someone like you watching out for me, I meant it." I felt myself start to blush and looked away. "And as far as what my parents did," he continued with a shrug, "oddly enough, I'm grateful. No, really," he insisted with a smile, seeing my face. "It was terrible yes, but if it hadn't happened the way it did, I would never have found my way here. I would never have learned who I really am. It was a long road, but it led me here, and for that I can be nothing but grateful."

I looked at him in awe. He truly was the most amazing person I'd ever met. To have gone through something so horrible at so young an age. I knew all too well how scared and lost he must have been – I'd seen it in Ryland's eyes countless times before. But Ryland had me; for Alex there'd been no one. Before I even realized what I was doing, I leaned forward, wrapped my arms around his neck, and hugged him.

"I'm sorry," I said softly, my cheek resting against the warmth of his neck.

He stiffened, and for an embarrassing moment I thought he was going to push me away. However, after what felt like two years – though couldn't have been more than two seconds – I felt his arms slide around my waist and his head sink into my shoulder. I breathed in the scent coming off his hair, which was sweet and musky with the tiniest bit of cologne. The headiness of it was invigorating, making my skin tingle and my pulse begin to pound.

I pulled back – though probably not as far as I should have – and looked up at him. "I'm sorry for earlier," I said, feeling like a total ass for whining about Jocelyn to someone who'd had it so much worse than I ever had.

Immediately his eyebrows furrowed. "Don't," he said, shaking his head. Then, without seeming conscious of the action, his hand came up and slowly brushed the stray hairs away from my face, softly grazing my cheek. My heart lurched and sputtered, and I prayed he couldn't feel my hands shake against his shoulders. Holding my eyes with a look that made my stomach tight, he continued, "Don't ever apologize for saying how you feel."

I opened my mouth to speak, but suddenly out of nowhere, he dropped his arms like they were lead weights and stood. "I need to get back," he said quickly, shoving his hands in his pockets and not meeting my eyes.

"Oh, OK," I said, trying not to seem let down.

"Can you find your way back?" he asked, walking past me.

He didn't want to walk with me?

"Sure, no problem," I said, which was of course a lie, but if he wasn't going to offer to take me back, I certainly wasn't about to ask.

He paused at the edge of the tree's canopy and looked back at me – or more accurately, looked at the ground right in front of me.

"Are you free later tonight? We really do need to talk about Ryland. Can you meet me at the rotunda, say around six?"

"Sure, six is fine."

With that, he walked back the way we'd come, only to break into a jog a few yards away from the tree.

9

Two hours, a ripped shirt, and a skinned knee later, I finally stumbled back into civilization, exhausted and frustrated. Alex's pace had ensured that I was unable to follow him, and I must have taken a wrong turn somewhere.

I had seen enough of the Irish woods to last me several years, and was beyond in need of a shower. Dirty and sick of nature as I was, even more troubling was the sudden and drastic turn in Alex's mood that afternoon. I couldn't believe I'd hugged him, what the hell was I thinking? Obviously I scared him away – or at least that was the only thing I could figure.

Though… he *had* hugged me back.

Regardless of what had happened to upset him, one thing was certain: I was not at all looking forward to seeing him again that night. I was terrified it would be as uneasy and awkward as the final few minutes of the afternoon had been, which would not be any fun at all.

As I reached the top of the short flight of stairs to Lorcan Hall, I saw a short blonde figure pacing in front of the large bay window in the Hall's main foyer.

"Chloe?" I asked, stepping into the invitingly warm hall.

"There you are!" she cried, running up and throwing her arms around my neck, "Alex was so worried!"

"I'm fine," I mumbled against her shoulder.

"He made me promise to stay right here and – mercy be!" she said, pulling back and seeing the state of me. "What happened?"

"Had some... trouble," I stammered, feeling like an idiot. "It's no big deal."

"Oh, you poor dear! Alex felt so awful for leaving you! I promised him I'd keep a watch out for you until he got back."

"Got back from where?" I asked, trying not to sound overly interested.

"The Order has called a meeting, but he - Oh! Mr Anderson!" she called, seeing him come down the main stairs.

"What can I do for you, lass?" he smiled, cheerful as always.

"Are you off to the meeting?"

"Aye, and it could run long by the look of it."

"Would you please tell Alex that-"

But before she could finish, Alex came around the corner, pulling on a jacket. "Chloe, I've got to go look–"

He stopped short as he saw me, acute relief washing over his features. Though relief quickly became horror as he got a better look at me. I self-consciously tucked my hair behind my ear in a vain attempt to look as though I hadn't just gotten the crap kicked out of me by Mother Nature.

"I am so sorry," he breathed, guilt stricken.

"It's fine," I said with my best smile, "I took a detour, that's all." I tried my best to sound convincing, but it was clear he wasn't buying what I was selling.

"I've got to go," he nodded over his shoulder, "they've called a meeting and we might be a while. I don't think we're going to be able to meet tonight. Tomorrow morning, same place? Classes start, so everyone else will be busy. We'll have all day."

"Sure, that's fine, don't worry about it," I said, hoping to ease some of the self-reproach he appeared to be stuck in.

He nodded, then looking me over again, added, "You should go sit down–"

"Don't you worry," Chloe cut in, wrapping her arm around my waist giving me a squeeze, "I'll get her all taken care of."

"Aye lad." Mr Anderson gestured to Alex, whose eyes hadn't left me. "We're needed yonder." Alex went without an argument, but looked back over his shoulder at me four separate times before turning down the main hall and out of sight.

So, he abandons me one minute, then feels horrible about it the next. Interesting… As much as I hated myself for getting any sort of pleasure out of someone else's discomfort, I had to admit that I rather liked the idea that he was worried about me. Plus, I was glad to see that he seemed to be over whatever funk had caused him to leave me in the first place.

With my spirits adequately lifted, I turned to Chloe. "I

should go shower."

"Yes, of course, you go and clean up. Then when you're done, come over to my room and we'll have dinner and a chat," she said, clasping both my hands in hers excitedly.

"Sounds great," I said, smiling.

I don't know that I've ever taken a shower that felt so good. Even the soap stinging my fresh scrapes couldn't lessen the warm relaxing joy for me. It was however, the first shower in which I had to clean leaves out of the tub when I was done. Fun.

After I dressed, I called my mom for the first time since we'd left for Ireland. I spent almost an hour telling her all about the school, and how well Ryland was doing, and assuring her that everything was great. Luckily, she didn't specifically ask how I was doing, nor did she bring up the subject of Jocelyn, for which I was immensely grateful. I would have hated to lie to her anymore than we already had, but honestly I had no idea how I was feeling about everything, and as far as Jocelyn was concerned, it was better she not know what had actually happened. Much as I had always wanted my mom to see Jocelyn for what he was, I couldn't bring myself to hurt her with the truth. She and Ry may have both been under a delusion, but it made them happy, which was good enough for me.

Once Mom was reassured and all her questions answered, I hung up, got ready, and then slipped on my shoes to go over to Chloe's room. However, as I reached the door I hesitated, my protective instincts rearing up. I hadn't heard a word from Ryland since leaving his room that morning, and I was anxious to find out if he was still doing all right. Wasn't that why I was here, to make sure he was OK? What if he needed me?

What if he didn't…?

Ignoring that last echo of a thought I went back to the phone, grabbed the card Alex had given me with his information on it, and dialed the number to his room.

"Hello?"

"Hi Ry." At least he was there.

"Oh, hey Becca."

"So how was your day? Did you have fun with the other kids?"

"Yeah, it was fun. Everybody's great here!"

"Good, I'm glad." Really, I was. Glad. "So, I was thinking I'd come take you to your first class tomorrow."

"Oh… um, sure…"

"What's wrong?"

"Nothing, it's just… I am supposed to meet some of the guys so we could walk together. A lot of us have the same classes, and…"

…and you don't want to look like the baby who had to bring his sister along to hold your hand. "Oh, yeah sure, that's fine." It really was. Fine. "I just wanted to make sure you knew where you were going."

"Yep, I'm good!"

"Good."

"I've got to go up and eat now, but I can come see you tomorrow after classes if you want."

If you want? Great. A pity visit. Fantastic. "Sure,

sounds good."

"OK, I'll see you then! Love you! Bye!"

"Love you t–" *click*

Bye...

Less than an hour later I was sitting cross-legged on Chloe's fluffy pink comforter, eating the last slice of pizza, while she sat behind me playing with my hair.

"I'd kill for hair like yours," she gushed, running her fingers through the curls she'd just let tumble off the barrel of the hot iron.

"No you wouldn't," I mumbled over the last mouthful of pizza, "Trust me, it sucks."

"How can you say that? It's gorgeous!"

"Oh, I agree, it's spectacular – when someone takes the time to do it. Otherwise it's a humongous pain in the ass. Most of the time it's in a ponytail or a frizzy bun."

"Aw," she said, stroking my mane like a cat, "it just needs some attention."

"Tell you what, chop it off, and we'll make you a wig."

"Don't you dare!" she gasped.

"Where did you learn to do hair?"

"Oh, I don't know, playing with my dolls, I guess. But I've always wanted a real person to practice on," she giggled, giving my hair a playful tug.

"You've never made-up your friends?"

"No, you're the first actual human head I've done. To be honest, I've never had many girlfriends."

"You're kidding!" I was shocked. "I would have figured you to be one of the most popular girls on campus."

She laughed. "No, not me. There was one other young female Holder who went through school with me, but she didn't care for my company. She didn't like being a Holder; thought it made her a freak. I, of course, was thrilled about it, so she and I didn't really get on."

"But what about the girls who aren't Holders? Didn't you get to know them?"

"I tried for a while, but when you have to keep so much about yourself a secret, it's hard to get close to anyone. Probably sounds odd, but I was happier to keep to myself."

"That doesn't sound strange at all," I said, glancing down as I rolled the hem of my shirt between my fingers. "Actually, I know exactly how you feel. I've never really had any friends either."

"How can that be?"

"I was advanced," I said, the last word tasting sour on my tongue. "I didn't move through school with the same group of kids like everyone else did. I was always jumping ahead and taking special courses, always the youngest in the class. By the time I was nine, the kids my own age didn't even remember who I was, and the ones I took classes with were too old to view me as potential friend material."

"We're a pair, aren't we?" she laughed, giving my shoulders a hug from behind. "But not to worry, because now you have me!"

"Yes," I agreed, ignoring the ache that came with the

knowledge that I would soon be gone.

"There! Done!" She hopped off the bed and grabbed a hand mirror from her dresser. "Have a look!" she said gesturing to the full-length mirror on the wall.

I followed her lead, using the two mirrors to examine her handy work. It was stunning! She had fashioned a series of interlocking braids that were incredibly elaborate, while at the same time loose and flowing. The woven strands transitioned seamlessly into a sea of bouncy curls that fell against the middle of my back. There were curled strands hanging loose at my temples and neck, and even a small jeweled pin in one of the locks. The whole thing looked delicate enough to fall to pieces at any moment, yet at the same time felt secure enough to withstand a tropical storm.

"This is amazing, Chloe! I feel like I should change," I said, suddenly feeling underdressed in my T-shirt and jeans. "When I get married, I am calling you up."

"Deal," she giggled.

"Not that that will be any time soon," I said, laughing at how her eyes lit up.

"You never know," she said with a dreamy sigh, resuming her seat on the bed.

"Oh, I'm pretty sure."

"No boyfriend, then?"

I chuckled, shaking my head. "I started high school when I was twelve and graduated at fifteen, which meant the only boys I knew were anywhere from two to six years older than me."

"That's not such a difference."

"Trust me, it is. Maybe when you are twenty-two and

twenty-six it's no big deal, but a fifteen year old seeing someone who is a nineteen or twenty? The US has laws against that," I laughed, sitting down next to her. "What about you? Boyfriend?"

"No, not yet." She fell backwards onto the bed and put her hands over her heart. "But I'll find him. He's out there, I know it!" Her tone reminded me of the way a kindergarten teacher would read the "and they lived happily ever after" line to a room full of doe-eyed toddlers. Suddenly, as if remembering something, her eyes widened and she sat up. "Anyway," she said quickly, turning to face me, "how's your brother doing? Does he like it here?"

Ignoring both the remaining sting from Ryland's continued dismissal of me, and the fact that she was deliberately changing the subject, I answered, "He loves it, more than loves it. I don't know if he'll ever come home."

"That's great!"

"Yeah, it is." I smiled, but I lacked enthusiasm.

"What's wrong?"

"Nothing," I sighed, rolling a loose thread between my fingers.

"You can tell me," she said, with what sounded like real concern.

"It really is nothing," I said, suddenly realizing that I actually wanted to talk to someone about it. "It's… well, I guess I never expected him to take to it here so fast. Don't get me wrong, I'm glad he did, it's just that this is the first time he hasn't… needed me." I looked down, feeling silly.

"Oh," she said leaning over and giving me a hug, "of course he needs you!"

I returned her hug out of courtesy, expecting it to feel stiff and awkward like hugging an elderly aunt you barely know. But to my surprise it wasn't. It was warm and comforting and actually made me feel better. It was shocking to think that I'd only met this girl a little over twenty-four hours ago, and she already felt like someone I'd known for years.

After a long moment she let go, and said with a smile, "It's his first day, he's just excited. You have to know he still loves you."

"I know. It's not that, it's more..." I paused, not sure how to put it into words. "For as long as I can remember I've had to take care of him. Protect him from everything; from mean kids who would follow him home from school shouting and teasing him, to doctors and teachers who wanted to put him away. I haven't even gone to college yet, mainly because I was terrified to think of what might happen to him if I left. I'm overjoyed that he is finally happy and with people who understand him and make him feel at home, I really am. But now that I don't need to constantly worry and look out for him, I'm not sure what to do." As soon as I finished, I realized how horrible I sounded. I was coming across like some self-centered psycho who would rather her brother be miserable so long as it meant she had something to do. God, why did I have to tell the truth? Why didn't I just lie and say,

"Yes, Ryland is great and I couldn't be happier" like I had to Mom? It wasn't even a lie. "You must think I'm horrible," I mumbled, not looking up.

I felt Chloe take both my hands in hers and give them a squeeze. I hesitantly glanced up to see nothing more than compassion and sympathy in her eyes. "You know what I think?" she said gently. "I think you are an amazing sister." I smiled, if only out of relief that she didn't think I was nuts. "I also think," she continued, "that you have spent enough of your life putting other people first. You've spent years worrying about Ryland. If he is doing well on his own, then maybe it's time to start worrying about yourself. What do you want to do?"

"I don't know. I guess I should head home soon. Mom is alone now, and…" I stopped at the sound of Chloe's sigh.

"You're missing the point," she smiled. "I don't want to hear what you think you *should* do, I want to know what you *want* to do. Your Mum is a grown woman. I think she can handle herself. And I think what she wants most of all is for both her children to be happy. *Both* of her children." She squeezed my hands again. "Not only Ryland. Now, stop worrying about everyone else for a minute and tell me what you want."

I took a breath and thought for a second. What did I want? College? A real job? That's what normal girls my age had, so is that what I should want?

"I don't know," I answered honestly.

"That's all right," she grinned. "The first step is thinking about it."

As she gave me a warm smile and stood, gathering up

the rest of the hair paraphernalia and putting them back into her dresser. I tried to wrap my mind around the idea of doing something only for myself, and while it was a pleasant thought it was also oddly terrifying and more than I was ready to ponder for the moment, so I looked for a new topic of conversation.

"Do you think they are done with their meeting yet?" I asked, eyeing the clock on the wall and realizing how late it had become.

"The Order? Hard to say. From what I heard, there was a lot to go over. They'll discuss Ryland of course, which could take a while, plus Min's guards have been tampered with and they need to decide what do to about that…"

She continued, but for some reason my mind hung on the "guards" comment. "Wait." I stopped her. "Min's what?"

"Hmm?" She stopped, thrown off a bit. "Oh, the guards?"

"Yeah, what is that? Min is the older lady you were telling me about, right?"

"That's her. Her ability allows her to cast spells and charms, one of which is a guard charm she can place around places to protect them. She always keeps several around the school for the safety of the students."

"And someone has been tampering with them?" I asked. "Like, trying to get in?"

"Oh, no, I'm sure that's not it," Chloe said, obviously seeing that I was anxious. "Besides, Min knows the moment something interferes with any of the charms she casts, and can fix or reinforce them almost instantly. Not to worry," she assured me with a smile. "Whatever it was, it'll have been resolved by now."

"Sure," I said, letting my anxiety loosen just a bit. It was good to know that they had special security in place, though the idea that someone was messing with it was bothersome. Regardless, supernatural Holder protection had to be better than the security most schools used, so I figured I couldn't really complain.

Still, I couldn't help but wonder why someone would want to break in...

"So what now?" Chloe asked with a sigh, glancing around her room for a new activity.

"Actually, I should probably get to bed. It's late and I'm supposed to meet Alex in the morning."

"Where are you two going?"

"I don't know; I'm meeting him in the rotunda at the end of the main hall."

"The Inner Chamber!" She bounced off the bed wringing her hands together in excitement, "He's taking you to the Inner Chamber! Oh, just wait till you see it, it's amazing!"

"The what?" I asked, pulling on my shoes.

"They call it the Inner Chamber, it's where the Order meets and where they store all the artifacts, and books, and of course, the Iris."

"What's that?"

"Alex will tell you all about it," she said, shooing me out of the room, "Now go get some sleep!"

"OK, see you tomorrow," I laughed.

"Have fun!" she called after me.

I waved over my shoulder before turning down the hall to my room, wondering what this chamber had that could possibly be so great. I had no idea, but whatever it was, if a girl who could literally see the future thought it was awesome, I figured it must be pretty cool.

10

The next morning, I had made it all the way down to the main entryway – without getting lost, I might add – on my way to meet Alex, when I heard someone calling my name.

"Becca, lass!"

I looked over toward the lounge area adjacent to the main foyer, to find Mr Anderson waving to me.

"We don't need a second opinion! You lost, take it like a man!" a second voice chided.

"We need a second opinion because you're a rotten cheat, and I don't trust you far as I can throw you!"

I entered the lounge area, where Mr Anderson and the bald-headed man from the office eavesdropping incident yesterday were standing side by side in the corner of the room, looking down and pointing at the floor.

"Here now, lass," Mr Anderson said seeing me. "Come over here, and tell us which is closer."

I stepped up to see what they were hovering over, to find several square-shaped folded pieces of paper scattered across the floor. Two of which seemed to be almost exactly the same distance away from a small red dot taped to the floor.

"Bocci?" I asked, remembering a similar game we played in gym.

"In Italy it's bocci, in Ireland it's bowls," the bald man said, extending his hand toward me. "Duncan Reid, Miss Ingle, it's a pleasure."

"Becca, please," I said, shaking his hand. He had large hands though he was very skinny, and had a slight accent that I couldn't quite place.

"Now," he said, mockingly apologetic, "if you could do us a favor and put this poor, blind fool out of his misery and inform him that he's lost–"

"No you don't!" Mr Anderson yelled, pushing Mr Reid away from me. "She'll do it on her own, with no help from the likes of a cheat!"

"I am not a cheat! You are a sore loser, sir!"

"Well," I mused, looking it over, "the corner of the one on the right is a tiny bit closer."

"Ha ha!" Mr Reid laughed, clearly the owner of the right square.

"That's because you moved it!" Mr Anderson insisted.

"You want to see me move it," Mr Reid said, exacerbated. "I'll move it!"

At that moment all the paper squares came flying up off the floor and straight into Mr Anderson's face like a flock of attacking seagulls. They then started to hover around him, slapping him in the face, poking him on the nose, ruffling at his hair. I gave a yelp, and looked up to Mr Reid, expecting him to go to his friend's aid, but he simply stood there watching and chuckling, looking vastly amused.

Then it dawned on me. "Are you doing that?" I asked, as Mr Anderson began swatting at the flying papers as he would a swarm of bees, cursing under his breath.

Mr Reid nodded. "It's what I do. Did no one tell you? I'm a Kinetic, I can move objects without touching them."

"Oh, so that's why he thinks you cheated?" I asked, watching the assault on Mr Anderson, with wonder. "Can you move anything, or does it have to be something light?"

"Anything," he said. "Here, have a seat."

No sooner had he finished the sentence than a large upholstered armchair slid across the room, stopping just behind me.

"You're not worried he'll retaliate?" I asked, taking a seat while trying not to laugh at Mr Anderson, who was becoming winded.

"Him? No, he's good as useless," said Mr Reid clearly enjoying the show. "He's an Imparter. All he can do is put words in people's heads. Talk to them without physically talking. No real threat in that."

"I'll show you a threat!" Mr Anderson panted, still trying to fight off the attack.

Mr Reid was silent, but his eyebrows rose a few seconds later, looking mockingly scandalized. "Well," he said, obviously having just received an imparted message from Mr Anderson, "that wasn't very nice. There is a lady present, you know."

"Aye, and you're lucky for that!"

"What did I tell you two about dragging innocent bystanders into your nonsense?"

The flying papers fell to the floor and we all looked over to see Alex in the doorway, thumbs hooked in his pockets, shaking his head.

"Reid cheated!" Mr Anderson said, hunched over, catching his breath.

"Of course. As always, you lost, so I must have cheated!"

Alex caught my eye and motioned for me to follow him as he turned to go. I walked past Mr Anderson and Mr Reid, carefully stepping around the strewn paper squares, leaving the men to their argument. It sounded as though they might be squabbling until dinner, which was why I was shocked when, just as Alex and I turned the corner, I heard Mr Reid ask, "Do you want to go again?" to which Mr Anderson replied, "Of course, why not?" Alex chuckled under his breath, shaking his head.

"Are they always like that?" I asked.

"Are you kidding? You should see them on Scrabble night," Alex laughed. After a moment, he continued more soberly. "I'm glad you came down. I was worried that, after yesterday..." He grimaced, looking guilty.

"It's fine," I assured him. "Really. No big deal. I made it back in one piece, and last night I hung out with Chloe."

As we approached the rotunda he pulled a set of keys out of his pocket and began flipping through them. "I hope she isn't bothering you," he said glancing up at me.

"Chloe? No, not at all. Why?"

"She's a wonderful person," he said, singling out one of the keys on the ring. "I only ask, because I know how excited she is to have another girl around, and I don't want her to overwhelm you. I love her like a sister, but she can be a little overzealous at times."

"No, she's great," I assured him. "I can definitely see what you mean, but honestly, I like it," I told him a bit sheepishly as we arrived at the only door in the rotunda. "I sort of missed out on all the typical girlfriend stuff when I was growing up."

"Well, in that case you're in luck. If there is anyone on earth who can get you caught up on all things girly, it's Chloe."

"I believe it."

"All right," he said, sliding the key he'd selected into the large lock on the door. "You ready?"

"Um, sure, I guess. What are we doing?"

"Remember on the plane when I told you there were some things I wanted you to see?" he asked with a smile as he held the door open for me.

I stepped into a large circular room with an antique marble floor and a high-domed ceiling. There were tapestries on the walls that I could tell were very old, as well as shelves filled with books and artifacts, each one looking far too valuable to even as much as breathe near, much less touch. Everything in the room felt as though it was from a different era. Even the metal lighting sconces on the walls looked like they had at one time held torches and had since been wired for modern lights. The whole thing was like stepping into another world;

all we needed was a round table and some knights, and we could be in Camelot.

"This is incredible," I breathed, tilting my head back and admiring the domed ceiling.

"We call it the Inner Chamber, and only a few people have access. It's where all the sacred artifacts are housed, and where we hold meetings of the Order – or we used to anyway. Lately we've been going to Jocelyn's office so we don't have to stand the whole time," he said, gesturing to the lack of chairs.

"Chloe mentioned that, what is it?"

"The Order? A small group of Holders all dedicated to... Well, let's just say a common goal. Jocelyn is in charge, and then there's myself, Mr Anderson, Mr Reid, Taron, and a woman named Min Stetz, who will actually be joining us here in a minute. There are a few others who help us on occasion, but they don't reside here year round like the rest of us."

"And what does this 'Super Human Squad' do?"

"This what?" he laughed.

"Come on, 'Order' is a bit stuffy, don't you think?"

"Yes, and Super Human Squad sounds like a really bad cartoon," he teased, as we began to slowly walk around the parameter of the room.

I nodded, giving him that. "So, what does the Order do?"

"Long ago, Holders used their abilities for the good of everyone. They were often peace keepers, or healers, always using their powers either discreetly or not at all. But," he paused, taking a breath and growing serious, "over the last few centuries or so, with our numbers dwindling, and the world growing, it became more about keeping our secrets, and putting an end to our only enemy; a man named Failghe Darragh."

"Who is that?"

"Darragh is an extremely powerful Holder. A Holder who believes that we are an advanced race, superior to average humans."

"Aren't you?"

"Maybe, maybe not. It depends on how you define 'superior'. It's arguable that the lion is superior to the field mouse in most respects, but doesn't mean that all the field mice should be removed to make room for more lions."

"Wait." I stopped, turning to face him. "He wants to remove all the humans?"

"He wants the human race to be as he believes it should be: under Holder control. And if we let him, he could do it. Very, very easily."

"So, this Darragh really believes that he can somehow snap his fingers and run the world? I can't see how that would even be possible. People aren't stupid, they'd wouldn't just surrender and let him take over."

"No, people wouldn't. If, that is, they had any idea what was happening to them," he said, as we resumed our slow pace around the room. "Darragh is a smart man. He knows how to bide his time and work discreetly. He has multiple abilities, one of which is reading and controlling the thoughts and minds of others."

"Like Jocelyn?"

"Yes, except that Jocelyn is a good man. He would never use his ability to manipulate others, or force his way. He doesn't even read minds unless it is absolutely necessary. To be able to manipulate the thoughts and actions of others is one of the most powerful abilities a Holder can have, and isn't something that should be taken lightly."

"So, he really could take over if he wanted to? If you all let him?"

Alex nodded. "All he would need is access to one or two world leaders, or even simply to a large group of average individuals, to start a chain reaction that would be almost impossible to stop."

"Has he ever tried?"

"He's attempted things on a smaller scale here and there over the years, but we keep a close watch and have been able to control the situations. Though it's been a long time since he's made any sort of move, which leads us to believe he is waiting for..." he paused, glancing at me then quickly away. "That he is planning something."

"You told me on the flight here that Holders only have one ability each, but now you say that Darragh has multiple?"

"Yes. Darragh is the only exception. He is more than seven hundred years old, and over the centuries has learned ways of increasing his power. One of which is stealing and merging the abilities of other Holders to his own."

"And that's bad?" I asked, hearing the disdain in his

voice as he explained.

"It's unnatural," a female voice said from behind us.

I turned to see a short woman standing at the door. I recognized her as the woman from yesterday in the hall, though now that I wasn't trying to hide I was able to get a better look at her. She was sporting the same frizzy hair, but now most of it was tied up in a scarf. She had a long blue dress on, with bracelets and rings all over her wrists and hands. Something about her reminded me of those Russian Matryoshka dolls that all fit inside one another.

"Becca, this is Min Stetz," Alex said smiling as he walked over to her, placing a hand on her back. "I asked her to come and share her wisdom."

"Bah, wisdom," Min said, waving her hand dismissively.

"Min is our *máthair ghlac*," he said, bending down and giving her a kiss on the head. Then, looking up at me with a smile, translated, "Surrogate mother. And she's very modest. She knows more about our histories and artifacts," he motioned around the room, "than anyone."

Min reached up and grabbed his chin and shook it, then gave his cheek a gentle slap, like an affectionate grandmother might do to her grandson.

"She is also our resident sorceress. Her ability is called Alchemy, meaning she can cast charms and spells, and mix potions. She is also the one who forges and charms our Sciaths."

"Yes, and I also read *saols*," she said, giving Alex a wry look.

"What's a *saol*?" I asked.

"A person's life energy; their aura," Min replied, still looking at Alex. "Is there something you neglected to tell me?" she asked him, slyly.

The color in his face seemed to pale just a bit. "No," he answered, shooting her a look full of meaning that I couldn't decipher.

"All right then," she said, with a "we'll discuss this later" look.

He cleared his throat. "I was telling her about Darragh," he told Min, a little louder than needed.

Min shook her head sadly. "Unnatural," she said again. "No one should have more than one gift. That is not the way it was meant to be. Would you steal the head of another because you wished to be smarter? Would you take the legs of a man because you wished to be faster? Darragh was gifted with an ability as the rest of us were, but that was not enough for him. He could not see his gift for the blessing that it was, he only saw power. And he wanted more. Even if it meant he had to take it."

"How does he do that?" I asked.

"We don't know for sure," Alex said, "but we do know that the Holder he takes from doesn't survive."

"He kills them?" I whispered.

"He has to, there is no other way," Min said. "In order to take the ability of another, you must take their life force. The two cannot be separated."

My stomach turned when I thought about how cold a man like that would have to be. If that was the way he treated others of his own race, what would he do to the hundreds of thousands of humans he felt were beneath him?

"If he has every ability there is, how do you stop him?" I asked, wondering if they were fighting a lost cause.

"He does not have every ability," Min said. "He has many, that is true. More than we are aware of, I am sure. But there are many he does not yet possess, including the one he wants most of all."

She motioned for me to follow her as she made her way over to a large table on the opposite side of the room. There were several items on it, the largest of which was a black box in the center with a clear glass lid.

"The Iris," she said, resting her hand on the box. "This is what he wants. The one thing he cannot have."

I looked in the box to see a large circular medallion, about half an inch thick and six inches in diameter. She'd called it the Iris, and I supposed it did look something like an eye; the design on the face consisting of three circles, one inside the other. The outer and innermost circles – which on an eye would have been the whites and pupil – were pewter and had intricate Celtic knots engraved all over the surface. The middle "iris" circle was shiny and black, and made of glass, or possibly a smooth stone, I couldn't tell.

"What is it?" I asked, leaning forward for a closer look.

"It's called *Dubh Inteachán*; the Black Iris. It was forged over two thousand years ago by one of the most powerful Alchemists in history," Alex said, stepping up behind me.

"It was said," Min began in what I can only imagine

was her best "come gather around the campfire" voice, "that he dreamt one night of a time far in the future, when the Holderkind would face a great enemy. In his dream there was a great battle, in which all the Holders were killed. He believed that his dream was a sign. It took him over a year of constant work, but finally the Iris was completed."

"So, what does it do?" I asked.

"Well…" Alex paused, scratching the back of his head and glancing over to Min. "We're not really sure."

"Not sure? It sounds like kind of a big deal; shouldn't you maybe look into that?"

"We can't know for sure what it does until it's awakened and used."

"OK…" I prompted, when neither of them continued, not enjoying the sudden feeling that they were deliberately not telling me something.

"You see, child," Min said, as Alex glanced down looking… nervous? "The Iris was designed so that only one Holder would ever be able to use it. The Iris's creator feared that it would fall into evil hands if left unprotected, so he put an unbreakable charm on it that contained a foretelling. He said that one day a great Holder would be born whose ability came neither from his mother or father, and he would be called *Bronntanas*, meaning the Gift."

"And, that's the guy?" I asked.

Min shook her head. "His son. *Mac an Bronntanas*, or Son of the Gift. He is said to be a mighty warrior with unrivaled courage and enduring spirit. He will be the greatest and most powerful Holder the world has known. The Iris will recognize him instantly, and they will work as one, overtaking any enemy in their path, ensuring the survival of the Holder race."

"OK," I sighed, closing my eyes for a moment. "Let me see if I've got this. You're looking for this all powerful warrior guy so he can come and wake up the Iris and use it to get rid of the Darragh guy?"

"Yes," Alex said, as Min nodded.

"And Darragh is looking for this guy too so he can kill him, steal his ability, and use the Iris for himself?"

Alex hesitated. "Um, well... yes. Or at least that's what he wants," he stammered, wringing his hands together. "But we're going to make sure that doesn't ever happen."

I'm not sure if it was the worry in his tone or the constant gauge of my reaction in his eyes, but my hands started to tremble and I felt my heart rate begin to climb.

"Wait a minute," I said, as the pieces began to come together in my mind. "When you asked me to meet you here, it was because you said we needed to talk about..." Suddenly, all the little hints and half thoughts I'd been hearing over the last few days fell into place...

...let's just say he's special...

...Ryland's case is very unique...

...he isn't ready for such a large burden...

...just a boy...

...we really do need to talk about Ryland...

Like a splash of cold water in the face, it was all clear; and the realization left me so furious and hurt that I could barely find words.

Alex's hands came up in an effort to calm me when he

saw my eyes pop open. "Let me explain…"

"Ryland? That's what this is all about? He's not some heroic warrior! What the hell are you thinking? He's ten!" I was shouting now, but I didn't care. "You lied to me!" I yelled, taking a step back from Alex. "You promised me that coming here was what was best for him, and now I find out that there is some psycho Holder out there that wants to kill him for his ability! How the hell is that what's best for him?"

Alex stepped forward and took hold of my hand, begging, "Becca, please, I didn't mean to–"

"No!" I shouted, ripping out of his grasp. "You," I breathed heavily and pointed at him. "You promised me…" I couldn't finish, afraid my voice would break as the betrayal sliced me like a razor. "You stay away from me," I growled at him, ignoring his pained expression, "and stay away from my brother!"

11

Less than a minute after leaving Alex and Min in the Inner Chamber, I was weaving through clusters of green and white school uniforms, dodging backpacks, and on my way to Ryland's dorm.

That bastard! I trusted him!

Why was I so surprised? What did I expect? Wasn't this the way it always was? Wasn't there always some ulterior motive? Oh well, it didn't matter. We were leaving, that much I knew. No way in hell was Ryland staying here even one more night if I had anything to say about it.

I ran up the steps to Ryland's dorm, burst through the door, and stormed down the hall toward his room. This would be easy: I would tell Ryland to pack his things, we'd go back to Lorcan together – I was not letting him out of my sight – where I'd pack mine, I'd call us a cab, and we'd be at the airport by 1.00. As far as I was concerned, the sooner we were out of Ireland the better.

"Ryland," I yelled, pounding on his door. "It's me, let me in!"

No answer.

My heart started to race. "Ryland, I swear to God, if you're screwing with me–"

"He's got a class," a small voice said out of nowhere, making me literally jump up and yelp.

"Sorry," the boy said, shrinking back a step. "H-he's in class."

I took a deep breath, pressing my hand to my thumping chest. Damn it, class. I'd completely forgotten.

The boy looked up sheepishly. "You're his sister, right?"

"Yes, Becca," I nodded with a sigh.

"Can I leave this for him?" he asked, pulling an envelope from his pocket.

"Yeah, sure," I said, taking a step away from the door.

The boy wedged the envelope in the crack between the door and the frame, poking it a few times to make sure it wouldn't fall.

"Thanks," he said, turning back one more time to look at me before taking off down the hall.

Once the boy was out of sight, I gave into my nosier instincts and grabbed the envelope out of the door. Written in pencil on the front was:

Ryland

I printed you a better one.

- Con

I opened the – thankfully unsealed – envelope, and pulled out a photograph of Ryland standing arm-in-arm with three other boys about his age. One of them I recognized from my visit to his room yesterday morning, the other two I'd never seen, but it didn't matter as none of them were the person I was focused on. My eyes were glued to the little redhead in the center, who had the biggest smile I'd ever seen on his freckled face. A smile that went all the way to his eyes, lighting him up from the inside out. I stood there for a long moment, feeling all my anger and pent-up aggression trickle out of me as I stared down at the photo – its message ringing in my head, loud and clear.

Ryland was happy here. For the first time in his life, he was *happy*.

With something between a sigh and a huff, I slowly walked back toward the front doors of the dorm, not realizing I still held the picture until I stepped outside and felt the first drops of the coming storm on my face. Not thinking to return it, I slid the photo into my pocket to keep it safe, and sauntered back across campus, barely noticing the rain. By the time I climbed the steps to Lorcan, hair stuck to my face and wet strands dripping down my back, I felt more like a zombie than a person. All I wanted was to crawl into bed and never get out, yet as I stepped up to the door of the hall I couldn't bring myself to go in. I followed the covered porch around the side of the building, and found a stone bench against the far-east wall.

I sat, looking out over the dark and wet landscape, deeply resenting the fact that my anger had dissipated. Anger was good. It was familiar. I knew what to do with it. Moreover, I knew how to make it work to my advantage. Screaming, shouting, fuming – that was what I knew. But now that my anger had dissolved like sidewalk chalk would in the current downpour, the only feelings I was left with were hurt and confusion – two things that I'd never done well with.

I pulled the picture back out of my pocket, looking again at Ryland's smiling face. What the hell was I supposed to do now? How could I take Ryland away from the first place he'd ever enjoyed being in? How could I let him stay knowing there was a crazy Holder out there just waiting for the chance to kill him? If I took him away, he'd hate me, but wasn't hating me and being alive better than loving me and being dead? I rubbed my hands up and down my arms with a shiver, more torn than I'd ever been, and hating it.

I'm not sure how long I sat there looking blankly into the rain, but it felt like a while. It was long enough for the two o'clock bells to chime from across campus, and long enough for my soaked hair and shirt to dry of their own volition.

I had no idea where she'd come from or how long she'd been watching me, but suddenly Min's voice asked me softly from a few feet away, "May I sit?"

"Shouldn't you be teaching somewhere?" I said weakly.

"I have only two classes this semester, both are held on Tuesdays and Thursdays," she informed me. "May I sit?"

I nodded and she sat, folding her hands in her lap. After a quiet moment she looked down at the bench where I had set the picture of Ryland and his friends and slid it over to face her.

"Do you know the other boys?" she asked.

"No," I answered, glancing down at the picture again.

"Brian and Connor Jones," she said, pointing to the two boys on the right. "Brothers from London. And that's Wally Couit from the south of France. Brian and Wally were in my literature class last semester, Connor the year before. Good boys." She slid the photo back over beside me and looked out over the grounds. "Ryland is happy."

I wasn't sure if she was asking, or simply making an observation based on the picture, but either way, I wasn't about to be caught in a trap. "Yes, he is. And how happy will he be when he finds out that there is a man out there who has been waiting hundreds of years to kill him? How happy will he be when he finds out that the only reason he was brought here is so that a bunch of people he doesn't know can use him for an ability he's not aware he has."

"That is not true," she said, calmly turning to face me.

"That's certainly what it sounded like."

"I know you will find this hard to believe, but the best thing for Ryland is to be here, where he is protected."

With a flare in my chest, my anger was back. I stood and rounded to face her, while she sat calmly looking up at me. "Why all of a sudden, does everyone else get to decide what's best for him? Who do you people think you are? I have always looked out for him! Always taken care of him! And now I'm supposed to just hand his welfare over to a bunch of people I hardly know, including his 'father' who ran out on him less than two weeks after he was born? I have always known what is best for him! People like you have been trying to take him away almost his entire life, and I have always been there to save him, and I'm sure as hell not going to stop now, just because Ryland's feelings might get hurt!"

"Shush, shush, shush," Min hushed soothingly, sliding over on the bench, taking my trembling hand in hers and pulling me back into the seat.

"I can't let him get hurt," I said weakly, slumping down next to her, exhausted.

"And you think that taking him away is the best way to do that?" She patted my hand, which she still held, and lifted my chin with her free hand, forcing me to look at her. "Ryland is safer here than anywhere else in the world, that is why we brought him here. Darragh can get to him anywhere else – anywhere but St Brigid's. Neither Darragh, nor any of his accomplices, can enter the school grounds. The guards I cast have made sure of that.

I was immediately reminded of my conversation with Chloe the night before. "Yeah, from what I hear, someone has been trying to find a way through your guards."

Min sighed. "Yes, that is true."

"Is it one of them?" I demanded, already fairly certain I knew the answer. "Is it someone after Ry?"

To her credit, she did not bother denying it. "We believe so, yes."

"And you still expect me to believe he's safe here? This only *proves* he's not safe!"

"On the contrary," Min countered calmly, "it only proves how safe he is. Yes, someone has tried to breach my guards, and yes, we suspect that person's intention was to get hold of Ryland, but the most important thing is that they were unsuccessful. My guards not only held, but also served to alert us to the threat, allowing extra precautions to be made. I have not only strengthened the charms protecting the school, but I have also added one to Ryland's dormitory. No one can remove him from it, or from the campus itself against his will – not even you," she smiled, chucking me under the chin. "He needs to be here, where we can protect him properly. Taking him away will only add to the danger. Moreover, we have no solid proof that the attempted breach had anything to do with Ryland at all. Of course we must act on the side of caution, but there is yet a strong chance that it was only a harmless accident."

I wanted to believe her, but fought it. "What about the Iris, you only want him…"

"Yes, we have been waiting for the one who can use the Iris, but the fact that we have him does not mean we expect him to use it now. He is not ready for any of it yet, we know that. The only thing we wish to do right now is test the prophecies we have been counting on so heavily. We want to give him the Iris, so that we can confirm that all is as we have so long believed it to be. Ryland will not find out about his ability, or the Holders, or the prophecies, or any of it."

"What, like he's not going to ask what's going on?"

"We will speak to him briefly beforehand, and tell him what he needs to know. Holders have been hiding from people for centuries. Believe me when I say we are prepared for his questions. Then, when the test is over, he will go back to life as usual."

"He has to find out about everything, eventually."

"Precisely – eventually. He will learn slowly, along with the other Holders his age. Then, in a few years, after Ryland is fully awakened, he will join us when and if he is ready and willing. He is young and has time; he will not have to find out everything in a matter of days as you did. I am surprised that you are taking everything as well as you are. Alex was right," she said. "You do have a little of the Holder in you, how else could you have absorbed so much in so short a time?"

"Yeah, well I may have reached my limit," I said.

"Don't worry, there is no more to tell. A few details here and there perhaps, but aside from that, you know all that we know at this point. The rest is all yet to be seen."

"But what about Darragh? You said that you thought he was planning something, and that he had to be stopped. It doesn't sound like you have a lot of time to just sit around waiting."

"We are prepared to wait as long as we have to. Forcing Ryland into something he is not ready for doesn't do anyone any good. We have been waiting hundreds of years for this. You can rest assured that the entire situation will be handled with the upmost care. You just need to trust us. Ryland is safe here."

The desire to believe her was getting the better of me, but I beat it back once again. "Why didn't Alex tell me? He promised to tell me everything. He promised that..."

my voice died off as I looked away, well aware that my remaining hurt at Alex's betrayal – or at least what I had at first assumed was a betrayal, but now seemed more like an irrational leap on my part – was clear in my voice.

"He *did* tell you everything. He may have saved the most troubling information for last, but he couldn't possibly tell you everything at once. And would you have come here at all if he had? Alex handled everything as best as he could, and he truly does care about what happens to your brother. He kept us all up very late last night proving that."

"What do you mean?"

"Most of the Order wanted Ryland tested with the Iris right away, but Alex insisted that he be given at least two uninterrupted weeks to adjust to his classes and his new life here, before we hold the teSt He was adamant that that's what you would want, and he wouldn't take no for an answer."

"He did that?" I whispered, feeling like a total ass for yelling at him the way I did.

"Without him, Ryland may have very well been tested today."

"Oh, God I was so horrible." I hung my face in my hands.

"Don't worry, he'll understand," she assured me, patting my knee. "You believe this is truly what is best for Ryland."

Again, I couldn't tell if she was asking or making an observation, but I nodded. She smiled, patted my hand once more, and stood.

"One more thing," she said as she turned to go. "Try to take it easy on Alex. He has had a much harder time these last few days than he lets on."

I wanted to ask what she meant, but the look on her face told me she wasn't planning on saying anymore about it, so I simply said, "I will."

She smiled and walked off, leaving me on the bench alone.

"Trust us," she'd said.

Could I really do that? Could I really trust a bunch of people I barely knew with Ryland's safety? Did I really have a choice? Honestly, I knew the answer was no. If I wasn't willing to give these people a chance, then Ry's safety would be all up to me, and how could I protect him from something I didn't understand?

I couldn't.

Surprisingly, the moment I made that small realization, the smothering pressure on my chest lifted slightly, and deep down I got the renewed sense that this really was what Ryland needed. I still had a mountain of reservations, but it was clear now that running wasn't going to be the answer. I promised to always do what was best for Ryland, and – much as I was uncomfortable with it – it seemed that at the moment, that meant doing nothing at all.

I stood and stretched, feeling much better, at least when it came to Ry. However, I was feeling increasingly awful for the way I'd treated Alex this morning, especially knowing what he'd done for Ryland last night. I stood and stretched before making my way back indoors, happy to get out of the damp chill. When I arrived at my room I found a brown postal box waiting for me at the foot of my door. I took it in with me and tossed it on the bed, before removing my musty shirt and jeans that still smelled like rainwater in favor of a cozy pink sweatshirt and black yoga pants. I washed my face, brushed and braided my hair, then turned my attention to the mysterious box.

The postal code told me it was from Mom – she must have posted it almost as soon as we left – and I opened it to find goodies galore. Three of my favorite magazines, a box of Oreos, a five pound bag of peanut butter M&Ms, a new tube of lip gloss, my fuzzy slippers that I hadn't had room in my suitcase to pack, and a card with instructions to share the loot with my brother, even though I was sure he'd gotten his own box. Last but not least, way down at the bottom, I found one of my favorites – three boxes of Kraft Velveeta macaroni and cheese – which gave me an idea.

I slid off the bed, pulled on my slippers, and went up to Alex's room, praying both that he would be there and that he wouldn't turn me away, though I couldn't say I'd blame him if he did. I knocked timidly three times then stepped back, wringing my hands together in front of me. I counted ten-Mississippi's before I heard footsteps, then five more Mississippi's before the door opened and I saw Alex – who looked horrible. Pale, drawn, and so tired it was almost hard to believe he was standing.

"Becca?" I don't know if he could have sounded more shocked. It was as if he'd never expected to see me again.

Though I suppose that was my fault. Immediately he was beseeching, "Becca, please believe me, I never–"

"No." I stopped him, guilt scratching at my stomach. "You don't have to explain. I'm sorry. I shouldn't have yelled at you. I know you weren't trying to... I just..." I didn't know what to say.

Fumbled words or not, they seemed to have done the trick as he smiled. "You don't have to apologize, I understand."

"Maybe you haven't noticed, but I can be a little over-emotional at times," I smirked.

"No. I don't believe that for a minute," he laughed.

"Have you eaten yet?" I asked, hoping to have the chance to make up for my horrible behavior.

"No." He narrowed his eyebrows in a silent question.

"Good!" I said, perking up. "Give me twenty minutes, then come down to my room... that is... if you want to," I added in a milder tone, not wanting to force him.

"I'll be there," he said.

12

"What about McDonalds?"

"Yep. Actually, I'm going to go out on a limb and say that the ones here are better," Alex said, leaning over and placing his empty bowl on the coffee table. "They have curly or 'twisty' fries, and onion rings. Not to mention the 'euro-saver' menu."

"Ha! As in, the dollar menu?"

Alex and I had spent the last hour sitting on the couch in my room, eating, talking, and laughing. I'd been throwing tons of random – and probably stupid – questions at him about how Ireland differed from the US, while he humored me with as many answers as he knew. The latest round of queries regarding food and restaurants had sprung from the Velveeta Mac and Cheese peace offering I had made us for dinner.

"That was really good." He nodded toward his empty bowl. "Thank you. You didn't have go to the trouble."

"It was no trouble, I was going to make it for myself anyway, and I couldn't have eaten the whole box on my own." I paused with a grimace. "OK, that's a lie, I totally could have. But I shouldn't, so really you did me a favor."

He laughed. "Well, thank you. You should have asked Ryland over, I'm sure he'll be jealous when he finds out what he missed."

"No," I sighed, pulling my legs up under me. "He likes to eat with his new friends. Besides, Mom sent him a box of stuff too, so no way is he getting any of mine." That last part was supposed to be a joke, but it came out a little too somber.

"Are you OK?" he asked, noticing my change of mood.

"Sure." I smiled, hoping it didn't look forced. I might have been a bit down with regards to Ry, but I was not about to turn into the whining ninny I'd been with Chloe the night before. I opened my mouth to change the subject, only to find Alex pensively studying me.

"Speaking of Ryland," he said, as though he were afraid I was suddenly a giant bubble and might pop at any moment, "there is something I wanted to talk to you about."

"Go ahead," I said. "I promise I won't freak out," I added, sensing that was his fear.

"It's about Jocelyn."

My nostrils flared, but I kept my cool. "In that case I promise to try not to freak out," I amended with a smirk, only half-kidding.

"Jocelyn thinks that he and Ryland should meet before we test Ryland with the Iris."

"Min mentioned something about testing him, what exactly is going to happen there?" In my defense, I really was curious. It wasn't just a ploy to avoid the Jocelyn subject for as long as possible. Not entirely, anyway.

"As far as the test itself, not much. We will bring him to the Inner Chamber, put his Sciath on him – or what will one day be his Sciath – just to be safe, hand him the Iris, and see what happens."

"See what happens? You don't know what will happen?"

"The prophecies say that he will activate it, but we're not sure what that means. There's no need to worry," he said, seeing the look on my face. "Abilities in general are subtle. Ryland will more than likely not even be aware anything is happening. Min will be watching his *saol* to see if there are any changes, and Jocelyn will monitor his subconscious thoughts to see if anything is triggered there."

"Earlier you said that Ryland would be a mind-reader like Jocelyn, but now you make it sound like you don't know what his ability will be."

"That's because we don't. He may turn out to be a Reader like Jocelyn – his hearing thoughts is a strong indicator that he will be – or he may have an ability all of his own. Or he may be normal and it's the use of the Iris that makes him special. We don't know specifically what we are looking for, but when it happens, it should be obvious. Or so we've been told."

"Nice to know you guys have a plan," I quipped. "I'd hate to think you were playing all this by ear."

"He'll be safe. I'll make sure of it."

"Can I be there?"

"Actually, it was decided by all of us that you should be there. We think it will make Ryland feel more at ease. We don't want him to be any more nervous than he has to be. Which," he continued hesitantly, guiding us back to the original subject, "is also why Jocelyn thinks it might be a good idea that he and Ryland meet before then. If the day of the test is also the first day Ryland sees his father... well, like I said, we want him to be as relaxed as possible."

I sighed, pursing my lips, knowing there was nothing I could do. Or at least nothing I could do in all fairness. I mean, I'd known this was bound to happen eventually, and – much as I hated it – I couldn't stop Ryland from meeting Jocelyn. Even if I tried, he was bound to meet him after I was gone, and if it had to happen I'd rather be nearby.

"When?" I asked after a moment.

"In a few days. It will be two weeks before the test, and–"

"Yeah, thanks for that," I interrupted. "Min told me that was you, and... well I wanted to thank you."

He smiled and looked down. "It's what was best for everyone." I noted a little bit of tension in the air before he cleared his throat and continued his previous thought. "The test will be a week from Sunday, and you and I can take Ryland to meet Jocelyn sometime this week."

"No," I said shaking my head. "Ryland can go, but not me."

"You don't want to be there?"

"Oh, I want to be there all right, but something is

telling me that it would be better if I wasn't. Ryland is going to have to start doing these things on his own, and I think we all know it'll go a lot smoother without me and my temper in the mix," I said with a grin.

"You might be right," Alex chuckled, though it was clear there was something else on his mind.

"What is it?" I asked.

He hesitated, looking slightly awkward. "You don't have to tell me if you don't want… I was just wondering, what happened, exactly?"

At first I wasn't sure what he meant. "With Jocelyn? You don't know? I'd assumed everyone here knew all about it."

"He's never mentioned it, and it's not something that the rest of us talk about."

"Well I guess it's not something to be proud of, is it?" I couldn't hide the bitterness in my tone. Everyone here worshiped the ground Jocelyn walked on. Of course he wasn't going to inform his fan club that deep down he's a commitment-phobe and a deadbeat dad.

"All I've ever known was that at one time he was married to his Anam, and had two kids: a girl and a boy."

"Wait, married to his what?"

Alex shifted in his seat, looking incredibly uncomfortable. "His Anam," he said reluctantly, then anticipating my question, continued: "It's umm… it's nothing. Just a… sort of a bond…" He scratched the back of his neck, looking away. "Tell you what, you can ask Chloe about that one, she's something of an expert."

Ah. Must be a girly thing.

"Well," I said, hoping if we moved on he would relax, "there isn't much to tell." I looked down at the couch cushion, not sure what to say. I didn't mind telling him, but I was oddly embarrassed, as if he might think less of me if he knew my own father didn't think enough of me to hang around. Hugging my knees to my chest, I decided to go for it, and hope for the best "He left us," I said, though I couldn't quite look up at him, resenting the emotion I felt building up in my throat. I sat there silently waiting for it to pass, while Alex waited patiently, knowing I would continue when I was ready.

"We lived in Maine when I was a kid. Jocelyn worked as a European history professor at the University of Maine and my mom was a nurse. When I was seven, Mom got a great new job at a children's hospital in Pittsburgh. She was about to have Ryland and the hospital said she could start right after he was born. The day Mom and Ryland came home from the hospital we started packing, and two weeks later, Mom, Ryland and I were on our way to Pennsylvania, expecting Jocelyn to follow us in a few weeks after his semester at the university officially ended. The day we'd expected him to arrive, Mom got a letter in the mail. She'd gone into her room to read it, and didn't come out. By that evening, my aunt Linda, Mom's sister, had come to stay with us for a while. I only saw Mom a few times over the next few days, and when I did she looked sick. I assumed she had caught a cold or something, and needed Aunt Linda to take care of Ryland and me so we wouldn't catch it. The only thing I couldn't figure out was why Jocelyn hadn't come yet. Aunt Linda was actually the one who told me that he wasn't coming at all. A few days later, when Mom was finally well enough to come out of her room, she tried to explain to me that Dad had gotten a new job running a school somewhere far away, and that it was what he'd always wanted, and that we should be happy for him, and not to be sad, and that maybe someday he'd come and visit me. I bought it too, until I read his letter. Mom and Aunt Linda were out on the porch talking one afternoon, and Ryland was sleeping in Mom's room. He woke up and started to cry, so I went to get him, and saw the letter on her dresser. It said that he'd been offered a position to run a private school in Ireland, and that it was an opportunity he couldn't pass up. He'd also assured her that, while his time with her would always be something he looked back fondly on, that he'd lately come to realize that 'family life' wasn't something he was suited for." I heard the animosity in my voice growing, but I didn't care. "Then of course he went on to say that he was really doing this for her, so she would be free to find someone who could give her what she deserved, and so on and so forth. All the same bullshit lines that people give who feel bad for doing something, but not bad enough to not do it. To this day my mom doesn't know I read it."

I paused again, my eyes having not moved from the couch cushion, as I couldn't risk letting Alex see me get emotional over a man so undeserving of my time. Though thankfully, the more the conversation leaned toward my mother, the more the hurt began dissolving into anger.

"It *killed* my mother," I stressed, finally looking up at Alex, wanting him to see the amazing Jocelyn the way he deserved to be seen. "She has never been the same. She loved him more than anything, and he tossed her aside like she was nothing; like we all were nothing. She didn't deserve that."

"None of you did," Alex said softly.

"And now, I come to find out that this whole time he actually had the ability to erase memories and control minds? That he could have saved her all that pain? Yeah, I know he doesn't believe in doing all that, but come on, you can't tell me that would have been worse than what he did? He could have made her believe anything he wanted! He could have given her a chance to be happy, to move on and have a life. If he didn't want to be with her anymore, he could have at least given her a chance with someone else. He owed her that much."

I stopped and ran my fingers through my hair, giving it a shake. I was trying very hard to remember that the man sitting in front of me, listening to me with such warm sympathy, had been walked out on by both of his parents, and that I was really in no position to be complaining.

"Anyway," I said to break the silence, though I was mortified that my voice cracked, "I'm going to opt out of 'family time'."

"Are you sure?" I could tell he wasn't trying to force me – like, say, Mom might have – but simply making sure I wouldn't come to regret my decision.

"Definitely," I nodded. "Ryland will be fine, and you'll still be there, right?"

"I'll be there in the beginning. If Ryland is all right, I'll step out into the hall and leave them alone, but I'll stay nearby. I'll make sure Ryland knows that I won't be far."

"Thank you," I said softly, truly grateful for how wonderful he'd been to both Ryland and I since we'd left home. Looking back, I really couldn't imagine having to do all this without him.

I held his eyes a second or two longer than I should have, trying to decipher what I saw, and wondering what he saw in mine. I'm not sure how long we sat there, but it was long enough to raise the hairs on the back of my neck and make my palms grow hot.

In desperate need of a distraction I reached down for our empty bowls, intending to take them to the bathroom sink. However, at the same moment I reached for his, he moved to hand it to me, causing us to collide. Instead of leaning back immediately, we both froze, our chests pressed against each other and – more notably – our mouths only inches apart.

I could feel his shaky breath on my cheek, and all I could think about was what his lips would feel like pressed against mine. Then suddenly, as if he'd read my mind, he began to slowly lean forward.

He was going to kiss me!

My hands started to tremble as I closed my eyes and tipped my head up. I felt his breath on my lower lip, tasted his warm scent on my tongue, felt the slightest brush of his nose against mine, and then–

Knock! Knock! Knock! "Becca?"

Ryland! Damn it!

We both turned our heads toward the door, and from the corner of my eye I saw Alex blink a few times, then stand calmly, take the bowls from the table, and walk into the bathroom, leaving me sitting on the couch in a – dare I say hot-and-bothered – stupor.

"Becca, you there?" Ryland called again from the other side of the door.

"Yeah, it's open," I called, rubbing my hands over my face.

He came through the door, all smiles, "Hey! Oh hey, Alex!"

I looked over to see Alex was indeed back from the bathroom.

"Hi Ryland, how's it going? You like it here so far?" Alex asked grinning, as though nothing had happened.

"It's awesome!" Ryland plopped down on the couch, right where Alex had been all evening.

"Glad to hear it. I've got to run, but I'll see you soon, OK?" he said, looking decidedly at Ryland and not me.

"OK, bye."

With that, Alex tuned and opened the door, stopping only when I called to him, "Will I see you tomorrow?" I realized that I probably sounded needy, but I sure as hell wasn't about to let him leave without so much as a nod in my direction after almost kissing the guy.

Almost... Damn!

He turned and met my eyes for the first time since leaving with the bowls. "Of course," he said, as though there could be no other answer.

He shut the door behind him with a soft click, while Ryland began digging through my goodie box from Mom.

"Aw! You got peanut butter M&M's, I only got plain! Can I have some? I'll give you some of mine. Becca?"

"Hmm?" I asked, still looking at the door. "Can I have some M&M's?"

"Sure," I said, lying back against the couch. "Whatever you want."

13

If there was one thing I learned over the next few days, it was that Ireland was nothing like the US. I guess I should have suspected that, but for some reason my subconscious had it figured that since the people in Ireland spoke English it must be a lot like home.

It was not.

Sure, there were similarities; they did (basically) speak English, though there were some euphemisms I was unfamiliar with, like "trainers" for shoes, and so on. My personal favorite was "feck". As you can imagine, the Irish dialect caused the "e" to sound a lot like a "u", which sorry, but I got a kick out of. Hearing that – *ahem* – word thrown around in casual conversation by everyone from professors to students was hilarious, and it took me several days – and a lot of suppressed giggling – to get used to.

The food wasn't much better. I have always been a picky eater, and unfortunately the Irish cuisine wasn't doing it for me. In the cafeteria's defense, they did try. The school hosted students from all over the word, and I could tell that the culinary staff did their best to cater to everyone, what with "Italian Day", the "Eastern Buffet", and the "American Specials". But, try as they might, putting a sign over something that says "American", doesn't inherently make it so. For instance, the "American Grilled Cheese" was grated hard cheddar, melted between two slices of rye soda bread.

No thanks.

I was anxious about breakfast as that had always been my favorite kind of food, and was happy to find that most of it was the same sort of stuff I was used to – eggs, bacon, toast, pancakes – except of course, the baked beans. Who in their right mind came up with the idea to serve baked beans for breakfast I'll never know, but it isn't a tradition I'll be adopting any time soon.

And then there was the weather! After a few days I started to wonder if an umbrella shouldn't be added to the national flag, as I'd never seen so much rain in my life! There wasn't a day without it, and you never knew when it might pop up. Sure, there were your typical storms that were easy to see rolling in, but sometimes a shower would sneak up, soak you before you had a chance to run, and then be gone again like it had never been.

Strange euphemisms, weird food, and crazy weather aside, my stay at St Brigid's was turning out much more enjoyable than I would have ever imagined. I'd expected to be little more than Ryland's sister, but everyone made me feel so included and at home it was as though they were honestly happy to have me. Min always greeted me with a smile, Mr Anderson and Mr Reid held a permanent seat for me in whatever the daily game was, and Chloe was always happy to spend as much time with me as she could. Honestly, if she weren't taking a few of the college-level courses that St Brigid's offered, thus requiring her to go to class once or twice a day, I'd probably never be alone. Alex was worried that it bothered me, but I actually liked it. It made me feel wanted, and Lord knows I wasn't getting that from Ry. The only time I even saw him was in the morning before he left for classes, and even that was only because I made a point of going to his dorm on my way back from breakfast each day to say hi. Normally I wouldn't have been so clingy, but after those first few days I realized that if I didn't make the effort I very well might not see him again until he graduated. Mr Popularity certainly wasn't going to any lengths to seek me out. Which, I had to keep reminding myself, was good, even if a little annoying.

The one person who didn't seem to want me around was Taron. He continued to ignore and/or sneer at me in derision every chance he got, but it didn't bother me, as he was a jerk. I didn't care how long he'd been with Jocelyn, or how trustworthy Alex said he was. To me, he'd been nothing but a gigantic ass, and I would continue to consider him as such until he gave me a reason to do otherwise – and I wasn't holding my breath.

Last, but by no means least, there was Alex. I'd worried that after our almost-kiss, fantastically frustrating as it had been, that things would be awkward between us.

However, when we'd met the following day he acted as though it had never happened, which was a relief…

… and, kind of annoying.

But as my only options were to either ask him outright about it, or ignore it and move on, I chose the latter. Better to be happy and enjoy what time with him I had, than to ruin everything by being needy.

We hung out together every day, without fail. Most days he would find me playing, judging, or just watching the Anderson/Reid game of the day. So often actually, that I came to expect him and started to look forward to that more than the game itself. He would arrive no later than four, and join us for a while. Sometimes he would play a round or two of whatever sport or contest we had going, then eventually he would casually ask if I wanted to take a walk. Sometimes we would in fact walk, while other times we'd find a seat somewhere and talk, or go to the cafeteria and grab dinner. But no matter what we ended up doing, it was always, hands down, my favorite part of the day.

The afternoon Alex didn't come to the lounge at his usual time was the first day since we left Pittsburgh that I hadn't seen him. I forced a smile through the last round of checkers, no longer in the mood, pulled on my jacket and walked out onto the porch, not really sure what to do with myself. Or more accurately, avoiding what I knew I *should* be doing with myself, which was go to the computer lab, finally make a decision about which school to attend in the spring, and send my enrolment forms in. I'd been thinking about it a lot over the past few days, and the fact of the matter was I was out of excuses. It was clear that Ryland was happy, and thanks to security updates from Min and a few conversations with Alex, I was actually beginning to believe that he was indeed safe here as well. Mom and I talked every few days, and I could tell that she was also doing well on her own and wouldn't need my help at home anymore. Everyone was happy, and there was nothing holding me back.

So why couldn't I do it?

Why couldn't I bring myself to take the twenty minutes and send in an enrolment paper? Why did I suddenly get a knot in my stomach every time I thought of going back home and starting a real life for myself?

I sat down on the wide stone railing that ran along the edge of the porch, straddling it, with one foot almost touching the stone floor of the porch, while the other was dangling over ten feet off the ground. I noticed a piece of branch from a bush, laying on the railing just in front of me, and started absent-mindedly picking the tiny leaves off of it and piling them up on top of each other. When the twig was bare, I tossed it over the rail and stared at the tower of leaves, admiring the fact that I'd gotten it so high. But then, all of a sudden, the top leaf began to slowly lift off the tower, and float in the air. The second leaf followed, then the third, and the fourth, until all the leaves were hovering in the air, only inches from my face. I blinked a few times, sure I was seeing things, but when I looked again there they were, bobbling gently in the air, like Christmas ornaments on a swaying branch. They hung there for a moment longer, then began to move again, arranging themselves into letters, and then words: May I join you?

I whipped around to find Alex standing a few feet behind me, smiling.

"Did you…?" I turned back to the floating leaf-message only to find it gone. Of course it was gone – it had never really been there.

"Sorry," Alex chuckled, as he came around to sit next to me on the rail, "didn't mean to scare you."

I gave him a wry grin as I brushed the leaves away. "All right… that was pretty cool."

"Thanks," he said, crossing his legs up under him and shifting to face me, "I try. I'm not bothering you, am I? You seemed pretty deep in thought."

"No, just thinking about school," I told him, happy to have something else to put my mind to.

"What do you mean?" There was a sudden seriousness in his tone that confused me.

"I'm going to send in my enrolment paperwork soon, that's all."

"Oh," he said, reaching down and pulling some long palms off of the tree growing just under his spot on the rail. He began twisting and tying them together in his hands. "Where are you going to go?" he asked, not looking up from his work.

"Well, that's part of the problem, I'm not sure yet. Probably Princeton. It's in a suburb which I like, and it's really pretty. Lame reasons to choose a school, I know, but it's Princeton after all. Hard to go wrong."

"Hmm." He nodded, still watching his hands. He hadn't even glanced up while I'd been talking, and I started to worry I was boring him. "Everything OK?" I asked.

He looked up at me, but didn't quite smile. "Yeah, sure."

Looking for a new subject I saw a few of the scattered leaves from the twig on the rail between us, and got to thinking.

"What do you see?" I asked, curious. "When you cast something, I mean. Do you see what you make other people see, or do you see what's really there?"

"Well," he said, looking thoughtful, "both, really. Mostly I see what I cast, but I can still see reality."

"You see both at once? Doesn't that give you a headache?" I was getting dizzy just thinking about it.

"No, not at all, but then I'm used to it. Here, I'll show you."

Everything around me went blurry and when it cleared, Alex and I were unmoved – me straddling, while he was cross-legged – only now we were on a long white-sand beach, seated on a smooth driftwood log. The sun was setting on the horizon, while the waves rolled back and forth, licking the shore only a few feet from where my toes dangled.

"Wow," I said under my breath in amazement. "Where's this?"

"A beach in the South of France. Taron and I were scouting near here last year."

"I guess scouting does have its perks," I laughed, looking around. "So, you see all this?" I waved at the scenery.

He nodded. "I see everything that you see, but for me there is also reality. I can still see the school, and the grounds over the top of everything else, but... I don't know, it's hard to describe... it's almost as though I can see *through* them to the alternate reality that I cast."

"Show me."

He smiled, seeming happy. I wanted to understand, and in an instant things around me shifted and suddenly I could see it all too. We were still on the beach, but now I could also see vague shapes and outlines of the real world that I hadn't been able to see a moment ago. Lorcan Hall, the rail we were on, even the outlines of each of the stones in the floor of the porch were there, but the actual objects themselves were transparent. It was as though everything in reality was made of clear glass and you could only see the edges and shadows of the shapes.

"I can always see reality, but it's also easy to ignore if I want to," Alex said.

"What about other people? If someone were to walk by us right now, would they see all this?"

"Only if I wanted them to."

"Would I even know if someone walked by?"

"You wouldn't see them but you could still hear them. Listen." The sounds of the ocean, which I hadn't even registered were there, suddenly disappeared, and I could hear people – students and teachers – off in the distance, returning to their rooms for the night, or maybe heading to dinner. "I can create sounds, and cover the visuals of reality, but I can't cover the sounds of the real world.

I can drown them out when possible," he said as the sound of the ocean came back, covering the distant sounds of the campus, "but any noise within a normal conversational distance, I can't do anything about."

"So, if I had said something in the hall the other day, I would have been busted?" I asked, remembering the way Alex was able to hide me.

"Definitely," he agreed. "We both would have."

The beach faded away as Alex turned his attention back to the palms he was casually braiding.

"Looks like tomorrow is the day," he said after a while, glancing up at me, "For Ryland's meeting I mean."

"Oh… right." I'd been wondering how much longer they'd wait.

"We can go get him in the morning. That is, if you want to go. I figured you'd still want to take him, even if you weren't going in."

"I do," I nodded, feeling guilty. "Honestly, I do want to go in with him, you know, just to be there for him, but… I can't."

"It's all right, I'm sure he'll understand. And for his first meeting maybe it's best that he does it alone."

"Maybe. Still, I feel like I'm letting him down. And I feel horrible for making you do something that I should be doing."

Alex looked up at me then with eyes so deep they might well have been endless. "I don't think you have ever let anyone down, Becca." The warmth in his voice made the back of my neck get hot, even with the chill in the air. "And don't worry about me," he added a moment later, "I am more than happy to help."

As I looked into his eyes as he said those words, something fell together for me. He *was* more than happy to help; I'd seen that countless times over the past several days. But it wasn't just that he was always helping me, he was always helping everyone. Taking care of everyone, the way that someone would care… for family. This was his family, where he belonged. Min, and Chloe, Anderson and Reid, it was even clear that he regarded Jocelyn as a father figure although I'd never actually seen the two of them together. He'd adopted them all as the family he'd never had. Though, I could also see that it wasn't just the people, but the Holder idea in general. From the way he'd spoken about the first time Jocelyn told him that he wasn't the only one who was different, to his vast knowledge of the Holder stories and histories, it was clear that this was truly who he was.

"This is your home, isn't it?" I asked quietly. I knew the question didn't really make sense, but I could see he knew what I meant.

He nodded slowly, his eyes never leaving mine. "It's the only one I've ever had."

Again for what seemed like the hundredth time since I'd met him, I was in awe. Instead of allowing himself to be defined by his horrible childhood – as so many people would have done – he took the opportunity offered by these people and this life to start over and make his own identity. Little as this realization may have seemed, it explained so much. None of the other Holders spoke fluent Gaelic besides Jocelyn, who I knew had learned as a child, but Alex did. Not only did he speak it, but his use of it always impressed me, like his flawless accent, or the way he would seamlessly slip in and out of Gaelic when describing or naming something he was particularly fond of, as he had done when introducing me to Min, calling her *máthair ghlac*, or surrogate mother. At the time it had seemed odd, but now I understood; it was the language of his heart.

"It's who I am," he finished, as though he could see the realization in my eyes.

No, I couldn't let him think that. Much as I admired his adopting and identifying with a new life, it was his ability to do so that was truly remarkable. His strength of character and courage in the face of everything he'd gone through – that was what made him who he was.

What made him amazing.

I shook my head, still holding his eyes. "That's part of who you are, but you are so much more than that."

He held there, both of us still as the building itself, and, I couldn't speak for him, but I would have been happy to stay there the rest of the night. Without willing it to, my mind went back to the night in my room when he'd come so close to kissing me. He hadn't tried anything like that since, but that didn't mean that I couldn't, right? It would have been easy, all I had to do was lean forward a tiny bit. Should I? Did I really have the balls to–?

Alex took a deep breath, breaking my train of thought, and the moment itself.

Damn it! OK, no hesitating next time...

He uncrossed his legs and slid down to the porch while I worked at regaining my composure. He brushed off his pants and tossed the clump of palms he'd been fiddling with onto the rail where he'd been sitting.

"What is that?" I asked, picking up the palms, which he had twisted and tied into an intricate knot shaped sort of like an X.

"Nothing," he said with a shrug. "It's called a St Brigid's Cross. Chloe showed me how to tie them. I make them all the time, just for something to do. Grass works the best."

Obviously he thought it was no big deal, but I was impressed.

"Let me run and get my coat and we'll go to dinner. I told Chloe she could meet us over there, I hope that's all right."

"Sure, that'd be great," I said, though I would have preferred it to have been just the two of us.

"I'll meet you up front," he said walking off and disappearing into the building.

When I was sure he was gone I hopped down off the rail and slid the little cross into my jeans pocket, for the first time actually admitting to myself that I was seriously falling for this guy.

Falling hard.

And if I didn't watch myself, I might not be able to get back up.

14

"You should come, Becca," Ryland said as we approached the hallway that led down to Jocelyn's office. "What if he asks why you didn't come?" Alex and I were walking him to his first ever meeting with his father, and every step he took seemed just a tiny bit slower than the last.

"He's not going to ask, Ry."

"You don't know that." He began dragging the toe of his foot along the stone floor with each step.

"I'm pretty sure, buddy."

"We've been here for almost two weeks, and you haven't seen him yet, you should come. Alex, shouldn't she come?"

He may have been right. I'd not seen hide nor hair of Jocelyn since our encounter in the hallway on my first day – which Ryland of course knew nothing about – and I wasn't sure how to feel about that. The idea of avoiding him altogether had been fine before he'd had the gall not to recognize his own daughter and make me feel like an idiot, but now I was done with hiding and avoiding. My only goal now was to show him that I didn't give a damn what he thought, and the only way to do that was to see him. Or at least that was what I said my plan was, though as aloof and detached as I tried to be I still wasn't quite able to give in to Ryland's pleading for me to join him.

"Listen," I said, stopping him and turning his shoulders to face me, "there is nothing to worry about. Alex is going to be with you, and I will be right down the hall." His eyebrows furrowed reluctantly, and I decided to change my game plan. "You've been talking about meeting your dad for years, and now you are going to chicken out?"

"I'm not chicken!" He crossed his arms over his chest.

"Looks like you are."

"Am not!"

"You better go down and tell him that Ryland's too scared to come," I said to Alex over Ry's head.

"No! You're scared, I'm not scared! I'm not scared of anything! Come on!" he turned to Alex. "Let's go."

"Nice," Alex whispered with a laugh.

"I'll be in the lounge when you're done." I grinned, to which Alex nodded, then chased after Ryland who had stomped off without him, more than happy to prove me wrong.

I turned back up the hall, trying to push past the knot that had formed in my stomach at Ryland's accusation. Was he right? Was I scared?

No. Fear is a reaction to the unknown, and I knew exactly what would have happened if I'd gone in with him to the meeting, and it wasn't something that Ryland needed to see. In any event, no way would I ever admit to being scared of anything that involved Jocelyn.

Luckily the lounge was empty, and I pulled one of the oversized armchairs up to the bay window and sank down into the soft, worn leather. Just as I was seriously considering taking a nap, I heard Chloe's singsong voice coming down the main stairs.

"There you are! I was knocking at your room not a minute ago! I got a new shipment of magazines today, come up and have a look at them with me!"

"I would, but I can't now, maybe later."

"You waiting for someone?" she asked, leaning over to look out the window.

"Ryland is in with Jocelyn, and I told him I'd be here when he gets out."

"Oh… the big meeting." She sat down on the ottoman at my knee. "Was he scared?"

"A little, but he'll be all right."

"Sorry," she said, standing. "I'll leave you be."

"No, stay," I insisted. "I could use the company. Besides, there is something I've been meaning to ask you." Ever since my talk with Alex about my parents, I had been meaning to take his suggestion and ask Chloe about the Anam thing he had mentioned, but as Chloe usually did most of the talking, I hadn't had a good opportunity.

"What's that?" She leaned forward, resting her elbows on her knees.

"What's Anam?"

She stiffened, instantly nervous. "What? Why? Where did you hear that?"

"Alex mentioned it, and when I asked him what it meant, he said to ask you."

"Wait, Alex said to ask me? Are you sure?"

"Yes... he said you were an expert. Is something wrong?" Why was this such a big deal to everyone?

"No, it's only that this was the one subject Alex forbid me to talk to you about... but since he was the one who told you to ask me–"

"*Forbid* you? Why?"

"He didn't say, but I assumed it was because of your parents. I know that's a bit of a touchy subject."

"Oh. We had been talking about my parents when it came up, so I guess that makes sense."

"But Alex said it was OK?" She was getting really excited now.

"Yeah, I guess it is."

"Oh my goodness, I can't believe I'm the one who gets to tell you!" She jumped up, resituated herself, pulled the ottoman closer to my chair, and tucked her hair back behind her ears. I bit back a giggle, thinking that she looked like a preschool teacher about to tell a fairytale to a bunch of dewy-eyed toddlers.

"Anam," she began, as though it was the most wonderful word ever uttered, "is Gaelic for soul, and it's what we call the special connection or bond that can happen between a Holder and a normal human. The legend says that thousands and thousands of years ago, when the Great Goddess of Ireland was creating all the people of the world, she blessed each of them with a tiny bit of her magic. This magic became the person's soul. It is what gave them the ability to love, to see right from wrong, to laugh, and hope, and dream, and care for one another. Once all the people were created, the goddess chose a small group of her favorites to give special powers to. These people would become Holders. But when she tried to give each of these people their special gift or ability, she found that the power of their soul was too great, and there was no room for the extra magic. The goddess had to remove a piece of each Holder's soul to make room for their gift. Then she took the removed bit of soul and made it into a new regular human, so that none of her magic would be wasted. And so there would always be one special person out there for each Holder – someone who is the missing part of their soul – and when they find each other," she sighed, laying her hands over her heart, "it's like magic. All it takes is a single touch for your soul to recognize its missing bit. They say the connection hits you like lightning, and you're never the same again."

"Oh. I've heard of stuff like that. You know, Plato thought that at one time humans had four arms, four legs, and a head with two faces. He said that Zeus was threatened by their power, and split them all in two, condemning them to wander the earth looking for their other half."

"Oh," she said, flipping her hand dismissively, "that's just silly. I'm not just spinning tales, this is real. Min has known many Holders it's happened to. She can even tell if a Holder has found his or her Anam without even asking. The change in the Holder after coming into contact with their Anam is so profound, that it's actually apparent in their *saol*. She says she can see it plain as day. Though sadly, she hasn't been lucky enough to find her own."

"You mean there is no guarantee that you will find this person?"

"No, in fact these days most Holders never meet their Anam and spend their lives alone. It's a bit of a curse really. The only person a Holder can ever be truly happy with is their Anam."

"So you're saying that most Holders are destined to be miserable? Oh, yeah, sounds great."

"No, no, not miserable. That's the good part I guess; you don't fully know what you are missing until it happens, and then once it's happened, you don't have to worry about it."

"And it's always a Holder and a regular person?"

"Always."

"What about the regular person that the Holder is bonded to? Do they get any say in all this?"

"They don't have to return affection or interest, but they almost always do."

"OK," I said, trying to wrap my mind around this. "So, a Holder meets this one special person, and then bam, they just fall instantly in love? Seriously?"

"Oh, but it's so much more than that!" She leaned forward, placing her hands on my knee. "It's having someone who understands you, and is there for you no matter what. They say it's like finding something you lost that you can't live without, but didn't know that you lost until you find it. It's said to be the most completely fulfilling, all-encompassing, incredible love imaginable, and heaven and hell as my witness, one day it will be mine! I know my Anam is out there somewhere," she said, a faraway look in her eyes. "And if I have to meet every single man on earth, I am going to find him! I don't care how long – what?" she asked when she saw my lips pressed together in an attempt not to laugh. "I'm serious!" she whined with a grin, swatting my leg.

"Oh, no, I can see that," I laughed. "It's just that I'm pretty sure I've seen this movie before," I teased. "Now, either the boat's going to sink and he'll die, or you'll eat some fruit, pass out, and he'll have to come and kiss you to wake you up."

She crossed her arms and glared at me as I giggled, though as offended as she was pretending to be, she wasn't quite able to hide her smile. "You laugh if you will, but it's true."

"You are really excited about all this, aren't you?" I sighed, sobering.

"You have no idea," she sighed, tipping her head to the side and closing her eyes.

It was easy to see why Alex had called her an expert. Hopeless romantic might have been a better description.

"Wait," I said, suddenly remembering. "Alex had said that Jocelyn had been married to his Anam?" Chloe nodded, sobering slightly. "So… my mom is supposed to be Jocelyn's Anam?"

"That's what we've been told," she said timidly, wringing her hands. She could evidently see that I wasn't happy with the idea.

"That can't be," I said decidedly. "If everything you just told me is actually true, then there is no way."

"This is probably why Alex didn't want me bringing it up until you were ready."

My blood began to boil. "Jocelyn left us, he left her! If this connection is so important and profound how could he…?"

"I don't know." She stopped me, raising her hands apologetically. "I don't think anyone is sure about all that, you know, with your mother and Jocelyn and all. He never talks about it, and of course we don't ask. I'm only telling you what we have always believed. Maybe you could ask Min sometime, she might know more about it having been here for so long."

"Right." I closed my eyes, and took a deep breath. "Sorry, I didn't mean to yell at you. I just… Sorry."

"It's all right," she smiled, giving my knee a squeeze. "No worries."

I sat silently trying to wrap my mind around the idea of a profound tie connecting Jocelyn to my mother, and quickly realized that I had no desire to think about it. It just wasn't true. It couldn't be. Either this whole Anam idea was just a story, or Jocelyn had lied about having a bond with Mom to, I don't know, create sympathy or something.

Luckily, before I could get too worked up over any of it, I heard feet slapping against the stone floor making their way toward us. A few seconds later, Ryland came barreling into the lounge, a big smile on his face, calling for me like he was trying to wake the dead.

"Becca!"

"Ryland! Keep your voice down! For God's sake, you're in a school!"

"Sorry." He rolled his eyes. "Hi Chloe!"

"There's the lad," Chloe said, patting the seat next to her.

"I just met my dad," Ry gushed, plopping down next to her. "Becca said I wouldn't go, but I did!"

"Did you now? And how was that?" she asked, shifting to face him.

"Great! His hair's red like mine, how come you never told me that?" he asked, turning to me. "You always told me I had red hair because I was weird!"

"I guess I forgot," I said, shrugging. Before he could retort, Alex's arrival at the door caught my eye. "Can you keep an eye on him for a sec?" I asked Chloe.

"Sure, sure," she said, waving me away. I left Ry to describe every detail of his meeting, while I went to get the scoop from Alex.

We walked down the hall a bit, making sure we were out of earshot before I asked, "How did it go?"

"Really well. He was reluctant at first, but it only took a few minutes for me to be able to slip out of the room without him even noticing."

"That's good I guess. Did Jocelyn tell him about the test, or anything like that?"

"He told him enough, though he made it seem very casual. Ryland probably thinks that it's something all the students here have to do, and no big deal, which is exactly what we want him to think for now. He knows you'll be there too, and doesn't seem worried."

"Good." That was a relief. The last thing I wanted was for Ry to once again feel nervous or out of place, especially when he had just started to fit in.

"Listen," Alex said, looking down, "I am leaving for a few days. There is a Holder who helps us occasionally: a Reader. He can sense other Holder's abilities and gauge their level of power. Jocelyn thinks it might be a good idea to have him here for Ryland's test, so Taron and I are going to go get him. But there's," he looked down again, hesitating, "there was something I wanted to talk to you about first."

"OK," I said, when he didn't continue.

"Well... I know you will be here for Ryland's test, but afterwards... I wasn't sure what your plans were. I know you had originally said that you would return home after Ryland was settled, but... well I was wondering if you might consider... staying."

"Staying here?"

"Yes. I know you mentioned starting school somewhere," he continued quickly, "but you also weren't sure where to go. St Brigid's has a lot of college-accredited courses you could take for a semester or two while you decide. Chloe's taking a few. I'm sure Ryland would like having you close. Anyway," he handed me a small booklet, "I got this for you to look at if you wanted. It has all the courses in it, and I was just hoping that maybe you'd think about it."

I looked down at the booklet, not really seeing it. I didn't need to see it. It took less than a moment's thought to make my decision. Hell, maybe I'd known all along, but needed Alex to bring it to my attention, or maybe it was Chloe's words from that first night telling me again to think about myself for a change. Either way, in that moment, I knew what I wanted.

I wanted this. I wanted Alex. I wanted our walks and talks. I wanted to be wherever he was. But it wasn't just Alex: I wanted it all. I wanted breakfast in the cafeteria, and crazy rainy weather, and girl talks with Chloe. I wanted random games with Mr Anderson and Mr Reid, and grandmotherly Min.

I wanted to belong.

I'd spent so much time thinking about how well Ryland was fitting in, that I hadn't realized that I was fitting in too. Hadn't thought that maybe we both belonged here.

"I know that it might be hard to be so far from your mother," he continued, talking faster than he usually did, "but if you go to Princeton in the spring, you wouldn't really be home anymore either way, and I'm sure she'd like knowing that you were with Ryla–"

"Thank you," I cut in with a smile. "I'll think about it." I took the booklet from him with a smile, knowing deep down that the decision was already made.

The look on his face took my breath away, and made my heart pick up in a way that was becoming all too familiar. Though, for the first time my swoony-joy was just a little tainted as Chloe's words echoed in my mind: The only person a Holder can ever be truly happy with is their Anam.

Alex was a Holder.

"I've got to get going," he said, unaware of my creeping disappointment.

"Sure, yeah," I said, crossing my hands over the booklet, hugging it to my chest. "Be careful."

He moved to leave, but paused, seemingly unwilling to go. Then slowly, he lifted his hand, and lightly brushed his fingers along my jaw and down to my chin. He smiled once more, almost wistfully, before turning and striding off down the hall.

I stared after him, waiting for the red to fall back out of my cheeks. I knew Chloe had said that a Holder had to be bonded to be truly happy, but who knew, maybe Alex could be happy enough with me for a while?

15

"Becca? Are you up?" Chloe called through my room door. "You're going to be late."

Ugh.

Was it seriously morning already? Impossible.

Alex had been gone for two nights, and I hadn't slept a wink and a half between the both of them. Ever since my first night here, I'd fallen asleep each night to the sound of Alex's feet gently thumping on the floor as he paced back and forth across his bedroom. I had no idea what was keeping him from a normal bedtime hour so often, and while I was curious to find out, I could never quite bring myself to ask. First off, I already felt a bit intrusive just listening to the sound the way I did, and didn't want him to think I was an eavesdropper. But moreover, I was afraid that if he found out I could hear him, he would stop, and – odd as I know it was – I was comforted by the audible proof that he was still nearby, even at night.

However, ever since Alex had left with Taron to get the Reader I had nothing but a yawning silence each night, reminding me that Alex was gone and that I was very much alone. It was dumb that I felt as lonely as I did, with Chloe right down the hall and Ry only a few buildings away. Though try as I did to ignore it, there was an ever-present weight on my shoulders that somehow I knew would pass only when Alex got back. Maybe deep down I was worried about him, or maybe it was his company I missed. I wasn't sure, but what I did know was that I didn't like it. It was uncomfortable and, honestly, made me feel like a weak and dependent little ninny, and I'd be damned if I was ever going to be anything other than self-reliant.

Plus, this lack of sleep thing was really getting old.

I cracked an eye open, only to be met by a blinding ray of sunlight streaming in through a crack between the drape and the window frame.

Son of a bit–

"Becca?" Chloe called louder this time. "It's past almost noon, are you even in there?"

"Yeah, hang on, I'm coming." I stumbled out of bed and over to the door, letting her in.

"Oh, dear! I knew it, you slept in," she said, as I slumped over the couch. "Alex and Taron are back with Cormac, and everyone is setting up."

Alex was back? "Setting up for what?" I yawned, ignoring the small burst of energy I got at the news.

"For the test. Ryland's test is this afternoon, remember?"

I rubbed my hands over my face. "Oh, hell, that's right. OK, hang on, let me get dressed."

Twenty minutes later – after Chloe sent me back to change twice, saying I should look "nice", then insisted on gelling and scrunching all the curl into my hair – we emerged downstairs to find everyone gathered in the lounge. Mr Anderson, Mr Reid, and Taron (oh joy) were talking with a man I'd never seen before, while Min was sitting by the door with Alex. As he looked up he gave me a smile that made my toes curl. I shook off the remainder of my unease, and stepped over to join them.

"Didn't want to get up this morning?" he asked with a grin.

"Chloe's been wearing me out the past two days," I teased, bumping her with my elbow. Cheap trick, I knew, but it was better than saying, "I was tired because it seems I can't sleep without you wearing a hole in the floor above my head" or something else equally crazy and looking like a total nut-bag. "When did you get back?" I asked quickly, hoping to change the subject.

"Late last night. That's Cormac Dullin," he said, motioning over his shoulder toward the stranger. "He's our Reader. He'll be able to tell us exactly what is going on during and after the test."

From what I could see, this Cormac person seemed a very pleasant man. He appeared to be in his sixties – though Lord only knows how old he actually was – and had that certain look an older person can sometimes have, where it is obvious that they were extremely attractive in their youth.

"Speaking of the test," Alex said, turning to me, "we thought it might be best to send Anderson over to get Ryland, if that's all right with you."

Mr Anderson was about the happiest, most laid-back

person I'd ever met, and much as I would have liked to be the one to bring Ryland over, I understood. If anyone could set Ry at ease, it was Anderson.

"Sure, that's fine."

"Well, I best be off to class," Chloe said, pulling on her coat, a small pout on her lips.

"You're not going to be there?" I asked. I guess I'd just assumed she would be.

"What, me? No, of course not. I'm not cool enough to play with the big boys," she sneered playfully at Alex.

"You know we love you," Alex said, wrapping an arm around her and kissing her head, turning my brown eyes green for just a second.

"Yeah, yeah," she laughed pushing him away. "All right then, good luck and I want to hear all about it tonight!" She waved and was gone.

"I ought to go and fetch the lad!" Mr Anderson said coming across the room, following Chloe's example. "Is everything ready?" he asked Alex, nodding toward the Inner Chamber.

"Should be. Becca will be here waiting for you, the rest of us will be inside."

"Righto." Anderson smiled, gave me a wink, then headed out into the windy afternoon.

"What did he mean 'is everything ready?' What's there to get ready?" I asked Alex.

"Come on, I'll show you."

We walked down the hall toward the Inner Chamber when suddenly I realized something. Jocelyn wasn't in the lounge. That meant he could be...

"Where's Jocelyn?" I asked, really not wanting to run into him without a large crowd as a buffer.

"His office," Alex smiled, probably guessing why I'd asked. "He had a few things to finish up before we start."

The large door to the Chamber was unlocked this time, and when we went in I saw that everything was as it had been the first time I'd been there, with one notable difference. The center of the room, which had before been open, now held a small table with two items on it. The first I recognized as the Iris, but the other was new – and hard to miss. It was an enormous gold cuff with a vibrant green gem set in the center. The cuff itself had to be over six inches wide, with swags of gold chains hanging from it, and gaudy decorative carvings all over the thick metal face.

"What's that?" I asked, pointing to the bejeweled monstrosity.

"That," Alex laughed, "is – or will one day be – Ryland's Sciath."

"What? You've got to be kidding! That thing wouldn't fit around his leg!"

"No, I'm serious," he said, though he was smiling. "You have to understand, it was forged centuries ago for a 'great and powerful warrior', not a skinny ten year-old."

"Ha!" I couldn't help but laugh. "It's hideous! It looks like something from the set of Braveheart. Is he actually going to have to wear that thing?"

"Only for today. We want him to have it on for the test, just to be on the safe side. After that, Min can reset the stone into something more appropriate. The stone is the only thing that really matters anyway, that's where the power is. Resetting can take a while, but like I said, Ryland won't need a Sciath until his Awakening, so we have plenty of time."

I giggled again, picturing Ry with this massive hunk of metal on his puny little arm. Poor kid would never be able to swim again, at least not without plummeting straight to the bottom.

"Becca?" Alex said after a minute.

"Hmm?" I looked up, still grinning, but sobered when I saw how serious he had become.

"Anderson and Ryland will be here soon and we should get ready, but I wanted to ask you," he looked down and scratched the back of his neck, which I'd noticed he always did when he was nervous or uneasy, "are you busy tonight? There is something I need to talk to you about."

"Sure. Is everything OK?"

"Oh, yeah, everything is fine," he assured me, with a smile that made my knees shudder. "I'll see you tonight, then."

"It's not going to hurt, is it?"

"It's not going to hurt," I assured Ryland, as we stood in the small rotunda outside the Inner Chamber. Jocelyn had a few last minute things to tell everyone before the test that Ryland couldn't hear. Mr Anderson had stepped in to listen, and Ry and I were waiting for him to come back and get us.

"And I don't have to do anything?"

"Nope, nothing. They are going to put this big bracelet on your arm, then give you a small metal circle to hold, and then it'll be over."

He kept fidgeting with his jacket button, nervously. "You're sure that's it?"

"That's it."

"Then why is everyone acting like it's a big deal."

"Who told you it was a big deal?"

"No one told me it is, but they keep telling me it isn't, and when something *really* isn't a big deal no one ever says it isn't, they just don't say anything. People only say things aren't a big deal when they really are."

I had to hand it to the kid, he was perceptive. "You're thinking too much," I said, trying to play it down. "I promise, you won't even know anything is happening. And wait until you see all the cool stuff that's in there," I added, trying to move his focus.

Before he could argue again I heard feet on the other side of the door and realized Mr Anderson was coming to get us.

"Everything will be fine," I said, stepping behind him, and placing my hands on his shoulders. "Just relax. You will be back in your room before you know it."

The lock clicked and the door swung open, and there was... Jocelyn. It wasn't Anderson at all. My hands tightened on Ryland's shoulder, but my mouth stayed closed.

His eyes were on me for a split second before they darted away. He stooped down on his haunches, to be eye-level with Ry. "Are you ready?"

"Yes," came the timid reply.

"Don't worry, it won't take but a second."

As Jocelyn backed against the open door, so that we could pass by, I did my best to keep my expression impassive, and ignore the way his warm affectionate tone with Ryland sent stabbing pains to my stomach.

Ryland took a step toward the door, but then spun around and whispered up to me, "Are you sure it won't hurt?"

I rolled my eyes. "Would I let anything hurt you?"

He dropped his head, resigned. "No."

"Then what are you worried about?"

He gave me one more tentative glace before turning back around, looking up at Jocelyn who smiled, and walking into the Chamber. I meant to follow immediately behind him, but paused, glaring at Jocelyn.

"If that thing hurts him," I whispered, chin up, looking him straight in the eye, "I swear to God, I'll kill you." Without another word, I stepped past him and through the door.

Min was already leading Ryland to the table in the center of the room, so I made my way over to where everyone else was standing and took a place by Alex.

"How's he doing?" he whispered, as I slid in next to him.

"Good. Better than me." Only after I said the words did I realize how true they were. Ryland was doing well. Nervous sure, but otherwise well. While I, on the other hand, had been putting on a brave face all day, but now that he was finally up there about to do this I was freaking out. What if he got hurt? What if it was too much for his tiny body to handle? What if he touched it and it blew up, or messed with his head, or turned him into some crazy–

The touch of a hand on my back brought my mental panic to a halt. I glanced to my side, though I didn't need to. I knew it was Alex.

"He'll be fine," he breathed, rubbing my back in small, somewhat shy circles, in an effort to comfort me. Had the situation been different, I probably would have melted into a puddle on the floor. As it was however, I was too much on edge. Ryland would be fine, deep down I knew that, but still, as much as I wanted to be calm, and as much as Alex rubbing my back did console me, it was impossible not to be nervous.

I focused my attention on the center of the room where Min was placing the huge Sciath on Ryland's pencil-thin arm. Jocelyn had locked the Chamber door behind us and was standing beside Min, while the new guy, Cormac, was standing on the other side of the table. Once the Sciath was in place, Min opened the glass case containing the Iris and pulled it out. She glanced first at Jocelyn, then at Cormac, to make sure they were ready. When they both nodded, she looked down at Ryland and held out her hand. The room itself seemed to hold its breath as she slowly placed the Iris into Ryland's waiting palm, and then…

Nothing.

Or nothing that I could see anyway. I looked around at the others to see if there was something I had missed, but they were all focused on the group in the middle of the room. I saw Min glance at Jocelyn, then at Cormac, then Jocelyn looked at Min. They were all shooting glances at one another, their looks slowly changing from expectation, to surprise, to incomprehension – but no one was saying anything.

What the hell was going on?

Finally I couldn't take it any longer. "What's happening?" I whispered to Alex, though I was sure the entire room heard me.

"I don't know," he mouthed, eyebrows pulling together in confusion.

"Well?" Taron asked aloud, for once making me grateful for his presence.

"I'm not sure," Min finally said, shaking her head. "Jocelyn, do you…?"

"No, nothing. Cormac?"

"No," Cormac sighed, "it didn't work."

"What do you mean it didn't work?" Taron barked, effectively ending my grateful streak. "It has to work. *It has to work!*"

"How can you be sure?" Mr Reid asked, more pleasant though still with a concerned tone.

"I am positive," Cormac assured them. "The boy has had absolutely no change in his ability, nor has the general power level of the room altered in any way.

"It's true," Min agreed. "His *saol* is also unchanged."

"How can that be?" Taron croaked.

"Perhaps there's been a mistake?" Mr Reid suggested "Could his Sciath be interfering?"

"He's too young."

"Age has nothing to do with it."

"He should be awakened."

"What if it's all been wrong…?"

"Was it done correctly…?"

Everyone was talking at once, yelling over each other, trying to be heard, but I wasn't listening. What was being said didn't concern me. All I was concerned with was the little boy still standing in the middle of the room, eyes darting around to all the yelling adults, growing more upset by the second. When his frantic gaze finally met mine, I waved him over to me. He timidly slid the Iris onto the table and ran over, hiding his face in my side.

"I'm sorry," he squeaked, as the commotion around us continued.

"No, buddy." I stroked his hair. "You did fine."

"It's not your fault Ryland, you did great," Alex added, laying a hand on his shoulder. He was now the only one in the room, other than Ryland and me, not caught up in the fuss.

"What happened?" I asked Alex, though it was more of a rhetorical question, as it was clear no one else there had any idea.

Ryland pressed harder into my side as the battling voices grew louder, and my temper began to grow with them. These bastards were scaring him! He'd done everything they'd asked, and they were making him feel like he was the one who'd messed up!

"Gentlemen!" Alex called, causing the room to fall silent. "Perhaps we should discuss this elsewhere?"

The expressions around the room grew soft, and in some cases even embarrassed and apologetic as they all finally noticed the trembling kid hiding behind my arm. Everyone nodded and relaxed, seeming to agree that this should be handled at another time – everyone except Taron. He was still up in arms, and wasn't about to let anyone derail his tirade. He snatched the Iris off the table and came stomping toward us.

"He will at least try it again," he snapped, reaching out to grab Ryland's hand.

"You get away from him!" I snarled from between clenched teeth, more than done with his obnoxious attitude.

"Taron," Alex said calmly, placing a hand on his arm, "we know how much you–"

"He's not leaving until he tries again." Taron sneered at me, shaking Alex's hand away and ignoring him.

"And I said no!" I pushed Ryland further behind me. "If you all can't figure out how to work that thing," I said, glancing down at the Iris in his shaking hand, "then that's your problem! He didn't do anything wrong!"

"Of course not," Min said, with a sympathetic smile to Ry. "You did fine Ryland, you are free to go. Thank you for your help."

"No!" Taron roared, reaching around me, practically shoving the Iris in Ryland's face.

"I said get away from him!"

I reached over and ripped the Iris out of his hand, intending to throw it at his flaky bald head. However as soon as my fingers touched the smooth pewter surface, everything around me disappeared and I was suddenly floating in a warm sea of light. All my anger and fear from a moment ago slipped away leaving me with a feeling so relaxed and happy it reminded me of how it feels to wake up in the morning knowing you have no reason to get up, so you snuggle down into the covers again.

Had I been upset? Why? Everything was wonderful, there was no reason to be mad.

Along with my sudden ease, came a heightened sense of sight and sound. In fact, all my senses seemed to be in overdrive. All around me there were colors swirling gently in and out of one another, and ribbons of sound that were so clear it felt as though I could reach out and touch them. In the distance I could hear voices, dozens of them, all interwoven into a single hum of nondescript sound, the same as you might hear in a large room filled with people all talking amongst themselves. All of the colors and sounds and voices blended together into a beautiful tapestry that not only surrounded me, but flowed through me, mingling and blending with my own lazy thoughts and feelings, velvet against my mind and tingling along my skin. I began to feel drowsy, and wondered listlessly how different this place really was from the world of dreams. Just as I was about to sink off to sleep, I heard an echo of voices that sounded like they were coming from somewhere nearby.

"We have to get it away from her!"

"Can anyone reach?"

"Duncan!"

I tried to listen, but couldn't focus. I was just… so… tired…

Then, like being thrown into an ice-bath after a sauna, I slammed back to reality, collapsing to the floor. I went to get up, but couldn't move. Tried to open my eyes, but it was no use. As I lay like a wet towel on the floor, all came back to me: taking Ryland to the Inner Chamber, yelling at Taron, the Iris, the test…

The test!

Everything I'd been hearing over the past few weeks started to spin in my head as my mind began to drift away…

"…a mighty warrior…"

"…only one Holder would ever be able to use it…"

"…recognize instantly…"

"…ensuring the survival of the Holder race…"

"…most powerful Holder the world has known…"

All of those echoes and more melded together, forming the last conscious thought to pass through my mind, changing my life forever:

It was me.

16

The first thing I was aware of was the comforting smell of herbs: anise, chamomile, and coriander, along with several others I didn't recognize. I wasn't sure where I was, but I could tell I was lying down and no longer on the floor. The lack of echo meant I was in a much smaller room than the one I could last remember being in, and the shuffling of feet told me there was at least one other person there. A pot was boiling somewhere behind me, and every few minutes I felt the pressure of cool hands checking the temperature of my forehead and cheeks. I lifted my hundred-pound eyelids to find Chloe sitting next to me, anxiously fussing with the edge of the blanket that was pulled up under my chin.

"Oh!" she jumped when she noticed I was looking at her. "Oh, Min! Min, she's awake!"

"Yes, yes, I see," Min said, coming into view, shooing Chloe out of the chair so she could sit. "Well now," she smiled down at me. "How are you feeling?"

"I'm not sure," I croaked over a dry throat. "OK, I guess."

"Here," Min said, holding something brown to my lips. "Eat this."

"What is it?" I asked, eyeing it.

"It will help."

That wasn't exactly an answer, but I let her put the small disk into my mouth anyway, figuring she was only asking to be polite and that I probably didn't have a choice in the matter. Thankfully, it was good, though a bit strange; like caramel, only crumblier.

As I chewed I glanced around trying to get my bearings, realizing that I had been moved to what looked like an office. There were shelves on several walls, some covered with books, while others held hundreds of glass jars and bottles. There was a small fire going in the fireplace immediately opposite the door, with several bunches of different branches and flowers hanging upside-down from the mantle, drying. The remaining walls were hung with scarves that looked as though at one time they had been vibrant and colorful but had since faded with age. Even the couch I was lying on had originally been green with little embroidered flowers, but the fabric was so worn in some places that it had turned a dingy beige and you could almost see through it to the stuffing underneath.

As I looked at the threadbare upholstery cloth it occurred to me how well I was actually able to see it; each thread and weave pattern was crisp and clear. Then I realized that all my senses were turned up a notch. Not only could I hear the pot boiling on the stove, but also the faint tapping of the seeds or berries that were being boiled as they bounced along the bottom. I could smell the potpourri of all the spices and herbs on the shelves, but could also pick each out individually, noting their small distinctions even if I didn't know what they were called. The whole world was brighter and more focused. Not to an alarming degree, but certainly enough for me to take notice. Like cleaning a window you didn't realize was dirty, and being amazed by the difference.

"Your *saol* is looking much better," Min told me, calling me out of my internal marveling. "Your strength should be back in full by tomorrow."

"What happened to me?"

"You activated the Iris!" Chloe said with something between excitement and concern. "But it drained your life energy."

"But..." I closed my eyes for a second, trying to force my sluggish brain to work. "Why would it do that?"

"It appears to be your vulnerability," Min said. "Do you know what that means?"

"Um... I guess. Alex mentioned something about weaknesses, and how every Holder has one, and that your Sciath protects you."

"Exactly. Though luckily it seems that your weakness is tied specifically to the Iris."

"Wait, what? I don't understand."

"A Holder's vulnerability is usually revealed the moment they remove their Sciath. For instance, if I do not have mine on, I lose the ability to cast charms. Were Jocelyn to remove his, he would immediately lose control over his mind-reading and be forced to hear the thoughts of everyone nearby. But you need to be in possession of the Iris for your weakness to affect you. It's very interesting," she added, almost to herself.

"No, not that," I said, shaking my head, wondering if I was in some weird dream. "What I meant was, I don't understand why you are telling me all this. I know about weaknesses and Sciaths and all that, but what does that have to do with me? That's all Holder stuff. I'm not a Holder."

"But you are," Chloe beamed, kneeling down next to me, her excitement growing. "You activated the Iris, or the Iris activated you I suppose, but either way it worked! Everyone thought it was Ryland, but it's been you all the time! You're the one the Order's been waiting for!"

I stared blankly up at her, growing more confused by the second. They thought I was the one they needed? "No!" I shook my head as if to clear it. "No, that can't be..." A small part of my mind remembered coming to that same conclusion just before blacking out, but honestly I'd been hoping that part had been a dream.

It had to be a dream, didn't it? It was Ryland. He was the one they wanted. I'd spent weeks worrying about him – worrying about all this power that he supposedly held, worrying about his safety and the man who was after him, worrying about his future and everything that was expected of him – only to now find out that it was me?

But then, that would mean... Ryland was safe. That he was normal. (Well, relatively normal, anyway.)

No one wanted to kill him.

No one wanted his ability for their own.

No one was depending on him to save the world.

He was safe.

Safe – because they all wanted me.

I should have been happy at the prospect of taking his place in all this, and there was a large part of me that was truly relieved. For the moment however, that part was easily overwhelmed by the dry lump of terror swelling in the back of my throat.

"I can't," I whispered, beginning to shake. "I don't know how... I... can't..." The air started to rush faster and faster in and out of my mouth, as my mind spun around itself, trying desperately to find something solid to hold on to.

"Shush, now, off with you!" Min scolded Chloe, chasing her up off the floor and away from the couch. "Look now, you've upset her!"

"I'm sorry," Chloe repented, biting her lip.

"Keep your giddy prattling to yourself, or I'll send you off! She needs rest, not you yammering away, scaring the life out of her."

"Sorry," Chloe whispered, sitting on an armchair on the other side of the room. "I'll be quiet, I promise."

"Now, now," Min said, turning her attention back to my panic attack. "Everything is all right – now," she said, placing a hand on my chest, stopping my weak attempt to sit up. "Breathe through your nose and relax."

"How can it be me?" I asked, ignoring her. "I'm a girl. You said that–"

"Yes, yes." She stood and reached over my head, returning with a cup of something that smelled both sweet and sour. "Drink this."

"No! Tell me what happened! Why did–?"

"I will tell you after you drink," she said, with a look even a toddler would recognize as a "grandma loves you but she isn't above spanking you" scowl.

I tried again to sit up, but couldn't quite manage it, so she held the cup to my lips. Once she was satisfied with the amount I'd managed to choke down, and my breathing and pulse had resumed their normal rhythm, she put the cup on the floor and sat back in her chair with a sigh.

"Yes, you are a woman. And yes, it is true that throughout history, female Holders have never been blessed with the caliber of ability that men have been. I myself am extremely powerful for a woman, though I still could not compare to a male Alchemist, even if he were only half my age. But the fact that something has never happened before doesn't make it impossible. You are the one we've been waiting for, that much is clear. And while we are sure of that, there is little else that we know for certain at this moment. Tomorrow, we are all to meet with Cormac, where he will read you and determine what it is you are actually capable of. For now, I have placed a charm on your Sciath that will block your ability entirely for everyone's safety."

"You don't know what my ability is? Can't you see it in my, you know... whatever it's called?"

"Your *saol*? No. While it did change significantly the moment you touched the Iris, it shows me only that you are a Holder – an immensely powerful one, at that – but it does not show me your specific ability. That is where Cormac comes in. In truth," she continued with a grimace, talking more to herself than to me, "we should have seen it. At the very least, that you were destined to become a Holder. All the signs were there, we simply weren't paying attention."

"Signs like what?" I asked, wondering if they were the same things Alex had mentioned.

"Your advanced placement in school, your maturity and protective nature, even your ability and willingness to accept and understand the idea of Holders in general."

"All that means I'm a Holder?"

"No, but it should have let us see there was a strong possibility."

"But, if I'm a Holder," I questioned, trying to put this all together, "shouldn't I have had an Awakening? Alex said Holders should awaken in their early teens."

"Should, should," Min sighed, shaking her head. "There is no 'should'. Especially when it comes to you. Your abilities are only a few hours old, and already the strongest I've ever seen, even stronger than Jocelyn's. In this way alone, already you are an exception, not even to mention your gender. Who's to say what other 'rules' we will come to find that you break. Never listen to 'should', because in your case I predict that many 'shoulds' won't be."

Her calm air and the fact that she seemed so unaffected by all this actually made me feel better. Maybe I was overreacting. Maybe it would all be OK. I did a quick check of my arms and legs and found that I was finally able to move them a bit, so I shifted on the couch readjusting myself into a reclined sit. Only after moving did I notice the odd weight on my right arm. Suddenly, Min's words from a short while ago came back to me: "For now, I have placed a charm on your Sciath..."

Oh no...

I slowly lifted my arm out of the crevice between my body and the back of the couch, praying that I didn't feel...

...that it wasn't...

God damn it!

"No, no way!" I moaned, staring down at the gigantic golden cuff that was locked to my arm. "You can't possibly expect me to wear this thing!"

The fact that Min actually had to get up and walk away to hide the fact that she was silently chuckling at my horror, wasn't lost on me. "I will reset the stone for you, but it will take time," Min said, fiddling with the stove, her smile still in her tone. "Until then, I'm afraid you have no choice."

"Oh, you've got to be kidding me," I groaned, rubbing my eyes.

"Don't worry," Chloe said, timidly emerging from her corner, glancing over at Min as though she expected a reprimand. When none came, she slid in next to me again, kneeling down and taking a closer look at my new, one-arm shackle. "It's not so bad," she said, with the same pained smile one would use to tell a good friend that their botched nose job looked great.

As I glared down at the horrid draping chains and deep-green gem, there was a soft knock on the door.

"May I join you?" Mr Anderson asked, poking his head into the room.

"Of course," Min said, nodding. "How is everyone?"

"All right, no cause for alarm," he told her, then smiled at me before stooping down next to Chloe. "There's the lass! Gave us a right good scare, you did!"

"What do you mean, 'how is everyone'?" I asked, suddenly acutely aware that Alex and Ryland were absent from this little party. "Where is Ryland?" I looked at Mr Anderson, then over to Min. "Is something wrong?"

"No, of course not, don't worry yourself. The lad's in bed."

"In bed? What time is it?"

"Just after five in the evening. You were out for almost three hours dear," Chloe said, patting my arm.

"Then why is he asleep so early? Is he OK?" I pressed.

"He'll be fine. He was a bit rattled of course, but it's nothing to fear. Jocelyn will explain things to him tomorrow. For now, he took the lad over to his room and put him into a deep sleep. All's well."

"Whoa, whoa! Put him to sleep? Like, screwed with his head?"

"It's perfectly safe," Min assured me. "This way Ryland will sleep well, without being afraid or having nightmares."

"Nightmares? He's not that fragile. Just tell him I passed out because I didn't eat or something, he'd probably get a kick out of it," I smirked, knowing that there were few things Ryland enjoyed more than having something embarrassing he could tease me about.

"Passed out?" Min said, as both she and Mr Anderson looked at me like I was out of my mind. "Becca," she asked, stepping closer, "what happened when you touched the Iris? What did you see?"

"I don't know, lots of colors and light. It was peaceful. Mostly, it made me tired."

"That wasn't tired, that was your life energy draining away," she said thoughtfully. "But was there nothing else? Could you see us? Anything around you?"

"No, everything else disappeared. Why?" I asked, their shocked gazes confusing me.

"That may have been all it was for you, but for the rest of us there was quite a bit more."

"What happened?" Chloe and I asked at the same time.

"In a word: chaos. The moment your fingers touched the Iris, a blast of pure energy shot out from around you, throwing us all backwards, forcing us against the wall. The continuous stream of unrestrained power pouring out of you dominated us all, making it impossible for us to control our abilities. Reid had items of all sizes flying around the room, Alex began casting random images, this one," she said, pointing at Mr Anderson, "was filling our heads with so much nonsensical chatter we couldn't think straight, and Jocelyn had to use every ounce of his concentration to avoid warping and erasing our minds."

"Seriously?" I whispered, stunned. Everything had been so serene and tranquil for me that I never would have imagined there could have been such a commotion only a few feet away.

"The only way to stop it was to take the Iris from you," Min continued, "but we were all pinned to the wall by the sheer force of it, and unable to reach you. Finally, Reid was able to gather his wits enough to kinetically pull the Iris out of your hand, stopping the effects instantly."

"Wow," Chloe breathed, giving my arm a squeeze.

But I was more worried than impressed. "And Ryland saw everything? My God, he must be terrified!"

"For a bit, but we took care of him, don't you worry," Mr Anderson said with a smile.

"As I said, Jocelyn has made sure he will sleep well tonight, and tomorrow he will have a talk with him."

"Will he tell him everything?"

"Difficult to say. We will all discuss it at the meeting tomorrow morning."

"Aye," said Mr Anderson, looking at Min. "Nine o'clock, in Jocelyn's office, and that includes you too, lass," he added, nodding to me. "Seeing as how you're one of us now. Cormac will be there too, for the Reading."

"But are you sure–?"

"Hush now," Min said, as she helped me sit up. "No more of that. There is nothing anyone can do tonight. All that matters now is that you get a good rest." Once I was soundly on my feet, she went to the table next to the stove and retrieved a small corked bottle filled with a gray-green liquid. "Here," she said, handing me the bottle, "drink this."

I looked at the nasty color of the bottle's contents and cringed.

"Come on," she waved. "I've got somewhere to go, and I'm not leaving until it's gone."

I groaned and uncorked the bottle. It didn't smell like anything, but I still didn't trust it. I plugged my nose and downed the whole thing in two gulps.

"Blah!" I coughed, handing her the empty bottle. "Here, gone."

"Good girl. Now get on up to bed, it won't take long for that to begin working."

"What was it?" Though, as I had already drunk it, maybe I didn't want to know.

"You need a full night's rest to finish healing. That will make sure you get it. Now go on. Chloe, take her arm and make sure she doesn't trip. Anderson, go along will you? In case she can't make it all the way?"

"Certainly. You're not coming?"

"No, I need to go check on..." she hesitated, glancing toward Chloe and me, "someone."

"Oh, aye," Mr Anderson said sadly. "Poor lad."

"You know about that?" Min asked him quietly.

He nodded. "He told me last week."

My vision started to blur as I felt the bottle of – whatever it was – seep into my veins and make my head and limbs heavy. Chloe felt me slouch against her and began to lead me toward the door, but I was still straining to hear the quiet conversation happening across the room.

"What does it mean?" Mr Anderson asked, his low voice becoming harder and harder to hear. "Was it a mistake? Will he be able to move past it?"

"I'm not certain of anything at the moment," Min answered.

Their voices sounded miles away now, and my eyelids had started to droop. Chloe guided me through the door, and we made our way down the hall while my exhausted mind struggled to function. Who were they talking about? Move past what?

I opened my mouth to ask, but couldn't quite make the words come. I heard the echo of Chloe's voice call for Mr Anderson, and the next thing I knew it was morning.

17

"So, how are you feeling?" Chloe asked me, as we sat in her room eating Pop Tarts the next morning.

"Well, that was the best night's sleep I've ever had, bar none. I don't know what was in that bottle Min gave me, but sign me up!"

"It certainly didn't take long to work," Chloe laughed. "You all but fell asleep on me in the hall! Mr Anderson had to carry you the rest of the way!"

"Yeah, I was wondering how I ended up in bed."

"You slept like the dead, I'm sure, but that's not what I meant. I meant how are you feeling with, you know...?" She left her sentence hanging, leaning forward excitedly.

She was referring to my newfound Holderdom, I knew that. I'd known the first time she asked, but had avoided answering, because honestly, I didn't know what to tell her. Especially considering that I knew she, of course, thought it was great. Chloe would have been thrilled to be in my shoes, finally getting a chance to play with the big boys, and couldn't imagine why I'd be anything less than ecstatic.

Deliberately avoiding the question again, I asked one of my own, "Have you seen Alex at all today?"

"Alex? No, why?"

"No reason. I just haven't seen him since last night and was wondering if something might be wrong."

Worrying would have been closer to the truth, but as it wasn't a feeling I thought I could do an adequate job of explaining, I didn't elaborate. There was more than likely no need to worry. Everything was probably fine. Still though, much as I tried to shake it, something felt off.

His disappearance alone wouldn't have been enough to really concern me if it hadn't been for the whispered conversation between Min and Mr Anderson I'd half-heard last night. I had no way to prove it, but something deep down told me they had been talking about Alex.

"Hmm," Chloe mused, pulling me out of my thought bubble, "now that you mention it, he didn't look well when he got me out of class yesterday, and told me what had happened."

"Didn't look well how?"

"Well, he was more than a little shaken up, but knowing now what actually happened in there to you all, that part isn't surprising. But beyond that, he was a bit pale, and tired-looking. Sick, maybe?"

"Could be," I supposed. Min had mentioned checking on him, and Mr Anderson had asked if he would be able to "move past it", so I guess being sick made sense. Still, that wouldn't explain the rest of the conversation, including the mention of a "mistake". However, in all fairness, my eavesdropping had occurred while I was more than half-asleep and I could just as easily have misheard.

In any event it didn't matter because, sick or not, Alex was sure to be at the Order meeting later, where I could ask him myself if anything was wrong. Until then, I had enough to worry about without obsessing over something that would likely turn out to be nothing.

"If you think I haven't noticed that you're not answering my question, you're sadly mistaken, lady," she said, cocking her eyebrows.

"Sorry, what was it again?" I asked innocently.

"How. Do. You. Feel?"

"OK, I guess," I admitted with a shrug, looking down at the gold cuff covering the majority of my lower arm – or my Sciath, as I supposed I would need to start calling it, though "embarrassing eyesore" was still more appropriate, as far as I was concerned.

"Only OK? How can you say that? It's fantastic!"

"Yeah, except it's really not," I said, flicking at the chains hanging from my arm.

"What do you mean?"

"I don't know. What if I can't do all the things everyone expects me to? What if I totally suck at this? You all have been waiting for this for hundreds of years, and everyone has such high hopes..." I dropped off, and rubbed my hands over my face. "I'm just not used to letting people down."

"Oh!" She jumped up, pulling me with her and wrapped her arms around my neck. "You won't let anyone down!

The fact that you have awakened the Iris alone is enough to keep most of them happy for the next fifty or so years," she smiled. "Don't worry, everything will be fine. You're overwhelmed, that's all. Just wait, you'll feel worlds better when you find out exactly what your ability is – speaking of which, you need to get downstairs."

"And then there's that," I said, slipping on my shoes and shuffling to the door. "What if my ability turns out to be something horrible, like laser beams shooting out of my eyes or something?"

"Laser beams?" she barked a laugh. "I think we need to take away your comic books! Should we call you Super Holder?"

"Really?" I sniped. "Comic book jokes, from a girl who can walk through time!"

"Yes," she allowed, still laughing. "But it's still a far cry from laser eyes."

"OK then, fine, it probably won't be lasers. But I could still get stuck with something boring, like being able to predict the weather, or maybe some messed-up Midas syndrome where everything I touch turns to... I don't know..."

"Gold?" Chloe suggested.

"Yeah, but we both know I'd never get that lucky. It'd end up being aluminum."

"Listen to me," Chloe said, taking both my hands in hers. "You are talking madness, and you know it. Everything will be fine, and even if it's not, we all love you and won't let anything bad happen to you. You know that, right?"

I nodded, letting her words unwind me just a little. "Thanks, Chloe," I said, hugging.

"Of course! Now, go get 'em Super Holder!" she said, grinning and giving me a playful shove into the hall. "I'll be here when you get out." With that, she closed the door, giving me no choice but to leave.

I made my way down the stairs and through the halls, walking as smoothly as I could, trying to prevent the chains on my Sciath from clanking against the hard metal cuff with every step I took. God-damned stupid thing! I felt like a cat wearing one of those bell-collars.

As I reached the doors to the office I heard two familiar voices coming from the adjacent hall, and found Mr Anderson and Mr Reid walking toward me. I sighed with a smile, relieved that I wouldn't have to walk into the meeting by myself.

"There, now!" Mr Anderson called with a smile as he saw me.

"Good morning."

"Oh, Becca," Mr Reid said, placing a hand on my shoulder as he arrived next to me "How are you? I stopped by Min's rooms last night to see you, but you'd already gone. Are you feeling better?"

"Much, thank you," I said, touched that he'd thought to come and check on me. The fact that Jocelyn had not bothered to do so – even though he'd had time to personally make sure that Ryland was taken care of – was not lost on me, but for the moment I chose to ignore it.

"Now then," Mr Anderson said as the three of us stepped up to the carved dark wood doors of Jocelyn's office, "let's see what our little lass has for us." He winked at me as he held open the door, allowing us to pass.

I hadn't given any thought to what Jocelyn's office might be like, but the moment I entered the room I realized that I should have, because I was in no way prepared for it. The look, the feel of it all, hit me as hard as the smell of a bakery would a starving man, and I was instantly transported back to my childhood. Back to the house in Maine where a little girl laid on the floor of her daddy's office, coloring in her coloring books, while he sat at his desk grading term papers. The dark wood bookcases, the wine-red drapes, the large mahogany desk with the high-backed leather chair; it was all so familiar. Different, but somehow exactly the same. This office was of course much bigger, but was set up was just as I remembered – desk facing the room, bookshelves on the left, windows on the right. The drapes were the same color, but these I could see were velvet, not the thin cotton they had been at home, and there was now a fireplace against the far wall where, in Maine, a TV had been.

However, for all the differences in appearance, both big and small, one thing was exactly the same. So much so that, if I'd have let it, it would have brought tears to my eyes.

The smell.

Musty leather from his books, sweet peppermint from the candles he'd always liked, and a musky tang from the same cologne he'd always worn. It was the smell that used to greet me every afternoon when I came home from school. It was the smell of the scarf he would take off and wrap around my neck and face when we'd been out playing in the snow for too long. The smell of him hugging me goodnight.

I quietly cleared my throat, forcefully shoving the unwelcome memories to the back of my mind where they belonged. Having regained my composure, I followed Anderson to the center of the room where there were two leather couches, as well as four armchairs. Min was on one couch with Taron, while Jocelyn was leaning against the desk, talking with Cormac. It wasn't until I took a seat on the second couch that I noticed Alex sitting in the armchair nearest the desk – and, no sooner did I see him, than my worries were overwhelmingly confirmed.

Something was very wrong.

He sat listlessly staring at the side wall, eyes sunken and bloodshot, his elbow on the arm of the chair while his mouth and chin rested against his closed fist. He was very pale, looking as though he hadn't slept at all the night before, and it was obvious he hadn't shaved that morning.

I felt an uncomfortable stretching in my chest that made me squirm in my seat, and I had an almost overwhelming urge to run over and give him a hug. What could be wrong? Was he sick? Could be, though he didn't look congested or feverish. He just looked… sad.

As I sat there watching him, everything in me seemed to cry out to help. Problem was, I had no idea what to do, much less what to do in a room filled with other people. I continued to stare at him, hoping he might look up and catch my eye so that maybe I could quietly ask him what was wrong, or at the very least give him a sympathetic smile.

Unfortunately, he didn't look up until Jocelyn's voice called all our attention to the front of the room.

"Everyone," he said, standing up straight, lacing his hands together in front of himself. "I think we ought to begin. There is quite a lot to discuss this morning, but before we move to that, Cormac thinks it would be best to start with the Reading."

My neck grew hot as I could suddenly feel all the eyes in the room on me, causing a ball of prickly anxiety to begin rolling around in my ribcage. Cormac took a step in my direction and I made a move to stand.

"No, no," he said, raising his hand gently. "Stay seated, please. No need to be uncomfortable." He smiled, taking the place on the couch next to me. "Now then," he said, as I shifted to face him, praying it wasn't obvious how nervous I was. "We will go slowly and I promise you won't feel a thing. Does she have a Block?" he asked, turning to Min.

"Yes, on her Sciath. I thought it best until we knew what we're dealing with."

"Indeed," Cormac agreed. Then, turning back to me, "Min has put what's called a Block on your Sciath, making it impossible for you to access your ability as long as it's there, did she explain that to you?"

"Yes," I said, nodding.

"A Block can also interfere with my reading, so we will have to remove your Sciath before we can continue."

"No argument here," I said, looking forward to being free, even if it was only for a minute.

Min came over and reached for my arm, but I pulled away from her, remembering what she'd told me about the chaos that ensued during yesterday's test.

"Wait," I said. "What about yesterday? All the crazy stuff that happened because I didn't have this on? What if someone gets hurt this time?"

"Aye," Mr Anderson agreed, looking as concerned as I was. "Duck and cover then, shall we?" to which I heard someone – probably Mr Reid – punch him in the shoulder.

Min smiled at me comfortingly, ignoring them. "Everything will be fine. The issues we had were the direct result of your unprotected contact with the Iris. Without it here, we are all perfectly safe."

"You're sure?"

"Don't worry," she said, reaching down again for my Sciath.

She undid the clasps, then looked to Cormac who took my free hand in his.

"Are you ready?" Min asked him.

"Yes, go ahead."

I held my breath as Min removed the Sciath from my arm, and the moment it was gone I felt a warm fuzziness come over me. It seemed to generate from somewhere deep inside me, continually flowing in lazy patterns throughout my entire body. I released the breath I'd been holding, happy to find the sensation pleasant and soothing, as opposed to overwhelming and violent like the experience yesterday had been to the others.

As I began to analyze this new sensation, I found that I could sense other fuzzy energy sources, just like mine, coming from other parts of the room. Some stronger than others, some closer or further away, but all made up of the same blurry flowing force. Stranger yet, was that they weren't anything that I could actually see or hear. It was more of a feel – like soft brushes against my mind.

"What do you feel?" Cormac whispered, excited curiosity in his sparkling eyes.

"I don't know," I told him honestly.

"But you do feel them?"

"Them? You… you feel it too?"

"I can feel everything that you are."

"What are they?"

His eyebrows creased in amused confusion. "I'm not sure. I've never encountered anything like this. Min," he asked without looking away from me, "can you remove the Block?"

"Yes, of course," she answered, surprised.

She held the cuff between her hands and bowed her head over it mumbling something under her breath. When she looked up again, Cormac nodded downward indicating she should place it back on my arm.

"Let us see if we can clear things up," he said softly, though I could hear his anticipation underneath.

The moment the cool metal touched my skin everything rushed into focus, and I sucked in a breath so sharp it made everyone in the room jump. The vague haziness was gone, as though a gust of wind had blown through, clearing away the fog. What was left were seven bright, distinct energy fields, each one located in a different spot around the room. Each one coursing steadily yet powerfully within itself, and each one leaving its own unique feel against my mind.

Then, like the crack of a whip, it came to me.

Seven.

Seven energy sources – seven people!

My eyes darted around frantically from face to face, trying desperately to see what I could so clearly feel.

"It's all right," Cormac said, giving my hand a squeeze, his eyes dancing with delight. "Close your eyes and try to relax. It is nothing you can see. Just… feel."

I took a deep breath and did as he said, closing my eyes and concentrating on each distinctive brush against my mind.

"What are they?" I whispered, hoping this time he would know.

"Abilities," he said.

"What?" I opened my eyes to find him smiling.

"Each one is the corresponding person's ability. Their power."

So, I could sense other Holder's abilities; that was pretty cool. Could have been worse, anyway.

I closed my eyes again, picking out the nearest ability – Cormac's as it turned out, since he was the one sitting closest me – and focusing on it. As I concentrated on the unique footprint the delicate swirls and waves of power created, I felt an odd sensation within myself. As though my own ability was trying to reach out and connect somehow with his.

"Go on," Cormac said, seeming to know what I was considering.

I allowed the flow of my ability to extend outwards until it melted into Cormac's, creating one long continuous flow between the two of us.

This time it was his turn to make everyone jump, huffing out a breathy, "Oh my!", as though he'd been punched in the stomach.

"I'm sorry," I said, quickly breaking the connection between us, pulling my own energy back inward.

The whole room was silent for a few seconds before Cormac began to quietly laugh, shaking his head. "No," he said, his stunned amusement growing, "don't apologize."

"Well, Cormac?" Jocelyn asked, after a few more moments of silence. "Is she...?" He didn't finish, but everyone knew what he was asking.

"Oh, yes." Cormac smiled, looking at me in amazement. "She most certainly is."

18

"For God's sake, man!" Taron growled with his usual charm. "What can she do? Tell us what you saw!"

Cormac was still sitting silently, looking at me with something between wonder and humor. I wished he'd stop, as it was getting embarrassing, not to mention that I was just as anxious as everyone else to hear what he had to say.

"I don't know what to call it," Cormac said finally, turning to face the semi-circle of expectant faces. "It's something I've never seen before." He looked to Min who was still standing nearby. "You may put the Block back on her now. Best to keep it there for the time being."

Min did as she was asked, taking my Sciathed arm in her hands and mumbling over it again. Just as the last syllable was spoken my new sense disappeared, taking with it the awareness of not only my own ability, but of everyone else's as well. The gentle brushes against my mind were gone, leaving me totally normal once again, and honestly, a bit lonely. Subconsciously, I reached out, searching for the presence of the abilities again, but they were gone.

Jocelyn stepped forward, growing impatient. "You mentioned abilities, Cormac," he probed. "Is she a Reader as you are?"

"I thought so at first," Cormac answered, leaning forward. "The way she senses – that is to say, the feeling of each individual ability – is almost exactly the way in which I sense abilities when I Read someone. Initially the only difference between us that I noted was that, while I must have physical contact in order to Read, she was able to sense everyone in the room simultaneously, with no need for a physical touch. But then I noticed the attraction between her own ability to the abilities of those around her. The draw there was most unique, and quite unintentional on her part. And that's when I saw it." He turned back to me, placing a hand on my knee. "Becca, do you know what you did there at the end? The connection you forged between us?"

"Yes... I think. What about it? I didn't hurt you, did I?"

"No, no, not to worry, I was only startled," he assured me. "But you know what I am referring to? When you made your ability one with mine?"

"Yes?"

"That is your ability," he said, his eyes sparkling with excitement.

"Wait, what?"

"In that moment, when your power melded with mine, you were able to use my Reading ability as your own – or would have been able to, if you'd realized what was happening. That is what she does." He addressed everyone. "She can borrow the ability of any Holder within her sensing radius – I'd say thirty feet or so – and use it as her own. Moreover, she is not limited to just one ability at a time. With all of us here, she could impart thoughts, cast images, and read minds, all the while flying every book on these shelves around the room."

Everyone else in the room was silent as they processed what Cormac had said, making me the only one to speak. "So, I can do anything that the people around me can do?"

"Exactly. And in turn, were you to be completely alone, you wouldn't be able to do anything at all."

"Wow!" was all I could think to say.

"She'll need to be trained," Cormac said to Jocelyn, who had begun to pace slowly around the room. "She will need to learn how to use and control each ability individually. Min can lessen the restraints of the Block gradually, that way she can learn slowly and become accustomed to the characteristics and feel of each ability."

"What about the Iris?" Jocelyn asked. "How does it factor into all of this?"

"I believe that the true power of the Iris is an ability to magnify a Holder's power." Cormac stood and begin to gesture with his hands as he spoke. "That is what I believe happened to the rest of us at the test. As the Iris was overpowering Becca, it was giving off residual power that heightened our abilities. Heightened them so much, in fact, that we were no longer able to control them, even with our Sciaths on. That is what I believe the Iris will do for her."

"Do you mean it will heighten her own ability, or the abilities she assumes from others?" Mr Reid asked, scratching his chin.

"Both," Cormac replied. "Take you for instance, Reid. If Becca were to use your kinetic ability as her own, she could only ever be as powerful as you are. The same goes for all of us – she can only be as strong at any one ability as the Holder she assumed it from. However, with the Iris in her possession, I believe she will be able use any ability to its fullest extent, no matter the power level of the original Holder."

"Jesus, Mary, and Joseph," Mr Anderson mumbled, and I couldn't help but agree.

I had access to basically every ability in the Holder universe? I was going to be able to read minds, and walk through time, and move things around without touching them, and cast images of anything I wanted, and loads of other stuff, all for the price of one? This was incredible. And way more than I'd anticipated, that was for sure. In any event, the "lame ability" worries I'd told Chloe about this morning were as good as gone.

I glanced over at Alex to try and gauge his reaction to all this, only to find him staring down at the floor, his mind somewhere else entirely. Wasn't he interested? Shouldn't he be happy at the way things had worked out? After all, he was the one who'd asked me to stay, wasn't he even the least bit pleased to find out that I'd have no choice but to stick around for a while? Granted, I'd been planning on staying anyway, but he didn't know that.

I moved my gaze back to the center of the room, trying to ignore the sudden queasiness in my stomach.

Jocelyn had stopped pacing and was once again leaning against his desk, with his arms crossed over his chest, ruby Sciath shining on his finger. Everyone seemed to be watching him, waiting for him to speak, assuming that he would know where to go from here and oddly enough I found myself doing the same. My hatred of the man notwithstanding, I had to admit he could command a room. Almost everything about him, from his strong air to his steady gaze, gave the impression that he was a man of experience and knowledge. It wasn't hard to imagine scores of men ready to get behind him and follow him into a battle of any kind, and I found myself wondering if he had ever been a soldier during his two centuries of life.

"It's clear this is uncharted territory for us all, and we need to make sure we proceed with caution," Jocelyn began, uncrossing his arms and resting his palm on the edge of the desk. "I agree with Cormac, Becca should be trained." As he said this, he looked straight into my eyes and as much as I wanted to look away, I refused to be so cowardly. After a tense moment, his eyes moved to the group and he continued, "We will work slowly, training her one on one, beginning with perhaps Anderson, or Alex – someone who's ability won't allow her to hurt herself or anyone else." I could have sworn I saw Alex squirm at his mention. "Agreed?" Jocelyn asked.

"Agreed," everyone replied, while I sat quietly, assuming that as the newbie I wasn't yet one of the decision-makers.

"Becca?" Jocelyn asked, looking at me again.

"Yes, fine," I said, impressed that he'd noticed I hadn't answered.

"Good," he said to no one in particular. "The second matter is that of the charms," he said looking up at Min. "There has been another attempted breach."

"What?" I asked.

"Another?" Anderson said shaking his head.

"So someone is trying to get in, then?" Mr Reid murmured.

"When did it happen?" Cormac asked.

"Last night," Min informed the room. "Just past twelve."

"Could it have been one of the students? Perhaps an accident?" Cormac suggested.

"No, not this time. It came from outside the campus boundary. Someone attempted to use a charm of their own to open a hole in the guard, but they were not strong enough. The guard held, and I have added another set of strengtheners just in case."

"What about Lorcan, has one been set here?" Jocelyn asked.

"Yes, and I've added Becca to the removal charm around the school proper as well. She cannot be removed from either against her will."

"Her will."

My will...

My stomach squeezed uncomfortably, and I was suddenly glad I'd only had a Pop Tart for breakfast.

"Good," Jocelyn said.

"Something will have to be done," Anderson commented after a moment. "We can't have Darragh's bloody scoundrels trying to bust our doors in every other day."

"Min," Jocelyn said, turning to face her, "are you confident your guards will continue to hold?"

"I am," she stated firmly. "The breach attempts thus far have been weak and unfocused; nothing that the charms can't withstand. I have also changed the guards to keep out, not only those associated with Darragh, but any Holder, no matter the level of their ability. It is the strongest charm I have. I am certain it will hold."

Jocelyn nodded. "Then I am confident that everyone is safe for the time being. I do agree that something must be done, but we will move slowly and cautiously, at least until we know exactly what we are dealing with." He shifted his weight back toward the center of the group. "Which brings me to our last order of business. It is apparent that the information we have regarding the Iris is not as accurate as we have always believed it to be, and therefore we must entertain the possibility that there could be more aspects to this that we are unaware of. That is why I propose that we awaken Ryland."

"Wait," I cut in over the collective murmur of agreement. "You want to what?"

"Awaken him," Min said, then to Jocelyn added, "I had the same thought, actually." Turning to me, she continued. "A Holder has an Awakening naturally when they reach young adulthood. Ryland is still a few years away from that, so what we will do is bring on his Awakening artificially. Force it to happen early."

"Force it," I stressed, not at all happy with that term. "That doesn't exactly sound pleasant."

"It has been done before with no problem at all. It only takes an hour or so, and then it is over."

"And why are you doing this?" I asked.

"To make sure there is nothing overlooked," Jocelyn said. "Considering that none of this has gone as planned, the safest thing for us to do is cover all our bases. The Iris had no effect on Ryland, but that doesn't necessarily mean he will not still be instrumental to us in some way, and if that is the case, it will be best for us, and safest for him, if we find out now. That way, if any extra precautions are needed, we are ready."

He might have just been playing me, what with the whole "Ryland will be safer this way" thing, but I had to admit, I was buying it. It did make sense to want to check and make sure Ryland wasn't harboring any secret abilities or random tricks, especially considering some ancient prophecy had been telling people for hundreds of years that he was. Moreover, if he was still in any danger from this Darragh guy, I wanted to know about it.

"All right," I agreed, "but I want to be there."

"That won't be possible," Jocelyn said.

"What do you mean it won't be possible?"

"I'm afraid he's right, dear," Min said with an apologetic smile. "The Awakening process is simple enough, but it involves an incredible amount of power, and as fragile as you still are your presence wouldn't be safe for either of you." Much as I hated being called fragile by anyone, the fact that it came from short little grandma-faced Min, made it slightly easier to bear.

Mustering as much composure as I could, I addressed Jocelyn directly, "What are you going to tell him?"

"Everything," he answered. "Or at least everything within reason. There is no need to scare him with details he doesn't need, but after what he witnessed yesterday, there isn't much of a way around it."

"And you really think it's a good idea to have a ten year-old running around reading minds?" I asked, glancing back at Min.

"Oh no," she said, "certainly not. Once he is awakened he will have a Sciath, which I will put a Block on just as yours has now. He will not have access to his ability until he is of an age and maturity to handle it."

Well that was a relief.

"How soon can you be ready?" Jocelyn asked Min, as he walked around the desk and retrieved a coat that was folded over the arm of his desk chair.

"It's Sunday," she thought out loud, "so if I begin today, I could have everything ready by Tuesday morning."

"Let's make it Tuesday afternoon then, just to be safe," he said, looking around at everyone as he pulled his coat on. "Say, one o'clock? We will see what happens, and hold off on any more decision-making until then."

Everyone nodded, then began quietly talking amongst themselves while they stood and made their way toward the door. I got up, glancing quickly at Alex, planning to take this opportunity to walk with him and ask him what was wrong. However, before I could take my first step I was stopped by Jocelyn's voice as he came up beside me.

"Becca?"

I looked at him, trying not to appear annoyed that he was keeping me from my objective. "Yes?"

"I..." he hesitated, looking down at his hands as he spoke. "I have to go over and pick up Ryland. I put him to sleep last night which means I have to go and wake him. After that I will bring him back here and will explain things to him." He finally brought his eyes up to meet mine. "You are welcome to be there as well if you wish."

Well if this wasn't the proverbial olive branch, I didn't know what was. Normally, I would have put more thought into my reply, but as, one, I really did want to be there for Ryland's discovery of all this, and, two, Alex was headed for the door and if I didn't hurry I would miss him altogether, I decided to be gracious.

"I'd like that, thank you."

"Good," he said, with a smile that almost looked shy.

"Should I meet you here?"

"Yes," he agreed, as we began walking toward the door, only a few paces behind Alex. "Twenty minutes should do."

We stepped out into the hall where I saw Alex had turned down the adjacent hallway while everyone else had gone straight ahead. Jocelyn gave me one final nod before following the larger crowd up toward the front of the building, while I hurried after Alex, hugging my Sciath to my chest so I wouldn't jingle like a Christmas elf.

"Alex?" I called when I was only a few feet away. I saw him stiffen at the sound of my voice, and it seemed to take him a second too long to turn around. "Are you all right?" I asked, finding it hard to hide the worry in my tone.

He gave me something that looked like a smile, though it didn't make it all the way to his eyes. "Yeah, I'm OK," he said, his voice dry and rough. "Just not feeling well, that's all."

"Can I do anything for you?" I asked, almost excited at the chance to help him after all he'd done for me these last few weeks.

He winced for a split second, almost as if my words hurt him – though it was probably just gratitude. "No, thank you. I'll be all right."

"OK," I said, disappointed. "I'm sorry about last night," I added after a silent moment, hoping he would remember that he'd said he wanted to talk to me and maybe suggest that we talk now. Cheap trick, I know, but I wasn't ready to let him leave. Something was telling me that he needed me. Consoling, or comforting, or maybe just a friendly ear, I wasn't sure, but whatever it was, I was more than willing to provide it. The one thing I was sure about, however, was that something was wrong with him – and that something was more than sickness.

"What do you mean?"

"I know you said you wanted to talk to me, and with the way things worked out, we didn't have a chance."

"Oh," he said, barely breaking a whisper. "It's fine."

"Maybe later if you are feeling up to it we could–"

"No," he said quickly, "it was nothing, don't worry about it."

"Are you sure?"

"Positive." He paused, glancing down. "It doesn't matter now."

He took a deep breath and looked back up at me with what I'm sure was supposed to be a smile, but was so hopeless it looked more like he wanted to cry.

"Are you sure you're all right?" I asked again, hoping he would decide to confide in me.

"I'll be fine, I promise." He took step backward. "I'm going to go lie down."

I nodded, well aware that the direction in which he gestured did not lead to his room. "OK," I said.

It was OK. It was damn-well fine. If he didn't want to tell me what was bothering him, I wasn't about to beg. And I certainly wasn't about to let him know how much it hurt.

"Feel better," I called after his escaping form, not even sure if he heard me.

I turned back toward Jocelyn's office, determined that I was not going to let something as trivial as the fact that Alex didn't trust me get me down.

And I most definitely was not going to cry.

19

Dejected and depressed, I returned to Jocelyn's office where I waited for him to get back with Ryland. Once they arrived, the three of us spent over two hours in Jocelyn's office, explaining the concept of Holders to an initially very confused, then very awestruck, Ryland. Jocelyn did the majority of the talking, while I listened and watched Ry for any signs of an informational overload-induced panic, worried we might end up scarring the kid for life. Though in hindsight my concerns were pointless, as I realized that you'd probably be pretty hard-pressed to find a ten year-old kid anywhere on earth that wouldn't love the idea of having – as Ryland called them – superpowers.

Jocelyn told him almost everything about Holders in general: the different abilities, how you get them, and all about the Awakening process. Ryland was also happy to find out that there were other Holder kids attending St Brigid's that he would be taking classes with, in which they would all learn more about their abilities, and how to use and control them – though he wasn't thrilled about waiting a few more years for that part. The only things Jocelyn didn't mention were the Iris, and anything about me other than that we'd recently discovered that I was a Holder too, and of course nothing about Darragh.

Lastly, Jocelyn had made sure to explain why it was very important to keep all of this a secret, and told him that he would have Min add a special charm to his Sciath that would make it impossible for him to divulge anything crucial to anyone who wasn't a Holder. Ryland wasn't happy about that, swearing up and down that he wouldn't tell anyone, but I agreed that the charm was for the best. Contrary to Ryland's assurances, secrecy has never been his strongest suit.

On the way out of the office Jocelyn handed me an index card with a building and room number on it, as well as a day and time.

"Introduction to Irish," he told me. "You'll want to familiarize yourself with the language, it will make things easier for you," he said discreetly, knowing Ryland was still within earshot. "Professor Altus knows you will be joining. Your first class will be tomorrow at ten. Then tomorrow afternoon, if you are up for it, Taron and Min will give you your first training session. They will meet you in the Inner Chamber at three."

"Taron?" I repeated with a grimace, not disguising my irritation. But come on, did it really have to be him?

"Taron's Discerning ability is the most subtle, it will be the best one for you to start with."

"Yeah, all right," I said reluctantly, and left.

I walked Ryland up to the front of the building where he gave me a quick goodbye, then ran up the walk and off toward his dorm, excited to meet with his friends for dinner. As I watched his silhouette disappear through the line of trees separating Lorcan from the rest of campus, I was relieved that he was taking everything very well. Honestly, he probably didn't even need me there at the meeting, but still, I was glad I had gone. It would have been really easy to chicken out again – umm… I mean, decline the invitation – to avoid spending more potentially irritating or awkward time with Jocelyn, but I am proud to say that I didn't. It may not have been the most comfortable situation, but as the focus for both Jocelyn and me had been Ryland, it wasn't all that bad.

The rest of the day was quiet and enjoyable, other than the funk I fell into whenever I thought about my conversation in the hall with Alex. It was that prickly, uncomfortable, slightly nauseating feeling you get when you are pretty sure someone is mad at you, but you don't know why, and are too nervous to ask. That feeling that makes you hold your breath every time you turn a corner because you are terrified they might be there, and if they are, what are you supposed to say, and what will they say, and what if they don't say anything at all, and you think that you probably shouldn't say anything either…?

Yeah, uncomfortable funk.

Though more upsetting than the funk, was the general gloom that came with it. I hated knowing that Alex was having such a hard time, and that there was nothing I could do to help him – or nothing he'd let me do, anyway. As horrible as it may sound, when I first realized that something might be wrong with him I was actually kind of excited. It wasn't that I wanted him to be sick or upset, but because I was happy at the idea of finally being able to really assist. To be there for him, the way he'd been there for me so many times over the last few weeks. But now that I knew he was hurting, and that he didn't even want to tell me what was wrong much less let me help him with it, I was left feeling sort of helpless. Not to mention terrified that I might have unconsciously caused whatever it was that had him so upset. It didn't seem likely, but given his behavior toward me it was the only thing I could figure.

I was relieved when it came time to leave for class the next day, if nothing else for the chance to get out of the building and away from my Alex worries for a while. I donned the official green and white school uniform I'd had to borrow from Chloe, threw my notebook and pen into my bag, slid the St Brigid's cross that Alex had woven on the rail into my pocket, pulled on my coat, and hurried out into the brisk October morning.

As I strode across campus, I let the crisp tang of the musky, pine-scented Irish air tingle in my nose, and exhilarate my already bubbling excitement. After all, what was cooler and more romantic than learning an ancient language? This would be great! And later I would have my first training session, though the fact that it was Taron definitely put a damper on my mood, but hey, it was better than nothing.

I made it to class just as everyone else was arriving and introduced myself to the professor, who gave me my book and workbook, as well as a folder filled with handouts and study guides that I'd missed so far in the term.

"It is so nice to meet you, Miss Ingle," Professor Altus said, smiling. "I was delighted when Professor Clavish called to tell me you'd be joining us."

"I'm sorry, who called you?" I asked, feeling as though I'd missed something.

"Professor Clavish, he's the one who registered you for the course."

"Oh, of course." I smiled. So Jocelyn didn't bother to take the ten minutes to sign me up himself as he'd implied. That was mildly annoying.

He pointed out one of the empty seats in the back of the room and I sat down, leaving my coat on so that no one would think the hideous hunk of gold on my arm was me trying to make a fashion statement. I opened my notebook, ready to dive into the beauty and elegance of the Gaelic language, until, that is, I looked up at the board and saw a huge chart analyzing the differences and uses of Class I and Class II verbs. And then it all came back to me. The reason I'd transferred out of French in high school. The reason my pitiful attempt to learn Latin on my own to impress colleges had imploded barely before it began.

Learning languages sucks.

It was overrated, complicated, and horribly boring. Sure the idea of being fluent in a foreign tongue was exciting and romantic, but the actual learning of said language was far from dreamy. I knew there were some people who really enjoyed it, and more power to them, but for me it was hell. How I'd managed to forget that on my walk over here was beyond me, but I certainly wouldn't be forgetting it again. Give me the paintings of cavemen. That I would be happy to learn. You see an etching of a cow – it's a cow. You don't have to worry about whether the cow is male or female, or if it comes before or after the verb, or how many cows there are – it's a cow. Unfortunately, there were no cave paintings or cows for me that day, only endless verb conjugation, and one excruciating hour later I was on my way back to Lorcan, more than happy to never return to Gaelic class ever again.

"Shouldn't he be here by now?" I grumbled, as Cormac, Min, and I sat in the Inner Chamber waiting on Taron, who apparently had better things to do than be on time.

"I'm sure he'll be along shortly," Cormac said calmly.

"He'd better be. I need to go and check the potions on the cooker," Min said, growing restless.

"Just take the Block off now and go," I suggested, knowing that was the only reason she was there.

"It will be safer to wait," Min persisted.

"Come on, I won't do anything, I promise."

"It may be beneficial," Cormac chimed in, "to let her get reacquainted with the sensation of feeling the different abilities before she attempts to use them."

Min looked at the pendant watch hanging from a long chain around her neck, for what seemed like the hundredth time in the last fifteen minutes. "All right," she sighed, reaching over for my arm. "I'll come back to put it on again, make sure you don't leave this room until I return."

"Hello, there," came a call from the Chamber door.

"Anderson," Cormac replied. "What brings you to our little party?"

"Taron can't make it, so here I am!"

"I get to train with you?" I asked, overjoyed at this turn of events. Not only did I not have to spend an afternoon with Taron, but I'd take Imparting over Discerning any day of the week!

"Aye," he said, rubbing his hands together eagerly. "We'll have a good time of it, we will!"

"All right, I'm off," Min said, releasing my arm as the gentle brushing sensation of other's abilities came rushing back to me. "I'll return in an hour." And with that, she left.

I took a moment to re-accustom myself to the feeling of my new sixth sense, but at least this time there were only two other abilities in the room, and not seven like the first time.

"How do you feel?" Cormac asked.

"Good," I said, grinning. "It feels natural now, not weird anymore."

"Excellent."

"OK." I hopped up off of the window ledge I'd been sitting on. "What's first? What do I do?"

"Well," Cormac said, smiling at my excitement, "that is up to you. Start out however you feel comfortable. Stretch your legs a bit."

"Wait," Mr Anderson said, holding his hand out. "What about Jocelyn? He'll be stopping by, won't he? We don't want her accidentally latching on to him..."

"Don't worry, Min has made sure that won't happen."

"Wait, what?" I asked, feeling out of the loop.

"We had to take special precautions when it came to Jocelyn," Cormac said. "We have made sure that you will not be able to meld with or use his ability, even accidently, until you are ready."

"Why not, what's the big deal? You all worried that I'll start reading your minds?" I laughed.

"No, no, it's not that," Cormac said, growing serious. "I'm not sure you realize how far-reaching Jocelyn's ability actually is. He is one of the most powerful Holders in recorded history, and, like all Holders, his power increases with age. The vast majority of mind-reading Holders – even the fully empowered and awakened ones – can only read the thoughts passing through the average mind, and compel thoughts. Jocelyn however is in a league all his own. Not only can he read the thoughts a person thinks as they are thinking them, but can also look back into their memories, sifting through the millions of thoughts they have had over the course of their lifetime to find the exact thought or memory he wishes to see. Not only can he compel the thoughts of others, making them do anything he wishes, but he can change, create, and even erase memories, without the person having any idea it was done. And once a thought has been erased, it cannot be returned."

"But you said he can create memories, couldn't he just put back anything he erased?"

"The best he could do would be to recreate the memory, but it would never be the same as the original. If a thought or memory was only altered then he can set it right again, but once something is gone, it's gone for good. So," he chuckled, "you can see why we might be nervous about letting you have access to him in that sense, especially while you are still so new to this. You could try to read someone's mind, and wind up accidentally eradicating every thought they have ever had."

"And Ryland?" I asked, knowing his ability was less than a day from being fully awakened and suddenly fearing for all of humanity.

"Don't worry," he replied, guessing my fears. "The odds are that Ryland will be vastly less powerful than Jocelyn. At best he might be able to compel, but I doubt he will be able to cause any real damage. We won't know for sure until tomorrow, but I wouldn't worry too much."

"What about me? Can I just skip that one altogether? Sounds like that safer option..."

"You will learn it in time, but that won't come until much later, when you are ready. For now, we will keep to the abilities with a much smaller margin for error, like Imparting." He gestured to Mr Anderson. "Now, relax, take a deep breath, and explore."

I did as he suggested, taking a long breath in and out through my nose, and focusing on the abilities I felt in the room. Cormac's was easy to recognize due to our experiment yesterday, and since I'd already joined with his energy once I turned my attention to Mr Anderson.

Using my own ability I reached out to his specific touch against my mind, melding our abilities, just as I'd done with Cormac.

"Ho!" Mr Anderson said. "You did something there, didn't you?"

"I've connected my ability with yours," I admitted.

"What do you feel?" Cormac asked him.

"I don't know." He paused, looking slightly enamored. "It's warm, comforting. If I didn't know what it was, I might think it was only a change in my mood."

"May I?" Cormac asked me, extending his hand. I took it in mine, allowing him to read us.

"Did I do it right?" I asked.

"Oh yes," Cormac replied, "and quicker too this time. Was it difficult?"

"No, not at all," I laughed, thrilled at how easy and natural it was, "but will people always know when I am connected to them?"

"Perhaps at first, but with practice you will learn subtlety."

"Well, come on then, let's give it a go!" Mr Anderson said, seeming as excited as I was.

"OK, how?" I asked, looking expectantly at Mr Anderson. When his only answer was to look back at me in confusion, I began to worry. Was I supposed to be able to figure this out on my own? I could feel our connection, feel his ability flowing through me, but as for actually harnessing or using it, I was clueless. "What do I have to do?" I asked again, hoping he hadn't understood that I was looking for direction.

"I don't know," Mr Anderson said.

"What do you mean, you don't know?" I asked. "It's what you do."

"I can't explain it, I just… do it."

Well, that wasn't very helpful. I tried simply thinking the statement, "It's Monday". When that didn't work, I thought it louder, concentrating on Cormac's forehead. No good. For the next ten minutes the three of us stood in silence as I mentally shouted, screamed, whispered, and strained my way to a headache, trying everything I could think of to impart "It's Monday!" to either of the two men before me, all to no avail.

Undoubtedly seeing the tension in my face, Cormac placed a hand on my arm. "Relax Becca, there is no rush. We don't need you popping any blood vessels," he smiled, trying to get me to loosen up.

"I don't know what to do," I grumbled, irritated.

"You are trying too hard, you can't force it. Loosen up and allow it to come on its own."

I sighed – or huffed might be a better word– and closed my eyes, letting the knots in my shoulders unwind. Focusing only on what I could feel, not what I wanted to feel, I examined the two entwined abilities for some clue that I was missing. I gathered up some of the flowing energy, concentrating it in front of my mind, then gently thought through it, aiming directly at Cormac.

It's Monday.

"Haha!" he yelled, grabbing my arms and giving me a triumphant shake. "That's my girl!"

"She's done it?" Mr Anderson asked?

"Yes! 'It's Monday', clear as a bell!" he gushed. "Go on, try again."

"Aye, me this time," Mr Anderson said, not about to be left out.

I gathered up the ability in front of my waiting thought, and spoke through it, this time toward Mr Anderson.

I think I've got it.

"Holy Mother o' Christ!" he exclaimed, jumping back with a laugh. "Got it indeed!"

The remainder of the hour was spent practicing and learning control. I'd impart to Cormac, then Mr Anderson, then both of them at once. Then they began walking around the room and I would have to impart different thoughts to each of them as they moved, honing my precision, and trying not to cross the thoughts. At one point, I imparted to Cormac *I'm getting itchy*, while simultaneously imparting *My brain feels hungry* to Mr Anderson, but otherwise once I cracked the code, it went really well.

"I see we've made progress," Min said, calling our attention to the door as she entered. I'd been so focused on my imparting I hadn't even sensed her arrival.

"She's a regular Imparter if ever I've seen one!" Mr Anderson said, clapping me on the back.

"Indeed, she has done marvelously well," Cormac added.

"Good," Min said, nodding. "And Becca, do you feel all right?"

I feel great, I imparted proudly to all three of them, earning me a laugh from each.

"That's my girl!" Mr Anderson said, throwing his arm around my shoulders and giving me a gruff squeeze. "That is very impressive for your first time, and while I hate to bring an end to a productive afternoon–"

She stopped when she saw me suddenly look toward the door.

"Someone is coming," I announced, feeling the approach of a new ability.

"Can you tell who?" Cormac asked.

"No." I shook my head. "I do recognize it. It was definitely someone who was with us in the meeting yesterday, but there were so many abilities in the room I can't be sure who this one belongs to."

We all looked to the door as it swung open to reveal – Alex. I felt a sharp pinch in my throat as I tried to swallow, fixing my gaze on his chest, afraid to meet his eyes.

A book in his hand, he took two steps before freezing, obviously not expecting to find the room already occupied. "Oh, I'm sorry, I didn't realize," he said, turning to go.

"No lad." Mr Anderson stopped him, in his usual cheerful way, though I could also hear the note of sympathy in his voice. "We're on the way out, not to worry."

"Yes, in fact I am needed for an appointment," Cormac said. "Anderson, would you mind escorting me to Dr Van den Honert's office? I don't believe I know the way."

"Of course, of course," Mr Anderson said, following Cormac toward the door.

"You did a marvelous job today, Becca," Cormac said, with a gentle pat on my shoulder as he passed by me.

"Thank you," I replied, mortified that my voice shook.

The two men left, leaving Alex, Min and me in an eggshell of an atmosphere, none of us sure what to do next. Min made the first move, taking my Sciathed arm in her hands and replacing the Block, while Alex and I hung in a strange state of seeing each other without really looking at one another.

Finally, I'd had enough. If he wasn't going to break the tension then I would. For all I knew – or had solid proof of anyway – his recent mood change had nothing at all to do with me, and until I found out otherwise, I would go on as if nothing between us had changed. He might not reciprocate, but at least this way I was part of the solution as opposed to the problem.

I gulped back my unease and smiled at him, gesturing toward the enormous book he was carrying. "A little light reading?" I teased, hoping at the very least to see him smile.

He did smile, but it was that same sad, not quite real smile he'd given me yesterday, that made my chest ache. "Just bringing it back," he said.

He came toward us, as Min and I happened to be standing just in front of the bookshelf, and I held my breath, waiting for him to speak. My hopes were high when he hesitated for a split second as he passed me, giving me what almost looked like a real grin, before it turned into an awkward swallow.

I let out the breath, disappointed and torn. What could I do? I couldn't force him to talk to me. Should I let it go? Should I try again? I felt the woven cross in my pocket, pressing against my leg telling me yes, while the distant and withdrawn vibe coming off of Alex told me no.

I was at a total loss as to what to do, desperately trying to think of something I could do or say before he left, and I lost my chance. Though, as it turned out, I didn't have to think for long. Because as he passed by me again, on his way back toward the door, for the slightest moment...

...his hand touched mine.

20

It was just the slightest graze of his finger against the back of my hand, but the jolt it gave me – the pounding shockwave it ignited in my body – felt as though I'd grabbed hold of a livewire and couldn't let go.

Alex continued to stride quickly out of the room, having not even noticed the seemingly insignificant touch. A touch that had my insides screaming and reeling as they were sucked into tremulous rapids of emotion, that was cutting through me, breaking and unweaving the deepest pillars of my core, then stitching me back up again. And the thread – the bonding agent that was now holding me together – was Alex.

All of a sudden, it was as though Alex was part of me. A part I could barely remember being without. As though he'd always been there in the background of my life, and I simply hadn't realized it. In an instant he'd become my foundation; the canvas that my life was painted on, the idea of which was as subtle as it was all-encompassing, and as comforting as it was terrifying.

My God, what was happening to me?

I began to shake with cold, while my skin felt hot and feverish. I wanted it to stop but the ripples continued to surge on, shaking and rearranging me as they went, like clearing the screen on an Etch-A-Sketch only to draw the same picture again, but in a different color.

"Becca?" I heard Min call, realizing that she was all but holding me upright. "Becca, can you hear me? Just breathe, it will pass." She began to lead me out into the hall and toward her office, walking as quickly as my trembling legs would allow, all the while whispering words of comfort. "Keep breathing, we're almost there," she continued, as we arrived at her office door. "We don't want you passing out."

My mind continued to swim as Min guided my wobbling form through the door and over to the couch, setting me down to rest. She hurried over to her cabinet, grabbing a glass bottle and pouring its contents into a cup along with water from a teapot on the stove.

"Drink this," she said, handing me the glass, and taking a seat on the couch next to me. "The kettle's been off for a while so it is cold, but it will help."

I drank it down without even bothering to ask what it was, still waiting for my insides to be put right again. I looked up at Min, praying she would have a way to fix me, or at least an explanation, but I found her hand over her mouth, and her eyes dancing as though she were covering a grin.

A grin? What the hell could possibly be funny about this?

"Are you feeling better?" she asked, and now I was certain she was amused.

"A little," I said, my voice squeaky. "What was that? Why do I feel like this?"

"Feel like what? Tell me."

I got the feeling that she didn't need a description, but I tried to play along. "I don't know," I stammered, "different. Like..." I died off, not knowing what to say. The truth was it was like Alex was suddenly and inexplicably the center of my whole world, and all I could think about was going to see him and never being away from him, and a ton of other overly-emotional things that were way too cheesy and melodramatic for someone like me to ever admit to, so I stuck with, "... different."

She smiled knowingly, her obvious amusement really starting to wear on my nerves. "It's Alex, yes?"

I didn't answer, because I didn't need to. It was written all over me, I was sure. All I could do was stare, imploring her to be straight with me. Then, out of nowhere, she started to chuckle. "Poor Alex," she laughed to herself, shaking her head. "Wait until he finds out that all his worrying has been for nothing!"

I was at my wit's end. "Min!" I yelled through clenched teeth. "I need answers! What is wrong with me?" The tears were brimming in my eyes before I could stop them, and I was horrified at the realization that I was actually about to cry.

Thankfully, Min took pity on me, placing my empty cup on the floor, and gathering my hands in hers.

"He's your Anam," she said gently, giving my hands a pat. "That is what happened to you. That is why you feel the way you do. It is normal to feel strange and be emotional for a while, but that part will pass once your mind becomes used to the bond you've created."

I blinked, not understanding. "That can't be right,' I said. "Chloe told me about all that Anam stuff, and she said it had to be a Holder and a non-Holder."

"If Chloe is where you have been getting your information on the subject then there is more we will need to discuss than I thought," she said, rolling her eyes. "Chloe believes that the Anam bond is all true love, and fairy tales, and butterflies, but it is much more substantial than that." She paused, thoughtfully choosing her words before continuing. "Finding your Anam is like finding an extension of yourself in another person. Someone who will likely be very much like you in many respects, but also very different in others. Someone who complements you, balances you. They provide strength for your weaknesses, humility to your brashness, and comfort to your fears."

She stood and went over to one of the bookcases on the wall, pulled out a thick blue book and brought it back to the couch. The cover was worn, but I could see an image embossed onto the leather that looked familiar.

"Is that the Iris?"

She nodded, opening to a brightly colored page, then handing the book over to me. The page was covered in an ornate drawing of two people, surrounded by a frame of intricate Celtic knots and other decorative images.

The style reminded me of Egyptian hieroglyphs, the way the shapes were simple and the people were nondescript in gender, yet the level of detail and elaborate decoration reminded me of the icons of saints in Orthodox churches. The couple in the picture were standing with their bodies facing forward, while their heads were turned to the side, looking at each other and smiling. In the center of each of their chests was a gold circle with faded edges as if to represent light, but the figure on the left had a much smaller light than his right side counterpart. In the center there was a golden ray connecting the two lights, expanding in size as it went from left to right, almost as if the smaller light were feeding the larger.

"When a Holder," Min said, pointing to the figure on the right with the larger light, "finds the non-Holder they are destined for," she continued, now pointing to the other figure, "their spirits recognize one another, and the Holder is bound to that person forever." She touched the two lights and traced the frame encircling the couple. "The legend tells us that this bond was created when the goddess created new non-Holders from all the removed portions of the Holder's souls, but it has also been said that this was not merely an accident. Many Holders believe, myself included, that it was done intentionally, so that each Holder would not have to bear the burden of his or her ability – and they are burdens at times – without someone there to give them strength." She slid her finger across the golden light connecting the two spirits. "Give them love and support to lighten their load. Give them life."

"But, if all that is true, then I shouldn't have bonded with Alex. He's a Holder; I should have bonded with a non-Holder."

"There you are with that word again, what did I tell you about that?" she said, pursing her lips. "I won't try to explain it, because the truth is I cannot. All I know is that you and Alex are Anams. I am as certain of that as I am that I live and breathe. Your tongue can protest all it wants, but your *saol* cannot lie."

"So Chloe was right then, with all that love at first touch stuff?"

"Bah!" She waved her hand as if to shoo away my words. "Love is a cheap word. Anyone can say it, and few truly know what it means. But the Anam bond runs far deeper than that. It is the most profound connection one person can have with another, and it is not always, as they say, wine and roses. In fact," she continued, "it will be a good lesson for you."

"Lesson?"

"A lesson in trust and to let go of your need for control."

"I don't..." but my denial died on my tongue. "I've always been the strong one," I said, loathing the traitorous tears that again filled my eyes, but unable to do anything about them.

"Of course you were. You had to be. But occasionally letting go of control and trusting someone else to act when you cannot, does not mean you are weak – it means you are smart. Being bonded to another in this way is no easy thing. Trusting so completely, and having your happiness so dependent on another person, can be downright terrifying at times, but believe me when I say the rewards are worth the cost."

"That's all well and good, but I still don't understand," I said, pressing my temples to my forehead. "Chloe told me that a Holder can only be truly happy with their Anam, and even this," I saud, gesturing to the book in my lap, "shows a Holder bound to a non-Holder. Even if for some reason I'm bound to Alex, he can't ever be happy with me."

"The next time I hear you say the words can't, or shouldn't, or wouldn't, I'll smack you," she threatened, shaking her finger at me in full-on Russian grandma mode. "There are no rules. For the rest of us maybe, but not for you. How many times do we have to prove that for you to believe it?"

"Then what are you saying, that...?" I paused, remembering something she'd said earlier. "Wait, you said that Alex and I are Anams. What you meant to say was that he was my Anam, right?"

"I know what I said."

"But..." I stumbled over my own thoughts. "You didn't mean..." I looked at Min, but she only sat quietly, offering nothing, like a teacher waiting for her student to work the answer out for themselves. "We're each other's Anam? No, that can't be – yeah." I answered her glare. "I said it – can't be. He would have had to figure that out the first day we met! There is no way he has gone all this time, feeling like... like this," I said, pointing at to myself, "and not said anything."

"What was he to say?"

"I don't know, but something!"

"At the time he realized, you would not have understood, and since then you have been under a constant stream of information. He didn't want to add to your burden or overwhelm you."

"So what, he was waiting for me to just figure it out?"

"No, he fully intended to tell you, but that was before the test. Before we found out that you are also a Holder. Since then he has believed as you do: that a Holder cannot be bound to another Holder. That his bonding to you was a mistake, and that you are in fact destined for someone else."

"No," I said, shaking my head. "I'm sorry, I don't buy it." And I didn't. It was impossible that Alex wouldn't have given me some sign, some hint after all this time.

"You see what I say is true," she said, in the annoying way she had of wording a question as a statement.

"No, sorry, but I don't."

"Then you will see it soon enough, and you will realize how fortunate you are. The bond that has been forged between the two of you is like nothing our kind has ever seen. A Holder to a Holder, bonded on both sides; it has never happened before. But be mindful. In this bond you have a dual-edged sword which can cut deeper than its single-bladed cousin, but when wielded properly can be a fierce weapon."

"What should I do?"

"That is not for me to say. Where you go from here is entirely up to you. However," she said, coming over and putting an arm around me, guiding me to the door, "if I had to make a suggestion, I would say you should go and get a good night's rest."

"But I need to see him; I need to talk to him. You can't expect me to wait–" but I was silenced by Min's finger over my mouth.

"Much as I do not want Alex to suffer any longer than necessary," she said, continuing to guide me toward the door, "you are not in a state of mind at the moment for rational discussion."

"What are you talking about? I'm fine."

"You will be more 'fine' in the morning. Now go." She opened the door shooing me out. "Get to bed."

"It's not even seven o'clock!"

"Never mind that, you will sleep, trust me. No more arguments; get to bed."

"But I'm not tired!"

She glared at me. "Don't make me hypnotize you," she said, pointing again.

I eyed her warily. "You can't... wait, can you do that?"

"Maybe I can, maybe I can't. Do you want to find out?"

"Fine," I huffed, stomping off down the hall as Min closed the door behind me with what I swear was a chuckle.

"What does she know?" I muttered to myself on the way up the stairs. "There is nothing wrong with me, I'm fine!"

I got to my floor, and stood at the top of the stairs not wanting to go to bed – out of spite if nothing else – but not sure what else to do. My hand came to rest against my leg and I felt the small distinct lump of my woven cross in my pocket.

Alex.

I needed to see Alex.

I turned on my heel and ran up to his floor taking the stairs two at a time. Screw Min, what did she know? I'd never felt better in my life; I could do this. I jogged down the hall to Alex's door, and took a deep breath. This would be easy. I would knock, he would answer, and I would say...

I would say...

What would I say?

I stood there, locked in place, hand poised to knock, with no idea what to do next. A shuffling noise from the other side of the door sent a stab of panic to my throat, and I took off running down the hall, down the stairs and into my room before taking another breath.

I staggered into the bedroom and slumped over onto the bed, feeling the pricking of tears once again sting my eyes.

Dear God, this was ridiculous! When did I become such a blubbering ninny?

Maybe Min was right, I wasn't myself. If nothing else, the fact that I'd now been on the verge of crying – something I'd not done in, well, I couldn't remember how long – three times in one night, should have been enough to tell me all was not right in Becca-land and maybe I should hold off talking to anyone about anything emotion-related, much less Alex.

I changed into my nightclothes, brushed my teeth, braided my hair, and crawled into bed, hoping Min was right and sleep would come fast despite the hour. Though, much as I wanted to relax, I couldn't – not with Alex less than twenty feet above my head. Normally it was bad enough lying in bed knowing he was so close and yet so far, but his pacing the floor each night had always done its magic, singing me off to sleep. However, since my awakening as a Holder, he'd stopped his nightly march, leaving me in silence. And now with all these new feelings swelling inside me, making me want nothing more than to have him near, that silence was deafening. But the worst of all my newfound Alex-related sensations was the fact that now I could feel him. I could feel his actual physical being in the room. It was like a warm magnet, pulling deep within my chest.

I tossed and turned, unable to get comfortable, knowing that if Alex didn't find some way to fall asleep that there was no way I would, and hating that there was nothing I could do. Or nothing that I was mentally and emotionally prepared enough to trust myself to do, anyway.

Then again, maybe there was...

Remembering what Mr Anderson had said during our training session this afternoon I reached over and unclipped my Sciath, sliding it off my arm and setting on the bedside table. I felt the fuzzy, unfocused awareness come over me, which was a far cry from the crisp, defined sense I had when my Sciath was unblocked, but for what I wanted to try this would be fine. I felt the brush of

Alex's ability and reached out with my own, intending to join us. It was harder this time, my mental reach like trying to direct a cloud of fog as opposed to the clear band of force I'd already become used to. Finally, I was able to make the connection, shaky though it may have been, and felt his energy flow into me, entwining with mine. I relaxed immediately, relishing the feeling of the connection like I would a warm blanket tucked up under my chin. In turn, I felt the link between us begin to unwind him, though he likely had no idea what it was, seeing it only – as Mr Anderson had put it – as a comforting change in mood.

As I felt the tension slowly begin to drain out of him I snuggled down into my pillow, happy that, while I didn't feel ready to talk to him just yet, I was still able to offer him some sort of comfort. A drowsy curtain began to slip over the both of us, finally allowing the exhausted man above me to glide off to sleep, with me chasing at his heels.

21

"Why can't you be there?" Ryland asked, as we walked through fog on our way to Lorcan for his Awakening.

"Because, buddy, they said I can't. There's no reason to be scared, it wo–"

"I'm not scared."

"Right, sorry." I bit my lip to keep from smiling.

Truth was I'd been trying to find a way to weasel my way into the Awakening all morning, but Min was adamant that it was too dangerous. Apparently there was so much power required for the process that it would be nearly impossible for any Holder who wasn't actively participating to be in the room without extreme discomfort; much less a newbie like me. I would have been fine with the discomfort, but the idea that I could actually end up hurting someone forced me to accept that, like it or not, my attendance was out of the question.

"Who will be there?" he asked after a minute, tying to cover his nerves by making it sound like he didn't care, and was only asking to make conversation.

"Joc– Dad," I caught myself, "and Min."

"The old lady?"

"Yes, her name is Min. But they will both be doing things, so you may only see them at the start and at the end."

"What about the scary-looking guy?"

"OK, Taron," I stressed. "If you are going to be around these people you are going to have to start calling them by their names."

"You knew who I meant," he grumbled.

"Doesn't matter. No more 'old lady', or 'scary guy', or 'guy who talks funny'," I added, figuring I'd cover his nickname for Mr Anderson while I was at it. "Names, you got it?"

"Yeah, yeah."

We walked into Lorcan and into the lounge where Min, Mr Anderson, Mr Reid, and *Taron* were all waiting.

"There they are," said Mr Reid, seeing us enter. I felt Ryland shrink back a little when he saw Taron, but I led him into the room. "Are you ready?" Mr Reid asked Ryland.

"Sure," he said, with maybe a little too much bravado.

"There's a good lad!" Mr Anderson said, stepping up. "I've a class to be getting to, but I wanted to wish you luck!" He smiled, holding out a hand for Ryland to hit. "Taron?" He turned to the figure lurking in the corner. "You coming?"

Taron grunted, ever the charmer, and the two men stepped out into the cold. However at the moment my attention wasn't on them. It was on the already familiar warm, welcome pull in my chest, announcing the approach of someone on the staircase. A person who I could tell had already left his room this morning when I woke up, and I had not seen or felt all day.

Alex.

This was my shot. I'd already made the decision to talk to him today, being in a much better and less emotionally driven frame of mind, and was eager to get it over with so the butterflies in my stomach could find a new home.

But unfortunately it would have to wait just a little longer, because right now Ryland needed me.

"Is everything ready to go?" I asked Min.

"Yes," she nodded. "How about you?" The look in her eye told me exactly what she meant.

"Soon," was all I said.

"All right then," she said, looking down at Ry. "Let's go on back."

"Are you sure you can't come?" he asked, again pretending the answer was of no significance whatsoever.

"I'm sorry, Ry."

Min put a hand on his back and led him out of the lounge and down the hall while I watched, hugging my arms to my chest.

"He'll be fine, Becca," Mr Reid said.

"I know," I agreed. "I just wish he didn't have to be alone."

"Here," he said, turning toward the table with the checker board painted on it. "Why don't we have a round while we wait? It will take your mind off things."

I glanced out toward the hall, intending to tell him I couldn't because I needed to go and talk to someone, but paused, suddenly realizing that particular someone was gone. Alex must have left while Min was taking Ryland out and I hadn't realized. I peeked my head out into the hall to make sure, only to find it empty.

Damn.

Should I go look for him? Everything in me screamed yes, but deep down I knew it wasn't the time. Alex and I needed to talk – really talk – and I didn't want to have such an important conversation while part of my mind would be worried about Ry. Much as I hated putting it off once again, I'd promised Ryland that I'd be in the lounge waiting for him when he got out and that's where I needed to be; Alex would understand that. I could wait one more hour.

"Sure." I smiled at Mr Reid, who was arranging the game pieces on the board without so much as lifting a finger. "That would be great."

I sat down at the table, promising myself that once this Awakening was over and I was sure Ryland was OK, I would go looking for Alex, and not come back until I'd found him.

After seven rounds of checkers, only one of which I won – which I was certain was only because Mr Anderson let me – Min returned to the lounge.

"We're done," she said. "Everything went just as it should have."

"He's OK? Is he normal?"

"He's just fine. Cormac will need to confirm it, but as far as I can see his power level is completely normal. No stronger than, say, Anderson or Reid. He will be able to read minds and do some compulsion, but I doubt he will have anything beyond that."

"So, no erasing minds like Jocelyn, or hearing dead people or anything like that? He's just a normal mind-reader?" I asked, ignoring the oxymoron.

"Yes. Perfectly normal."

"Where is he?" I asked, having assumed Ryland would come back with her.

"Still in the Chamber with Jocelyn. I told him he wasn't allowed out until he finished every drop of the elixir I gave him. You can go in and see him if you want."

I hurried down to the Chamber where Ryland was sitting on a long table, drinking out of one of the jars I recognized from Min's office. Jocelyn looked up and gave me a stiff nod before stepping through the back door to his office.

Nice to see you, too.

"How'd it go?" I asked walking over to Ry, relieved that he seemed to be fine.

"OK," he said, peering down into the jar. "This is gross."

"Just drink it. Trust me, if it's from Min, it's good stuff." I leaned against the table next to him, noticing the new necklace he had around his neck. It was a lot like Alex's only his cord was brown leather and the stone in the center was red. "So it wasn't scary?"

"Nah," he said downing the rest of the drink. "Plus Alex was with me."

My head snapped up, "Alex was here?"

"Yeah, he said you didn't want me to be alone."

"He held his hand the whole time," came Min's voice from the door.

"He didn't need to," Ryland said, not about to let us think he'd been scared.

"No, of course not," Min said, smiling at him. "You were one of the bravest I've seen."

Ry looked at me proudly as if to make sure I'd heard, but I was looking at Min. "He was here?" I whispered. "I thought you said…"

"That it would be very difficult, yes. And it was. I told him as much before we began, but he would have it no other way." She turned to Ryland as I stared off, completely overwhelmed. "Now then, let's go and get you something to eat." She took the jar from him, and helped him down off the table. When they passed by me, Ryland poked my arm.

"You coming?"

"Becca has something she has to take care of up on the covered balcony first, I think," Min said, urging him on. "Maybe she'll come and join us later."

"OK, bye Becca," he said, following Min out of the Chamber, as I stared after them in a daze.

Alex had sat with Ryland so he wouldn't be scared. Despite all the strangeness between us he'd been there to take care of him when I couldn't. The swelling of emotion that fact caused in me was so strong that it was hard to breathe.

And, not just of nameless emotion… of love.

I loved him.

Yes, I was bonded to him, but that wasn't the same thing. Maybe to some people it would have been but as far as I was concerned the ideas were separate. My bond to him as my Anam had made it so my life would no longer be complete without him. It had rearranged my world, placing him in the center, fulfilling me in ways I hadn't realized I was empty. And yes, it had caused me to fall in love with him, and maybe that's where a large part of my love had stemmed from, but I also know it was much more than that. If I was being honest, my feelings for Alex had started long before the Anam bond had, even if I hadn't been ready to acknowledge them at the time. I didn't love Alex only because some supernatural connection told me I had to. I loved him because I knew him. Because I'd seen the man he truly was inside, and it never failed to amaze me. I loved him for his heart and his strength. For his endless compassion and his unbreakable spirit even in the face of everything he'd been through. I loved him because he was the person I wanted to be, and I was a better person just through the privilege of knowing him.

I'd only been to the covered balcony once before, but my feet seemed to remember the way all on their own and I was down the hall and up the stairs before I'd even realized I'd moved. As the door to the balcony came into sight, I felt the pulling in my chest and knew that Min had been right, he was out there. I gently reached for the handle and pulled open the door, surprised by how warm it was inside. The balcony was entirely glassed in as well as heated, but I'd still expected it to be chilly.

I stepped into the enclosure, shut the door softly behind me, and looked down to the other end, where Alex was standing in the corner with his arms crossed over his chest, gazing out over the thinning fog.

I slowly walked toward him, not sure where to begin. He tilted his head, glancing at me as I drew near, though he didn't turn to face me.

"Thank you," I said, stopping a few feet away from him. "For Ryland I mean. You didn't have to do that, I know it must have been hard–"

"It was nothing," he interrupted, trying to smile. "Just a little tiring that's all. Min says it will wear off in a few hours. Besides, he shouldn't have had to do it alone," he added, turning completely away from me, pretending to look out the back wall of windows, though I could see by his refection in the glass that his eyes were shut. "It was nothing."

"It was something to me."

I shouldn't have been surprised. Of course he would think it was nothing – because to him it truly was. He was always taking care of everyone around him, always giving. This truly was his family and he would do anything for any one of them, and the fact that he actually thought that it was unremarkable, only made it more so. I knew how much he loved Min and Chloe, and enjoyed the antics of Mr Anderson and Mr Reid. I also knew how close to his heart the scouting he did was, and how attached he was to the Order and his overall life at the school. And of course there was Jocelyn, who I knew Alex looked up to and respected as much as any son would a father, and it was more than apparent that each and every person in this little makeshift family loved Alex as much as he did them. And yet, as I watched him now, staring off into the falling snow, for the first time I could see how lonely he was. He didn't have what he truly wanted, what he needed. Even with all the people around him every day, when it came to the ways that mattered most, he was alone.

But it didn't have to be that way.

He had me.

I took a silent breath and steadied my shaking arms as I realized it was now or never.

"You're an amazing man, Alex," I said, watching the refection of his face. His eyes popped open but he didn't move. I took a step toward him and continued. "You take care of everyone, but who takes care of you?"

He cleared his throat, and it took him a moment to respond. "I don't need to be taken care of," he said quietly without turning.

"Everyone needs to be taken care of." I reached out my hand, placing it gently on his arm. He stiffened for a moment but didn't turn, so I stepped around in front of him. "Everyone needs someone," I told him softly, "and I need you."

He shut his eyes again and shook his head. "Becca, please don't do this to me," he breathed, begging.

"Do what? Tell you how I feel? You told me once never to apologize for that."

I waited for a response, but none came. He simply stared out into fog. Finally I couldn't take it anymore. I had to know what he was thinking, what he was *feeling*. I remembered the conversation we'd had on the plane the morning we landed. The conversation about Sciaths and – weaknesses.

Before I could think about it and change my mind, I lifted my hands, letting them slowly make their way toward either side of his neck. Seeing my movement he finally glanced down, and as my fingers touched the clasp of the cord, fear shot across his face and his hands flew up, pinning my wrists to his shoulders.

"No," he said, dread in his voice.

"Why not?" I asked, at the very least happy to have gotten a reaction. "It's only me."

"Yes, exactly. It's you," he said, keeping my hands firmly locked in place.

OK, that one hurt. I understood why he would be worried, but if he was so set on keeping his feelings hidden and me at arm's length then why was he still here? After all, he could have left. He could have let go of me and stepped away, I wouldn't have stopped him. But he did neither.

After a few moments his hold on my wrists started to loosen a bit. I don't think it was conscious on his part, but I found myself able to slide my hands out from under his. Again I went for the clasp of his Sciath, fully expecting him to stop me, but this time he didn't. I unfastened the clip and slid the cord from his neck, and waited. Waited for… well, actually I had no idea what I was waiting for. What did emotions look like? Would I actually see them? Or maybe I would hear something?

But nothing was happening. It wasn't until I looked up at him and saw the rock hard strain in his jaw that I realized what the problem was. He was holding everything in and keeping me out. He had said this was possible, but he'd also said that it was very hard to do. I probably could have waited him out, as it was clear he was already exhausted from attending the Awakening and wasn't going to be able to keep it up for long, but that wasn't what I wanted. I wanted him to want to let me in, not be unable to keep me out.

As I watched him battle to stay in control it was easy to see that he was losing. And yet as desperate as he seemed to keep me out, again I couldn't help but notice, he didn't leave. All he had to do was turn and walk away, and his internal war would be over.

I didn't know what he was feeling – and he seemed hell-bent on keeping it that way – but if I could do nothing else, I had to make sure he knew that he could trust me, and that I would always be there for him no matter what. I was slightly irritated that he didn't realize this already, but if I had to spell it out for him, then I would.

I reached up, took his face between my hands, and said the words that had been hovering at the back of my mind for weeks now. "Alex," I said, tilting his head, forcing him to meet my eyes, "I love you."

"Becca..." It was no more than a shaky breath, but it held so many different threads of emotion in it that I could barely tell them all apart. "You are meant for someone else."

"No," I said, beaming, hoping he would see the truth in my eyes. "I'm meant for you."

Before he could draw breath to argue with me, I pulled his face in to mine and kissed him.

The moment our lips touched he tensed, sucked a sharp breath, and grabbed my hips hands like iron, holding me at a distance. Undeterred, I moved my hands from the sides of his face to the back of his head, lacing my fingers through his hair, as his ridged mouth began to give way. Slowly, his lips parted and began moving in time with mine, sending my heart slamming into my ribcage. His arms slid, snaking their way around my waist, dragging me against his chest. Finally, I felt the remainder of his strain and tension snap with a shudder…

And that's when I saw it.

22

The flimsy wall he'd put up around himself collapsed like a tower of building blocks on a crooked table, and I was suddenly surrounded by swirling clouds of pure feeling. Every emotion that he was experiencing became visible, intertwining around us like billowing transparent waves of color – each wave representing a different emotion, and each emotion flowing with a different intensity. It was like nothing I'd ever seen before – like seeing into the soul.

The waves of joy and relief were two of the most prominent, and were laced with bright ribbons of contentment and trust. His confusion and skepticism were still there, as well as the remnants of grief and loneliness from the past few days. But happily, those darker emotional strands were quickly being swallowed up by the lighter colored positive waves of excitement and bliss. There were wispy curls of surprised delight, humored amusement, and peaceful submission, all dancing along the surface of the larger feelings like salty spray on the sea. But as much as there was to see, I had to admit, the wave ringing the loudest and shining the brightest was the one I was focused on, drinking it in like blessed water after a marathon.

It was his love.

Min had told me that he was bound to me, and how much he had suffered thinking we could never be together. The information had subconsciously led me to believe that he loved me, but assuming was nothing compared to knowing.

After a long, languid moment, our lips parted, and Alex rested his forehead against mine, shaking his head, causing mine to wobble.

"This can't be," he whispered, his voice not quite steady. "You shouldn't…"

"Don't let Min hear you say that," I teased, taking advantage of his pause. "She'll smack you."

"Min knows about this?" He pulled his head back, looking at me.

"Sure, she's the one who told me what actually happened to me yesterday."

"Yesterday?"

I nodded. "In the Inner Chamber, when you touched my hand on your way out."

"I… I don't remember… and that's when you…" he stammered, looking through me for a second.

I stood quietly, allowing him to think, and I watched in amazement as his internal pondering turned the bluish-gray wave of confusion that was still mingling in and out of his other emotions to lighten in color, turning to comprehension and finally, elation.

"So, this is real then?" he asked me, with so much joy in his eyes it made my throat tight. "You are really meant for me? We're meant... for each other?"

"Well, all I know for sure is that you are meant for me," I said, wrapping my arms around his waist, feeling my stomach give an excited squeeze, "but if you want me, I am all yours."

His eyes sparkled as he gently cupped my neck, tipping my chin up and capturing my lips again, giving me a very welcome non-verbal answer.

A minute later – or thereabouts, as I'd lost track of time, but whatever the actual total was, it wasn't long enough – Alex stepped back, but not before placing one last kiss on the hollow under my ear where my neck met my jaw. "Come on," he said, taking my hand and leading me over to a wide window seat.

We sat silently for a moment, neither of us sure what to say, when suddenly Alex started to laugh – a bit hysterically, actually – rubbing his hands over his face.

"How can this have happened? This is impossible!" He laughed, leaning back looking so relieved, he was almost slaphappy. "I'm not complaining or anything, it's just..." He looked over at me with unabashed wonder. "I would never in a thousand lifetimes have thought that this could ever happen."

"Yeah," I said, giving him a wry sideways glance "About all that 'thinking' you did – did it ever occur to you to just come out and tell me about all this?"

"Well, that depends," he said, grinning. "Do you mean before or after the Iris test debacle?"

"Either," I said, loving the playful smile on his face simply for the fact that it was there again.

"If we are talking about after, then no, there was no way I was going to tell you." I noticed some of the sadder strands of emotion flow back in to the cloudy cocktail floating around him. He must have seen my eyes wondering, because all of a sudden his ears turned red and a huge wave of embarrassment came billowing out into the mix.

"Right," he said with an awkward laugh, rubbing his neck where his Sciath should be. "I forgot you had that."

"You forgot? So, you can't see all this?"

"Nope."

I reached into my pocket and pulled out his Sciath, handing it over to him, fully expecting him to put it back on. He took it from me and looked at it a moment before laying it down on the bench between us.

"No." He shook his head. "I don't need it. I have nothing to hide. Not from you."

I picked up the necklace and reached around his neck, putting it back in its place. "I know you don't," I assured him, touched that he was willing to knowingly make himself so vulnerable. "But it doesn't need to happen all at once. We can work up to it."

Much as I loved being able to see what was going on inside him, I wanted him to be comfortable. I would never force him to go without it, and simply the fact that he was willing to was more than enough for me. I gave him a kiss on the cheek as I fastened the clip, and watched as all the wispy clouds vanished instantly.

"Now then, you were saying something about how you've spent the last few days lying to me..." I prompted with a smirk.

"I wasn't lying, I was..." The grin he started out with sunk as he trailed off, appearing at a loss for words. He sighed and leaned forward, resting his elbows on his knees, hands dangling between his legs. "I was in hell."

"You don't have to tell me," I said, when he stopped again. "It's OK."

"No." He looked up. "I want to. I want you to understand. I feel horrible for treating you the way I did – deliberately avoiding you, and pushing you off. I didn't mean to hurt you, but I didn't know what else to do. I had to keep you away until I could find a way to... cope."

He turned his head toward the opposite window looking at the landscape, but seeing only memories.

"When you activated the Iris, I didn't know what to think. After it was all over I lapsed into something like a trance. As if my mind couldn't process what had happened. Or maybe I wasn't letting my mind process it, I don't know. In any event, I was basically in a stupor until Min came to check on me that night, which is when my," he hesitated with an embarrassed wince, "somewhat hysterical meltdown occurred."

My hand found its way over to his arm, rubbing gently, my chest aching at what he must have gone through. He lifted my hand to his lips kissing my knuckles appreciatively, then brought it down, holding it between both of his hands.

"Min actually told me to try being with you anyway," he continued. "To act as though nothing had happened and see how things worked out."

"But you didn't want to do that?"

He shook his head slowly. "There was no way that would have ended well for me. Yes, I would have had you, but I would also have had to live in fear that on any given day you could meet your own Anam. Standing by and watching you bond to someone else isn't something I'd have ever been strong enough to do. But even if that day never came, I would still have to live my whole life knowing that you weren't as happy with me as I was with you. Whether you knew it or not, for you, I would have never been more than second best."

I nodded, silently agreeing with him. I'd once considered if Alex could be happy enough with me even though I wasn't – or, had assumed I wasn't – his Anam. Even at the time I could tell the idea, while tempting, would lead to nowhere good, and I wasn't even bonded to him then. I couldn't imagine how horrible the idea had seemed to him.

"Before she left that night Min tried to give me something to put me to sleep, but I wouldn't take it. I don't know, for some reason I was afraid to sleep, so I sat up all night long just thinking. The only conclusion I could come to was that it had all been a mistake. That you weren't truly my Anam, that I shouldn't have bonded with you, and that my feelings would go away – but somehow, deep down, I knew they wouldn't. The only shred of hope I had was that maybe the mistake had been with you. Maybe the Iris had reacted to something else entirely and when Cormac went to read you, he wouldn't find anything. Slim chance or no, it was all I had to hold onto. But then, the next morning, it turned out I didn't even need Cormac to tell me. The moment Min took your Sciath off, I knew. The way your face lit up when you felt the changing within you… it broke my heart."

"You looked so terrible that day," I murmured more to myself than to him, finally knowing why.

"Thank you," he said, throwing me a glance.

"You know what I mean." I nudged him with my shoulder.

He gave my hand an affectionate squeeze and continued. "After that, I did my best to keep you at a distance. It was just too hard. I was waiting for… I don't even know what. For my feelings to go away, maybe. For something to just make sense again." He paused, giving me a sneaky grin, "Though I will say, if I'd have known how things were going to work out, I'd have touched you that first day and saved myself some sleepless nights."

"Last night wasn't so bad." The words were out of my mouth before I could stop them, and I immediately looked away, biting my tongue.

He sat up, ending any hope I had of him having missed the comment. "How did you know that?" Before I could think up an excuse, he figured it out. "That was you? How did you do that?" he asked, turning to face me.

"I connected with you," I admitted, seeing there would be no way around it. "When I'd done it with Mr

Anderson in training that afternoon, he'd said it was comforting, so I thought I'd see if I could help."

"But didn't Min replace the Block after your session?"

"She did, so I took the whole thing off."

"Becca! You shouldn't have done that, it's dangerous!"

"But, you were upset."

The anger in his eyes softened, and then melted into something that made my skin warm and my stomach tight.

He leaned toward me with embers burning behind his gray eyes. "Well," he said, his lips just barely brushing mine as he spoke, "I promise you I will sleep very, very well tonight."

Just before he moved in – and I lost my focus completely – I leaned away. "Hold on now, you're not off the hook yet." I pressed my finger to his lips, pushing him back a bit. "I get why you didn't tell me after the test, and I can even see why you wouldn't have told me in the beginning, but that still doesn't explain why you didn't bring it up at any point in between. You had a good two weeks at your disposal, why didn't you just tell me?"

He looked away again, his ears turning red. "I…" He paused, clearing his throat and scratching the back of his neck. "I didn't want to tell you until…"

"What?"

He took a breath and looked up sheepishly. "I wanted you to love me." He held my eyes for a second then looked back down, his ears on fire. "But on your own, because you wanted to, not because you felt like you had to."

"You know I'm not the type to be pressured into anything."

"You mean to tell me," he eyed me skeptically, "that if I had told you that I was, not only hopelessly in love, but also irreversibly bound to you for the rest of my life, that you wouldn't have felt the slightest bit obligated to at least try to be with me? Then felt guilty if you couldn't make it work?"

"Maybe a little," I allowed.

"See? That's not what I wanted. I wanted you to be with me because it's what you wanted, and I thought maybe if we spent time together..." He cleared his throat again. "Anyway, I couldn't wait any longer, so I'd planned to tell you the night after the test, and hope for the best."

"Alex," I said, leaning over and forcing him to look at me, "I did love you. I may not have realized it at first, but I knew that before–"

"No," he said, holding a hand up to stop me. "It's OK, really."

"I'm serious," I insisted, not about to let him think that I was only trying to tell him what he wanted to hear.

"I know it may seem that way now, but really, it's all right." He brought his hand up, resting it on the side of my neck, grazing his thumb across my cheek. "What we've ended up with is more than I'd ever even imagined, that's all that matters."

As opposed to arguing with him, I reached into my pocket and pulled out the woven cross, holding it up for him to see. "Remember this?" I asked, though the look on his face told me he did.

"You kept that?" he breathed.

"I kept it, and it has been either in my pocket or on my bedside table every moment since that afternoon," I said. "So, don't you tell me that I didn't love you."

The next thing I knew he was kissing me with so much zeal that I actually had a hard time staying upright. His hands laced into my hair, and his throaty groan echoed in my chest, sending goosebumps up my arms and my eyes rolling back. Hours before I was ready, he released me, once again placing a kiss on that same spot under my ear, this time murmuring something against my skin that I didn't quite catch – though I was also fairly certain it wasn't in English.

He stood, pulling me up with him, taking my hand and leading me into the building, while I slid my cross safely back into my pocket. "I have to go down to Cormac's office, he's expecting me," he said, as we made our way hand in hand down the hall, stopping when we reached the top of the stairs. "It shouldn't take long, and then can we get dinner?"

"Sure," I said, so happy to be getting back to our old routine. "I should go check on Ryland anyway. Meet you in the lounge?"

"I'll be there," he said, rubbing his thumb across the back of my hand, then skipping off down the stairs.

I greeted my good buddies the stomach butterflies as they returned, carrying me down the steps to the first landing. They were around so much lately I was starting to think of them as pets, and idly wondered if I should consider naming them. However, my fluffy haze cleared somewhat as I rounded the banister and saw the agitated figure of Jocelyn coming up the stairs. He stopped as he saw me, looking me straight in the eye, his mouth a hard line.

"I need to have a word with you," he stated with no inflection whatsoever.

His words might not have given much away, but his expression told me one thing for sure...

I was in trouble.

23

If I'd been intimidated by Jocelyn, or even respected him enough to put any value on his good opinion, I might have been concerned. But as it stood, I wasn't. Whatever his problem was, I knew I hadn't done anything, and that this would turn out to be a mistake. Hell, I hadn't even been alone today, there was no way I'd done whatever he thought I had. Sure, I was planning to skip Gaelic class the next day, but it wasn't like it had actually happened yet, and unless he'd read my mind there was no way he could have known about it. And if he had read my mind, no matter what he'd seen, he was the one in the wrong, so either way I was good. Besides, if I came to find out that he'd read my mind, the conversation wouldn't get all that far anyway, because I'd be kicking his ass.

I followed him down to his office, not sure where this was all leading. Once the office door was closed behind us he stalked up to the front of the room next to his desk where he spun to face me, looking in no way pleased.

"It appears we need to have a discussion regarding your place here, and what it does and does not entail.

You may have arrived under the pretense that you were here to look after Ryland and wouldn't be staying. However, things have changed, and since you will be staying, there are some ground rules that need to be set."

"What are you talking about?"

"You are here to learn and to train."

"Yeah, OK…?"

"You will be a valuable asset to our organization and our cause, and the last thing you need is distraction."

"What?" I asked, beyond confused.

"You are not the type of person who needs to be… involved with anyone."

"Invol–" the word strangled in my throat as I realized what he was talking about. Immediately my mind went to the only other person who knew about Alex and me. "Did Min talk to you?" I asked, already plotting her demise.

"Min? No, Min has nothing to do with this." He clasped his hands behind his back and squared his shoulders, trying to appear as stern as possible. "You may not be aware of it, but my apartments are directly above this office and connected to the covered balcony on the east wall."

"You… you were watching us?" I half shrieked, both mortified and furious.

"No, I was not watching you, but yes, I did see you, and I want to make it very clear that nothing like that will ever happen again."

"Excuse me?" I whispered, barely comprehending what I was hearing. "Are you out of your mind?"

"I am very serious. A relationship like that won't end well for either of you, and that sort of distraction is the last thing you need right now. Your focus is to be on your training and the learning of our ways, and absolutely not on dating. Are we clear?"

"And I suppose the nature of our involvement is irrelevant to you? Even if I told you Alex had bonded to me?" And me to him, though I withheld that particular nugget.

"Impossible," he dismissed, and even had the blood curdling audacity to roll his eyes slightly, as though I was nothing more than a silly girl with a starry-eyed dream. "You're a Holder. It doesn't work that way. You will get your head out of the clouds and do what needs to be done, before any of this gets worse."

I felt my neck grow hot and my face flush as I looked at his aloof stance and stony expression. He expected me to just toss love aside, like it meant nothing. To throw it all away and focus on myself, not caring who I hurt in the process.

To be like him.

"So, let me get this straight," I said, trying to unclench my teeth. "I'm not allowed to be with Alex?"

"Alex has nothing to do with this, you have no business being with anyone, not with the way things have turned out regarding your ability. Alex is a good man, and I expect you to handle the situation like an adult and give him the respect of a courteous explanation, and then focus your attentions where they need to be."

In that moment, something in me snapped. "The respect of a courteous explanation? The respect of a *courteous explanation*?" I growled through my teeth. "What should I do? Should I send him a letter? Is that the adult thing to do?" He went rigid but didn't respond, his lips pressing back into their hard line. "You're the expert on ruining lives after all." I smiled cynically. "By all means, tell me what to do. Should I marry him first, would that be better? Start a family with him, then dump him flat? Make sure he really hates me?"

"How your mother feels about me has nothing to do with this."

"How she feels about you? If only!" I was shaking, I was so furious. "I wish she hated you! Dear God, you have no idea! But she never will. You dug your claws into her so deep that she'll go to her grave defending you, instead of finally realizing what a selfish coward you really are."

"There is nothing more I could have done to make it any easier on her!" he yelled.

"You have got to be kidding me! This, from the man who can literally alter memories and erase minds? You could have done anything you wanted! You could have made her forget all about you! You could have made her think she was the one who left you! Hell, even making her think you had died would have been better than a flat out rejection! You could have made it as easy on her as you wanted it to be, but you didn't! And don't give me any of that crap about not believing in interfering with people's minds, because you know damn well that there is nothing you could have done to her mind that would be any worse than what you actually did."

His expression hadn't faltered once since I started, nor had he attempted to speak. He just stood there rock hard, his cool impassiveness only fueling my fire.

"And now," I fumed, "you dare tell me who I can and can't be with? Who I can and can't love? You, who knows absolutely nothing about me? Expecting me to throw Alex aside so that I can focus on my own interests? I don't know what's worse; the fact that I have someone like you for a father, or the fact that you actually think I'm like you!" I finished, disgust heavy in my voice. I turned my back on him, stomping to the door, yanking it open.

"We're not done here." Jocelyn's voice as cold as steel came from behind me.

I glared over my shoulder at him as I yanked the door open. "On the contrary, professor, you and I are more than done," I spat, slamming the door behind me.

A few minutes later I was leaning up against the outside garden wall, arms crossed over my chest, still seething. The hot air streaming in and out of my flared nostrils turned to fog the moment it hit the chilly air making me look like an angry bull from a Saturday morning cartoon. I wanted to throw something, to scream, to jump up and down. Yet all I could seem to do was rigidly hold up the wall, hissing and cursing under my breath.

For ten years I'd dreamt of telling Jocelyn off. Of letting him know exactly what I thought of him, in as colorful a choice of language as I knew. Now that it was over, I waited for the endorphin rush of success. For the jump up and down, punching your fists in the air, take on the world victory dance, complete with Rocky-style theme music playing in the background. But thus far, all I had were throbbing temples, cold toes, a sore jaw from clenching my teeth, and the sound track of a bird cawing, that may or may not have been choking on something.

Not exactly what I'd imagined.

"It's cold out here," came the voice of someone I'd felt before I'd heard. "You should have a coat on," Alex said, eyeing my thin shirt and bare arms.

"I'm fine," I said, as he came up beside me. "My internal temperature is more than making up the difference."

"What happened?"

I huffed and pushed away from the wall, running my hands angrily through my hair which was now damp with fog. "Jocelyn and I..."

"I know," he said, when I didn't finish. "I actually overheard the tail end of it."

"You did?"

"Yeah, sorry. Cormac too. We were on our way to Jocelyn's office, and well," he gave me a sympathetic smile, "your voice carries. But don't worry, Cormac would never say anything. What I meant was, what started it?"

"What started it? Oh, nothing much, just Jocelyn basically forbidding me from being with you."

"What?"

"Yep. But don't worry, it's not you. I'm not allowed to be with anyone."

"He said that?"

"In no uncertain terms." I scowled down at the gravel pathway. "Who the hell does he think he is? What on earth makes him think he has a say in my love life?" I started kicking at the rocks, as my rage reared up again, clawing at my chest. "All of a sudden I'm a Holder, so now he owns me? The hell he does! He probably doesn't even remember when my birthday is, yet he thinks he can play 'father figure'? Fat damn chance! Any right he had to be the guy sitting on the front porch with a shotgun waiting for me to come home from a date was forfeited over ten years ago!"

"Were you all farmers in Kansas at some point?" Alex asked, suppressing a smile.

Suddenly I was actually picturing Jocelyn in overalls and a straw hat, sitting on a wooden rocker with a double barrel in his lap, and I started to smirk. I knew that was the point of his comment, but it still pissed me off. "I'm trying to be mad over here!" I snapped at him, still smiling in spite of myself.

"I'm sorry," he said gravely, putting on his serious face. "Go ahead."

But it was over. He'd effectively killed my tirade. I let my head hang down, blowing out the rest of my tension with a heavy sigh, glaring at him out of the corner of my eye.

"You did that on purpose."

"Maybe."

"Jerk!" I grinned, shivering.

He smiled, slipping his jacket off and wrapping it around me. "Anytime, leannán," he said stepping up behind me, hugging me against his chest.

"What?"

"Leannán," he repeated. "It's an endearment, like sweetheart or darling. Speaking of which, I hear you're in Gaelic class."

"Yeah, not for long," I grumbled.

"Becca..." he chided.

"It's so boring," I whined. "I got the text and the workbook, I'll just teach myself."

"No, you won't," he laughed, shaking his head.

"Excuse me!" I looked over my shoulder at him indignantly. "I happen to have graduated high school at fifteen, with a 5.0, and an ACT score of 31! I can most certainly teach myself a language!"

He continued to smile at me, amused. "I didn't say you can't, I said you won't. There's a difference."

OK, he was probably right, but I wasn't about to admit it. I changed topics. "Why do I even need it? You speak Gaelic, not to mention the oh-so-wonderful Professor Ingle," I sassed, using a bit more sarcasm than was really called for. "Can't one of you just tell me what stuff says?"

"What if we're not with you?"

"I'll call." I pouted, knowing I was going to lose this.

He sighed and leaned his head down so his mouth was next to my ear. "*Mo shaol anois tá brí toisc go bhfuil tú i sé, a ghrá mo chroí*," he murmured in a low, throaty voice, sending chills fluttering under my skin.

"Should I even bother asking?" I said, knowing he was probably making a point and wasn't planning on translating.

"Keep going to class, and you won't have to."

I leaned my head back to rest on his shoulder. "Somehow, I'm thinking whatever that was isn't going to be covered."

"Don't go, and you'll never find out." I could hear the grin in his tone.

We stood quietly for a minute, when something I'd been wondering about for a long time suddenly came to mind.

"Why don't you stick up for him?" I asked, a bit out of the blue. "You never do."

"What?"

"Jocelyn. I am constantly whining and complaining about him, and you have never once tried to defend him."

"You want me to defend him?" he asked as though I'd lost my mind.

"No, I've just always wondered. I know much you respect him. How much you look up to him. I've always known, and I understand. After what he did for you, you have every reason to think he's great, yet for all the times you've had to listen to me badmouth him, you've never, I don't know, come to his aid. I'm always waiting for it, but it never happens." The way it was turning out, the fact that Jocelyn had been responsible for saving Alex from the mental hospital and bringing him into this world – and by extension, to me – seemed like it might end up being his singular saving grace in my eyes.

"First of all," he said, spinning me around in his arms to face him, "you have never badmouthed him.

You've told me things that have happened, and how you personally feel. You don't run to anyone who will listen and slander him, you're far too good a person for that. You've even allowed Ryland to draw his own conclusions, never influencing or leading him with your own opinions. And yes, I do respect Jocelyn. More than any other man I've ever met, but that doesn't mean he's perfect. I don't know what happened with your family all those years ago, and I am in no position to defend him. And I certainly won't defend his not wanting us together, but I'm not too concerned about that. We'll have Min talk to him, and it will all work out, I'm sure."

"If you say so," I sighed.

"I do," he said giving me a peck on the nose. "Not to change the subject," he continued a bit reluctantly, "but can I ask you something?"

"Anything."

"Earlier, when you said 'Professor Ingle'... you did mean Jocelyn, yes?"

"Of course, who else?" He didn't answer, but something in his eyes made me wary. "Why do you ask?"

"Well..." He was obviously uncomfortable. "I wasn't sure, because Jocelyn's name – as far as I have ever known – is Clavish."

"What? No... no, that's not right. His name is Ingle... we are all Ingle."

He shrugged with a wince. "I assumed your mother had taken her maiden name or something like that."

"So," I backed away from him, pressing my fingers to my temples, "he actually changed his name? Why the hell would he do that?" When Alex's lip twitched, I could see there was something else. "What? What is it? Tell me!" I knew I shouldn't be yelling at him, but I couldn't help it.

"It's nothing," he said, raising his hands in an effort to calm me. "It's just that I don't think he changed his name. I've seen things with his name on them. Old things – much older than you. And his name was always Clavish."

I stared at him, completely dumbfounded for the first time in my life. "He took a fake name?" I breathed, embarrassed by how hurt I was. "He married my mother with a fake name?"

Alex pulled me in against him, rubbing my back. "I don't know," he said, kissing my forehead. "I'm sorry, I shouldn't have said anything."

"Yes, you should have." I wrapped my arms around his waist, resting my head on his chest. "I didn't mean to yell, it's not your fault. I just can't believe… why would he do that? What would someone…?" I shook my head, leaving the thought hanging. I knew the more I thought about it the angrier I'd get, and I'd had enough fuming for one afternoon. To hell with Jocelyn, whoever he was.

"You could always ask him, you know," Alex suggested.

"Yeah, I think we both know how that would turn out," I said glancing up at him with an evil grin, "and I promised my Mom I wouldn't kill him."

"I didn't mean right now," he laughed. "When you're ready."

"Pretty sure that will never happen."

"You don't give yourself enough credit."

"You give me way too much credit. We're not all perfect portraits of cool-headed rationality," I teased. "Do you ever get mad?"

"Oh, sure," he said. "There isn't usually anyone around to see it, but it happens."

"Well, make sure you find me next time, because I'm interested."

"Don't worry, I'm sure you'll piss me off sooner or later," he said with a chuckle.

"I look forward to it," I laughed. "Then, maybe I'll get the chance to do something for you, for a change."

"Ah, Becca," he sighed, lowering his face so his nose brushed against mine, raising the hairs on my arms. "You have no idea how much you do for me."

I looked up to find his stormy gaze holding me. "You have beautiful eyes," I sighed, loving the way his stare warmed my insides.

He froze for a second, before he smiled. "Yes," he chuckled. "I know."

"You *know*?" Not exactly the reaction I was expecting. "Most people would say thank you."

"I'm sorry," he amended, still grinning at his private joke. "What I meant was, you've told me that before."

"What?" I asked, completely confused now. "No I haven't." Sure, I'd thought about it, but I'd never actually said it. I most certainly would have remembered that.

But he nodded, his smile becoming shy. "Do you remember giving me back my pillow on the plane the morning we landed in Paris?"

"Sure."

"Do you remember what I told you when you thanked me?"

"Yeah, that I had already thanked you in my sleep..." My hands flew to my mouth as I remembered him acting strange that morning, and wondering if I'd said something else... "Oh God, I didn't..."

He chucked again. "You did." The gleam in his eyes told me that he was finding my embarrassment endearing, but I was far from amused.

"Was that it?" I demanded, slightly panicked. "Please tell me that was it."

"That was it, I promise. I slid the pillow under your head, you thanked me, and said," he paused, then quoted, "'You have the most amazing eyes. They're beautiful.'"

"Oh..." I moaned, squeezing my eyes shut and hiding my face against his chest.

"Don't," he laughed, leaning back and lifting my face. "You have nothing to be embarrassed about"

"Are you kidding me? I barely knew you, you must have thought I was a psycho!"

He grinned. "Actually," he said, leaning down until his lips brushed against mine, his scent filling my head, "it made my night."

He tilted my head up with his thumb and kissed me so tenderly that my embarrassment drained away instantly. I felt my neck flush and my pulse start to race and I realized it suddenly felt way too hot out for November. His lips continued to move slowly – so slowly – just barely touching my own, teasing me until my insides were screaming. After a few more seconds I couldn't take it any longer; I needed more. I brought my hands up to his neck and grabbed two handfuls of his collar and lifted myself up, moving my lips hungrily against his. With a gruff sigh, Alex grabbed my hips, and pulled me up against him. One of his arms wound its way around me, holding me tight, while the other hand slid up my back and neck, burying itself in my hair. The blood in my veins turned to molten honey as he opened his mouth and–

"Oh... My... God!"

Alex and I both froze, snapping our heads towards the front of the building, where Chloe stood, gaping at us.

"*Oh my God, oh my God, oh my God,*" she shrieked, like a cat having its tail stepped on, "How could you not tell me?"

"Oh no," Alex said, still breathing much heavier than usual. "I think we're in trouble."

"What do we do?" I giggled as she came stomping toward us, panting a bit myself.

"We run," Alex said with an evil smile, grabbing my hand and taking off in the other direction. I burst out laughing as we ran over the soggy pathway, with a screeching Chloe nipping at our heels.

24

The next afternoon I had to stifle a yawn during my training session with Mr Reid. It wasn't that I was bored; on the contrary, his ability was one that I had been the most excited to learn. It was that I'd stayed up way too late the night before, thanks to Alex. Sounds great, I know, but unfortunately it wasn't in the good way. In fact, Alex wasn't even physically there. He'd gone to bed (or as I would forever call it, bailed on me) right after we'd had dinner with Chloe – who, by the way, could run pretty damn fast when she wanted to – leaving me to field her neverending stream of questions about him and me. How it had happened, when I found out, when he found out, what it was like, how it felt when it happened, etc. After I'd answered everything I could, the cycle began again, in which she scolded me for not telling her I'd had a crush on him all that time, then swore up and down that she was going to let Alex have it for not telling her he'd bonded to me, then gushing about how lucky we were, and how cute we were, and how jealous she was, and repeat.

It was past one in the morning by the time she left my room, at which point I figured it was as good a time as any to give my mom a call. With the five hour time difference between Ireland and Pittsburgh it was only dinner time for her, and I was finally able to bring myself to tell her I was planning on staying at St Brigid's. She wasn't overly thrilled that I was putting off college for yet another year, but liked the idea of me taking some of the college courses St Brigid's offered, stating, "It will be good to have some credits so you can show whatever college you finally decide on that you haven't been slacking off since high school." Plus, she was happy that I would be there to keep an eye on Ry, and I know she was still thinking there was a chance that I would get closer to Jocelyn, though she didn't actually say it. I hadn't told her about any of my crash-and-burn encounters with the man called Dad, content to let her have delusions of father-daughter bliss if they made her happy.

I got to bed just after two, and being beyond exhausted when my alarm went off this morning had totally skipped my Gaelic class. But come on, I was really tired, and it was all crappy out…

…and I was tired…

Whatever. I would go next time, for sure. But even with the extra rest that skipping had provided me with that morning, I was still having trouble concentrating.

"Now, whenever you're ready," Mr Reid said, calling my attention back to the task at hand, "choose a book from the shelf and focus on it."

I picked out a small one with a thin green spine. "OK."

"What you want to make sure you do, is narrow–"

"For crying Holy Hell!" Mr Anderson moaned, throwing his hands up in frustration. "You've been rattling on for a year now! Just shut your trap, and let her give it a go!"

"I am trying to train her," Mr Reid argued. "Isn't that the point of these sessions? To train?"

"Aye, to train, not to talk her to death! At this rate, she'll know Kinetics by the time she's a grandmother!"

"Becca," Mr Reid asked me, deliberately ignoring Mr Anderson, "have you chosen a book?"

"Yep." I nodded, turning back to face the bookshelf, trying not to look amused by the banter.

"All right, go ahead and give it a try."

I melded Mr Reid's ability with mine, pleased with how easy it was getting. I focused my attention on the green book I'd chosen, reached out my hand and pushed the combined energy outward, extending toward the book. I gave a little squeal when I was able to make it wobble a little on the shelf.

"Good!" Mr Reid said, clapping his hands together.

"What'd I tell you?" Mr Anderson said. "The girl's a natural!"

"Now, just a little more…" Mr Reid encouraged me.

I pushed out a stronger wave of energy toward the bookshelf, causing the green book to fly into my waiting hand so quickly it was like I'd had it on a bungee.

"Marvelous!" Mr Reid exclaimed, thoroughly impressed.

"That wasn't hard at al–" But my thought was cut short as suddenly every book on the shelf followed behind the first one, whizzing through the air and knocking me off my feet. The next thing I knew, I was on the floor, buried in a pile of leather and musty paper.

"Oh, Becca!" Mr Reid called, digging me out, while Mr Anderson roared with laughter. "Are you hurt?"

"Just my pride," I assured him, crawling out of the dusty pile.

"You see!" Mr Reid rounded on the still laughing Mr Anderson. "If I'd have given her further instruction, that wouldn't have happened!"

"It's fine," I told him, brushing off my shirt. "I wasn't paying enough attention."

With a bang, the door to the Inner Chamber burst open, making us all jump. Min came running in, full of all-out panic.

"Jocelyn? Where is Jocelyn?"

"Office, why? What's wrong?" Mr Reid asked, as she ran to the door in the back of the Chamber that led to Jocelyn's office.

She threw it open without even bothering to knock. "Jocelyn, where are you?" she yelled.

"Here," he called, running in with Taron following right behind. "What's wrong?"

"Ryland's dorm has been attacked! The guard has been breached, I felt it."

My stomach gave a heave as her words rang in my ears. They'd finally gotten through. And because they didn't realize that I was actually the one they wanted, they'd gone after Ry instead.

"When?" Jocelyn asked, for the first time making me envious of his stony-calm, ever in control, demeanor.

"Only a moment ago, I came right away." I'd never seen Min so worked up, which wasn't doing much to ease the barbed wire wrapping around my lungs.

"Where's Alex?" Jocelyn asked looking around the room.

"Gone to get Cormac, he'll be here in a moment," Min answered again.

"How did it happen?" Mr Anderson asked.

"Didn't you feel them come through the guard around the school?" Mr Reid added.

"No, there have been no other breaches in any of my other charms or guards, not even around the campus as a whole. Someone had to have let them in."

"One of us?!" Mr Anderson cried, outraged. "No, it can't be!"

"Is that even possible?" Reid asked.

"No, that is what I do not understand! The only way is to create a bridge in the charm, and to do that you would need..." Min's voice died off, her eyes widening. "It can't be..."

As if on cue, Alex ran in panting. "Cormac's gone."

"What do you mean gone?" Jocelyn asked.

"Gone," Alex repeated, "his stuff too."

"Cormac," Min gasped, covering her mouth. "I... I gave him one of my books. He asked to see it last night, but I never thought..."

"Damn bloody traitor!" Mr Anderson spat.

"But why send someone after Ryland?" Alex asked.

"Maybe he lied about the boy's reading after his Awakening," Reid suggested.

"He's probably been lying from the start!" Anderson fumed.

"I should have kept a closer watch on him!" Min said.

"Never mind Cormac," Jocelyn cut in. "We'll worry about him later. Right now, Ryland's safety comes first," he said, leading everyone to the door. Pulling it open, he turned back and pointed directly at me. "You are not to leave this room until we come back. Everyone else, with me."

"No!" I screamed, my panic and my anger twisting inside me like a windup toy about to spring. "No way! I'm coming!"

"You will stay here until we return! That is not a request!" he bellowed.

Before I could argue, two hands gently but firmly grabbed either side of my face and turned me around. "Becca, listen to me," Alex pleaded, forcing me to look him in the eye. "We can focus all our attention on Ryland if we don't also have to worry about you. It's imperative that they don't find out about you."

"If Cormac is working with them, then they already know!"

"Not necessarily," he said. "Please, Becca, you have to trust us. We'll take care of Ryland." He must have seen the terror and reluctance in my eyes, because he quietly added, "Trust me."

I did trust him, more than anything, but I couldn't fight my nature. Everything in me was screaming to run to Ryland as fast as my legs would carry me, and now everyone expected me to just sit here on my hands and wait?

"Taron," Jocelyn ordered, not willing to wait for my answer, "stay here and watch her. She is not to leave this room."

Taron was outraged. "But you might need me! Alex can babysit her."

"We need Alex to conceal us. You will stay here, and do not let her out of your sight."

And that was it. Apparently, Jocelyn's word was law, whether Taron and I liked it or not. Alex kissed me on the forehead, whispering assurances that I was too panic-stricken to catch, before jogging out of the room with the rest of them, and a moment later, Taron and I were alone, staring silently at the door as it closed in front of us.

Without thinking, I ran toward the door, only to be yanked backward as a boney hand grabbed my upper arm.

"Where do you think you're going?" he snarled.

"Let go of me!" I screamed, clawing his hand, but it was no use. For a wiry guy he had a grip like the devil on a sinner.

"Sit down!" He threw me against the wall, but I had no intention of staying.

The moment his hand left my arm, I hopped up and made a bee line for the door to Jocelyn's office. Just before my hand reached the doorknob, Taron caught my arms – both this time – and hauled me back across the floor, kicking and screaming.

"I am not above tying you down. Now, you sit there!" He threw me back up against the wall. "And don't move!"

"I have to help him!" I shrieked, looking for something within reach to throw.

"Haven't you done enough?" he roared, finally earning my undivided attention. "If you'd have kept your mouth shut, your brother would have six people fighting to save him instead of five. But instead of being out there with the rest of the Order where I'm needed, I have to stay here and babysit you! If anything happens to Ryland, you have no one but yourself to blame!"

He stalked off to the other side of the room, still growling to himself, leaving me sitting speechless and humiliated.

Oh my God, he was right. He should be out there with the rest of them, but they were a man down because of me. What if something happened to Ryland because Taron wasn't there? Or what if someone else got hurt? Min, or Mr Anderson… or Alex?

Fear ran through me like a blade as I jumped up and ran over to Taron. "Go," I pleaded, grabbing hold of his arm. "Go and help them, I'll stay."

"Sure, you'd love that," he snorted, pulling away from me.

"Please," I begged. "Please go, someone could get hurt!"

"Jocelyn told me not to let you out of my sight, so that's what's going to happen."

"You're more worried about…" But my question

died on my tongue as I saw the answer in his face. He was more worried about doing what Jocelyn said than anything else. He'd gotten an order from his leader, and that was it. Much as I hated to admit it, I finally saw what everyone else saw in him. He was loyal. He might be a total ass, and his ability might be all but useless in a fight, but I could see he would stand by Jocelyn to the end. While I still didn't trust him in the least, I knew Jocelyn did, and right now that would have to be good enough for me.

"Then take me," I urged him, trying a new tactic. "We can both go, and I'll hide. You will still know where I am and you can help them while I stay hidden. I promise. No one will know I'm there." The small gleam in his eye at my suggestion gave me hope. "Please Taron, I won't try anything, I swear. You'd know if I was lying, right?"

I held my breath and put on my best obedient face, as he hesitated, looking me up and down. After what felt like hours, he huffed and glanced down at his watch.

"Fine," he clipped.

"Thank you!" I breathed, so relieved my hands were shaking.

"Don't thank me," he said, striding over to the long table against the back wall and opening the glass case holding the Iris. "I plan to blame this little excursion on you."

"What do we need that for?" I asked, as he slid the Iris into his pocket.

"Min didn't have time to reset the charms." He glanced upward indicating the room. "Chamber's not secure. It will be safer with Jocelyn."

Charms... I looked down at my Sciath realizing that Min had also forgotten to put the Block back on before she left. Now that I took a second to think about it, I could feel Taron's ability in the room with me and was surprised I hadn't noticed before. At any other time, I would have been thrilled to see that my ability to sense was becoming so natural that I could all but ignore it if I wanted to, however, at the moment that fact was furthest from my mind.

I ran to the door holding it open for Taron and we jogged down the hall, my pulse hammering alongside my mantra: please just let us get there in time... please let nothing have happened...

As I went to turn toward the main entrance, Taron called from behind me. "This way," he said, zipping his jacket. "They will be there already, we'll take a car, it'll be faster."

We ran down the side hall and out of one of the back doors to the parking lot behind Lorcan.

"Which one?" I asked, seeing a line of four St Brigid's vans lined up along the building.

"Doesn't matter, all the keys are in the glove boxes, just get in the first one."

I opened the passenger side door to find a pile of paperwork and old binders cluttering up the front seat. "What the hell? Whose stuff is this?" I asked, trying to shove it out of the way.

"How am I supposed to know? Everyone uses these, just get in the back," he growled, as he started the ignition. "Hurry up!"

I got in on top of the mess, crawling over it and through the gap between the two front seats. After reaching over and closing the door behind me, Taron took off out of the parking lot, the momentum throwing me into the row of seats behind him. I righted myself and leaned forward into the gap I'd just crawled through.

"Can't you just drive through the grass?" I asked as we turned onto the road. "His dorm's right there, it'd be quicker."

"Not without drawing attention."

"OK, then can we at least-?" but I stopped, as we suddenly made a wrong turn. "Wait, this isn't right!" I grabbed Taron's shoulder shaking. "It's back that way."

"*Srian*," Taron ordered, in what I can only assume was Gaelic.

"Wha–"

Before I could finish, a pair of enormous arms came around behind me, covering my mouth and pinning me against my seat. As I struggled vainly to get free, I saw Taron watching me in the rearview mirror, a disgusting grin framing his face.

"I told you not to thank me."

25

"Goddamned, dirty, back-stabbing, rotten son of a bitch!" I screamed against the gigantic calloused hand covering my mouth.

I could tell that the guy playing the part of the human seatbelt wasn't a Holder, but when it came to the art of restraining he definitely knew what he was doing. His left arm was like an iron band around my arms and chest, trapping me against the seat, while his right hand was smashed so hard against my mouth I couldn't even loosen my jaw enough to try and bite him. The only things I had that were free were my legs, and I made full use of them, slamming my feet into the back of Taron's seat, his side, his right arm, and any other part of him I could reach. With any luck he'd swerve and hit a tree and I'd be able to make a run for it before he got me too far away from the school. As I looked around, however, I realized we weren't even near the edge of campus.

Then I remembered: the charm. No one could take me off campus or out of any other buildings without my permission. I'd been stupid enough to leave Lorcan of my own free will, but no way would Taron be able to get past the school gates. Unfortunately, he knew this too, and had planned accordingly.

We pulled up to an old building on the other side of campus that I'd never seen before. The doors and windows were bricked over, and even though the shrubs and trees surrounding it had been kept neat it was clear the building hadn't been used in a long time. Taron parked the van along the back wall, next to a large pile of broken bricks that had been chiseled away from one of the doors. As soon as Taron came around and opened the back door, I felt the presence of another Holder there waiting for us. It was an ability I'd never felt before, and it was coming toward us from the inside the building.

"*Scaoileadh dá béal*," Taron ordered the guy holding me, as he pulled a rag out of his pocket.

Before I even had a chance to realize that the nasty sweaty palm was gone, Taron had leaned over me, shoved the rag into my mouth, and was tying the ends together behind my head. I thrashed my head from side to side trying to yell around the sour-tasting cotton. When that didn't slow him down, I shifted my hips and kicked him square in the stomach with every ounce of force I had, sending him flying backwards out of the van and onto the ground with a thud. He rolled over clutching his stomach, gasping and coughing, and I waited for my captor to look over at him, or maybe lean over to check on him – anything to make him lose focus for the split second I needed to wiggle free.

But it didn't happen. His grip on me never faltered, nor did it get stronger in reaction to my aggression. He was like stone, completely oblivious. What the hell was wrong with this guy?

"What the bloody hell took you so long?" asked the irritated voice of a tall man in a black leather trench coat.

It was the Holder I'd sensed. He pulled the still coughing Taron to his feet, then froze as he saw me.

"Where's the kid?" he barked at Taron.

"Calm down, Cail," Taron wheezed.

"You were supposed to bring the kid!"

"This is the one he wants, trust me."

"Well get her inside then, before someone see us," he said, glancing around, still looking more than skeptical.

"*A ghlacadh a cosa*," Taron ordered my captor.

He released me, sliding around to the door, allowing me a good look at him. At first glance, he seemed a normal man – albeit huge, but otherwise not unusual. It wasn't until I saw his eyes that I could tell something was wrong. He looked... dead. His eyes were glazed over and had no light in them, no awareness. He was like a zombie, doing exactly what he was told, with no other thought in his mind. It was one of the scariest things I'd ever seen.

I'd been hearing stories for weeks now about bad Holders stealing abilities, and evil Darragh, but for some reason they had seemed just that: stories. I'd believed they were true, but even so, subconsciously, they had always seemed far away. Like an erupting volcano: real and very dangerous, but not something I was ever likely to see in person. But now, looking into the cold, lifeless face of the man locking my feet together in his massive hands, I knew that whoever had done this to him was evil.

The feeling of barbed wire constricted around my ribcage as the realization fully sank in: they were going to take my ability.

And that the only way to do that… was to kill me.

I took a silent breath and reevaluated my situation. If I wanted to get through this then kicking and screaming was not the way to do so. There was no way I was going to be able to fight my way free of three grown men, therefore there was no point in wasting the energy trying. Besides, the more I struggled, the more likely they were to bind me, which would only make things worse. I was already gagged, if they decided to hog-tie me I was dead for sure.

I let them remove me from the van, only making a show of struggling so they wouldn't get suspicious.

"How long do I have?" Cail asked Taron, as they carried me into the dark building.

"An hour at least, but you won't need it," Taron told him.

"An hour! It's never taken less than two!"

"Only with a Drain, which is why we're using the Iris."

"You're sure it will work as well as a Drain?"

"Better. Trust me, I saw what it did to her. With the Iris she'll be dry in under a minute, then you'll have both her vial and the Iris to give the Master."

They set my feet on the floor and shoved me into a dark room filled with a bunch of rusty music stands. Before I could make it all the way up to my feet, they had shut and bolted the door. I tore the gag out of my mouth and crawled quietly over, leaning my ear against the crack between the door and the wall.

"Here," I heard Taron say, his voice low. "When you're ready, take her Sciath off and put it in her hand. Make sure you have the vial ready before you give it to her, and it will do the rest. Leave this book with the body, I took it off the old man. I've got to get back. I'll send the drone out as a decoy, to buy you some extra time, just in case. Don't forget to pick up the old man. I locked him in the utility shed by the south gate, you can drain him once you are a safe distance away. "

"What are you going to tell them?"

"That she used the Iris to overwhelm me and got away. Then they'll assume she ran into Cormac on her way to the dorm."

"Are you sure that will work?"

"As hotheaded as she is, they won't bat an eye," Taron said, his voice growing fainter by the second, telling me they were walking back up the hall. I pressed my ear harder against the crack, straining to hear as Taron continued. "As for the rest, you tripped the charm on the boy's dorm so they already know that something is going on, and they know that the old man is missing. When he doesn't come back and they find the Alchemist's book here, the story will practically write itself."

Their conversation drifted out of earshot, but it didn't

matter; I had a plan. I removed my Sciath, and set it down on the stone floor and stepped on it, bouncing up and down. Slowly the soft gold started to bend, collapsing under my foot. I picked up the now flat, deformed square and took it to the one bricked-up window and began bending it over the ledge. I had to lean all my weight on to either side, stretching the bevel setting that was holding the large emerald in place. I flipped it over, bending it the other way, then back again, over and over, weakening the metal, loosening the stone a little more each time. My hands were throbbing and my palms bleeding, but finally I had it so weak that I no longer needed the ledge and could continue bending it with my hands alone.

I heard footsteps in the hall and knew I was out of time. I dug into the loosened facet with my finger and yanked the emerald free, nearly cutting the end of my finger off. I hid the stone in my bloody palm, then took the now stoneless Sciath and started banging it against the bricks covering the window.

"Hey!" Cail yelled, barging in at the noise. "What do you think you're doing?"

He grabbed my arm, throwing me to the floor. He picked up my mangled Sciath and held it up laughing.

"You really thought you could dig your way out through a stone wall with this?" he mocked, tossing the lump of gold to the far corner of the room. "You're not as bright as you get credit for, love."

With my Sciath stone safe in my hand, I took a deep breath and braced myself. I didn't know how much time

I would have before he figured me out, but I knew it wouldn't be a lot. He knelt down in front of me and pulled the Iris and a small glass bottle out of his pocket. That must have been the vial Taron had mentioned. I didn't know what it was, but it gave off a strange sensation, as though something in me was being drawn toward it. It reminded me a little of the magnetic feeling I had whenever I was near Alex, only this feeling was in no way pleasant. It was like an uncomfortable sucking that I couldn't help but shrink away from.

"Now then," he said with a slimy sneer, "let's get this done, shall we?"

He grabbed my free hand, forcing the Iris into it, but this time the moment the Iris touched my fingers I was ready.

The feeling that coursed through me at contact wasn't at all like the first time. Now that I had my Sciath stone with me, the power of the Iris melted into me like butter into bread, mixing with my ability, giving me a rush like nothing I'd ever imagined. It was as if I were suddenly floating in space, looking out at hundreds of stars, each star a different Holder. I could not only sense Cail, but every Holder for miles and miles around, from the fully developed, to the weakest unawakened child.

I focused on the group nearest me, and easily recognized Min, Alex, Anderson, Reid, Jocelyn, and even Taron. He had made it over to them and was probably telling lies about me right now. I singled out Mr Anderson and shot my magnified ability out toward him like a lightning strike, melding with him almost instantly. Then I focused on every mind in the group, Imparting to them as loudly and quickly as I could: "It's Taron! It's Taron! He took me and the Iris! I don't know where I am! Please hel–"

But I was cut off as the Iris was ripped from my hand.

"What are you doing?" Cail yelled. "Why isn't it working?"

He set the Iris on the floor behind him and grabbed my shoulders looking me up and down, his eyes finally fixing on my closed fist. He tried to tear it open, prying my fingers apart, while I struggled, clawing and even biting. I managed to get a good solid kick to his shin, knocking him over and freeing me from his grip. I scrambled over to where the Iris lay, now unguarded, and snatched it up, knowing I would need all the help I could get. I scanned out again looking for the Order, and found them closer than they had been before. They were coming. They'd heard me and were on their way. All I had to do was buy them time to get here and everything would be all right.

I honed in on Mr Reid, merging with him just as Cail started to get up. The power enhancement of the Iris made my earlier short lesson feel like a Master's Class as I kinetically lifted a group of music stands as though they were nothing at all, hurling them straight at unsuspecting Cail. I continued to send stands flying, buzzing around the room like angry hornets, pummeling Cail to the ground, allowing me to crawl closer and closer to the exit.

As I reached the door, I heard Mr Anderson's voice echo in my head: "Hang on, lass, we're coming!"

Unfortunately, the wave of relief the news brought

me also brought the moment of distraction that Cail needed to throw one of the airborne stands into my arm, knocking the Iris from my hand, and snapping my connection with Mr Reid like a frozen twig. The stands fell out of the air in a shower of rusted metal, and before I could pull the door open and make a run for it Cail had a fistful of my shirt and was once again throwing me to the floor.

"You're going to pay for that," Cail growled, still panting, blood and sweat running down his brow.

With a malicious gleam in his eye he stomped down on my forearm sending an excruciating pain through it and forcing a scream from my throat. My hand wrenched itself open, the green gem rolling to the floor. Paralyzed by pain I watched helplessly as he kicked the stone out of reach and knelt down beside me again, Iris and vial in hand. He put the Iris back into my hand and I closed my eyes as the enveloping warmth – now, without my Sciath, exactly like it had been that first time – flowed over me leaving me drifting in the familiar sea of light. The sensation was just as I remembered it with one small difference. This time the pool of swirling contentment and far off sounds seemed to be draining away, as if someone had pulled out the stopper. I forced my heavy eyes open and saw the same dancing colors and light, but instead of floating lazily around me, they were being pulled away, sucked into the glass vial Cail was holding.

He was taking my ability – and with it, my life.

I tried to stay awake, but I was so tired. Every part of

me was so heavy, it felt like I was sinking into the stone of the floor. I struggled to find something to hold on to, but with every second that passed my mind drifted further away.

I thought of Ryland, and how much he'd grown. He'd be OK now. He finally had somewhere he belonged and people who would take care of him. He was safe. He didn't need me anymore.

The comfort that thought brought me was almost enough to make me surrender to the hazy, leaden weight pulling me down to the dark peace. But then, just as I was about to give up, I thought of Alex, and my heart tore from my chest. Alex loved me. He needed me, I had to hold on. Who would take care of him if I was gone? I pictured Alex's face and hung on to it. Pictured his smile, and his laugh, and the way his eyes sparkled when he looked at me.

Everything began to fade around me, but I kept that image in my mind until the last possible moment. Until I couldn't hold out any more. I took one last look into those fading blue eyes as they dissolved away...

And I let go.

26

I didn't wake up all at once. It wasn't the gradual shifting from the haze of sleep into the clarity of reality, or even the harsh jolt of awareness brought on by a nightmare or alarm clock. It was like being buried under a mountain of blankets, while someone slowly removed them one at a time. Each layer gone, brought me just the tiniest bit closer to the surface, returning my strength drop by drop. For a while I had to struggle to remain conscious for mere seconds at a time, and even then I couldn't move or even open my eyes. But if nothing else, I knew I wasn't dead. At least I really hoped not, or I was stuck in the lamest afterlife ever.

Eventually my periods of consciousness grew longer and became distinguishable from sleep, and my senses started to work again. I could hear the door open and close, and the occasional conversation, though those were rare and usually too hushed to make out. I could feel the bandages on my hands and the soreness of the wounds underneath. My ability also began to return and I started to sense the people around me. At first, it was only the slightest nudge here and there from the ability closest to me, barely noticeable. But gradually, as the layers continued to lift away, the nudges intensified, becoming the distinct and unique brushes of power I'd come to know and recognize.

Min came and went quite a bit, and Mr Anderson and Mr Reid were almost always nearby, but seldom came into the room. However, the person whose presence gave me the most comfort, and the one who garnered the majority of my attention, was Alex. Forever at my side, there wasn't one single time I'd woken up that I couldn't feel him next to me, holding my un-bandaged fingers, or gently stroking my cheek. Sometimes, when I couldn't feel anyone else around, he would talk to me, though unfortunately it was usually in Gaelic. But even if I didn't know what he was saying, the low tone of his voice and the graceful tumble of words were always a soothing balm on my tired mind.

Finally, after who knows how long, I woke up feeling strong enough to try and open my eyes. It felt like I was lifting up the back door of a Mack Truck, but after a few tries, I did it – only to find that thanks to my impeccable timing it was the middle of the night and so dark I could barely see anyway. What I could make out in the dim light was a small room with no window and one door. Luckily, my head was already tilted toward the right, where I could see Alex, sleeping on a rocker that was pulled up next to the bed.

I tried to call him, but couldn't even open my mouth, much less force air past my vocal cords fast enough to produce sound. I tried to move, to grunt, anything to get his attention, but it was no use. I lay there, looking at his darkened silhouette, so frustrated I wanted to scream – except I couldn't. I couldn't do anything. He was two feet away from me, but with the state I was in he may as well have been in the next room.

I was about to give up, hoping I'd have better luck tomorrow, when I realized that Alex's ability wasn't the only one present in my mind. While I couldn't see him in the room, Mr Anderson was also near enough – in the hall maybe? – for me to be able to feel his ability, which gave me an idea. I tried pushing my ability out to meet his, and was happy that it was easy to do so, especially given how ridiculously hard everything else seemed to be. I linked us together, and focused on Alex, hoping my plan would work.

Alex? I imparted quietly.

It did work, maybe even a little too much, as Alex sat up with a gasp, head whipping from side to side looking for the origin of his wakeup call.

It's me, I'm imparting, I said quickly. *I'm sorry, I didn't mean to scare you.*

He looked over at me, sucking in a harsh breath as he saw I was looking back at him. A second later he was leaning over me, his trembling hands on either side of my face, "Becca?" he whispered, letting out something between a laugh and a sob, "Y-you're awake?"

I tried to smile, but I don't think it worked. *Yeah, but it's too hard to talk, so I'm borrowing from Mr Anderson.*

"You're awake," he breathed with a shudder. "My God, you're awake..." He closed his eyes and rested his forehead against mine, fingers still shaking against my cheeks.

"I know it's late," I said, after a moment. "I'm sorry I woke you."

He pulled back shaking his head with a brilliant smile, tears shining in his eyes. "I'm so glad you did." He sat down on the edge of the bed, carefully gathering my nearest hand into one of his. "How do you feel?" he asked, his free hand lovingly grazing a trail back and forth from my temple to my jaw.

OK I guess. Not being able to move is annoying, but otherwise good. The wounds on my hands were actually pretty sore too, but I was afraid if I told him that he'd release the hand he was currently holding.

"You're weak," he said, his smile glowing as though that was somehow the best news ever. "You've been through a lot, give it time."

I'm not weak, I'm just tired, I denied, stupid as I knew it was.

"Awake for less than two minutes and already arguing with me!" he laughed, his face glowing.

Suddenly something dawned on me. *Wait a minute, how can I be using Anderson's ability? How can I feel anyone at all? Didn't Min Block me?*

"No," he said. "We decided that with the amount of control it took for you to use the Iris the way you did, that there was no need to replace the Block. You are firmly in control of yourself. You will still need to be trained, and she didn't remove the Block on Jocelyn, so you still won't be able to access anything he can do, but otherwise you are free and clear. But there is another question you're not asking," he said, grinning.

When I didn't answer – because I had no clue what he was talking about – he reached down below my field of vision, and pulled up a long silver chain that had something hanging from it, swinging back and forth like a pendulum.

If I'd had it in me to squeal, I would have.

It was my Sciath stone, cleaned and reset into a pendant. The deep green gem was visible from both sides, encircled by a thin silver ring that had a Celtic design carved into it.

"I thought you'd like it," Alex said, seeing my eyes light up. "Your old one was destroyed."

Yeah. Actually, I did that.

"You? Why?"

I knew they were going to take it off so they could use the Iris to drain me, so I broke it up to get the stone out and hid it in my hand. Then when they gave me the Iris, I was able to use it to call for help.

The amazement that lit his face made me want to look away, embarrassed, but since I couldn't, I tried changing the subject.

Where are we? I asked.

"One of the extended stay rooms in the school's infirmary," he answered, still smiling.

How long have I been here? I asked, not sure if I really wanted to know.

"It's Monday morning," he said with a wince. "So almost five days."

I hated the sadness that crept back into his features, so I tried to lighten the mood. *Wow, five days without brushing my teeth. Good thing I can't talk.*

He smiled at my lame attempt at humor, though the haunted look behind his eyes was still there as he leaned down to kiss my cheek.

But wait, five days? What about the nurses and doctors and stuff? What did you tell them happened to me? Should I know what you told them in case they ask?

"We told the head nurse the truth."

What, that I got my ass kicked by a magic rock? Somehow I'm thinking they didn't buy that.

He shook his head with a grin. "The head nurse here knows about us, and she's been the only one who's seen you. She isn't a Holder herself but Jocelyn always keeps at least one person on the medical staff aware of our... situation," he said with a wink. "Just in case there are any emergencies."

I have to admit, I thought I'd be worse off, I said, glancing down at my lack of wires, tubes, and other standard hospital paraphernalia. *Must not have been that bad.*

Alex's face sank, into a grave mask. "It was very bad, Becca. There just wasn't much that could be done for you."

What do you mean? Couldn't Min just give me some of her magic juice like she did the last time?

He shook his head, and even in the dim light I could

see some of the color drain from his face.

What happened, Alex? Please tell me. I hated to ask, seeing how difficult it was for him, but I needed to know.

He sighed, bringing his arm down from my face, wrapping my hand in both of his. "When we got to Ryland's dorm, there were no obvious signs of trouble. Min could tell that the guard charm around the building had been breached, but there was no one suspicious outside or in the hallways, and we found Ryland safe in one of the common areas with some friends. We split up, searching every room, restroom, even the roof, but there was nothing. We were reconvening outside, trying to determine what our next move should be, when Taron ran up and told us you'd gotten away." His jaw clenched angrily. "He told us that since Min hadn't replaced the Block on your Sciath, you'd been able to get a hold of the Iris and overwhelm him. He claimed you'd very nearly knocked him out, and that he'd come to the dorm to look for you, assuming that's where you would have gone. Jocelyn ordered us into teams of two, but just as we were about to go off and look for you, we got your message. We could hear you screaming in our heads… hear the terror in your voice…"

He stopped, looking away for a moment, then took a deep breath before continuing. "The look of shock and panic on Taron's face was as good as a confession, but we didn't have time to deal with him, knowing you were in danger. Jocelyn grabbed Taron by the collar and in the blink of an eye, pulled the information we needed right out of his mind. 'Aimirgin Hall,' he told us. 'There's an open door round back'. Then he did something I'd never seen him do. He told Taron to return to his room at Lorcan and stay there until he was sent for. Ordered him not to speak or attempt to contact anyone in any way."

And Taron actually did all that? Without trying to run, or anything?

"He had no choice. Jocelyn compelled him."

I thought he didn't believe in doing that sort of stuff?

"This was something of a special circumstance," Alex said, smiling sadly.

OK, so then what happened?

"Jocelyn, Anderson, Reid, and I all made a run for Aimirgin Hall, while Min went back to Lorcan to get us a car. When we were nearly there, Reid said he could feel you connecting with him, and we told Anderson to let you know we were coming as soon as he had you in range."

He did, though in hindsight maybe he shouldn't have, I said without thinking.

"Why?" Alex asked, as I kicked myself for bringing it up, well aware that Alex was better off not knowing the finer details of my "alone time" with Cail.

Nothing, it just distracted me for a second, I said, trying to play it off, but finding it extremely difficult to come off passé without the aid of facial expressions. *Sorry, go on,* I urged, hoping to thwart any further questioning on the subject.

He eyed me, but continued. "The man who had you must have heard us coming, because as we entered the building he came running out of one of the rooms trying to make a break for it. He had the Iris in one hand, and something else – we didn't know what it was at the time – in the other. Jocelyn was able to grab the Iris, and I heard Anderson and Reid wrestling him to the ground, while I ran into the room he'd come out of."

So you got him?

"No, he got away. Reid and Anderson thought they had him knocked out, but he must have come to and run off. That or he was faking to begin with, just waiting for an opportunity."

No one was guarding him?

"They were, but they all came running when they heard me... h-heard me find you." Alex paused, not really looking at me, but through me, seeing only the memories playing behind his eyes. "When Jocelyn came in, he tried to find a thought or any kind of sign in your mind, but there was nothing. It didn't even look like you were breathing." He continued to tighten his grip on my hand as he spoke, without appearing to be aware of it. After a long pause, he cleared his throat and closed his eyes, as if to push out the unwanted images. He cleared his throat once more and looked up, finally meeting my eyes with a weak smile. "Just as Min arrived, we were able to find your pulse. It was thin and weak, but we were thrilled – until Min found the broken shards of glass in the hall."

The what?

"When Anderson and Reid were struggling with the man in the hall, the glass bottle he'd been holding broke.

Neither of them thought anything of it, but as soon as Min saw the pieces of glass, and the remnants of your *saol* still hovering around them, she knew immediately what they were. It was a Spirit Vial. Min had read about them, but didn't realize that anyone had ever successfully created one. When we realized what it was... realized what had been in it... we didn't have much hope." He took another long breath, then ploughed on in a very matter-of-fact tone. "Min said that without being able to replace the life you'd lost, that there were only two possibilities. Either the tiny bit of energy you still had would be strong enough to regenerate and you would wake up, or you would simply fade away," he finished, his voice tight.

So, you've just been sitting here... for five days... waiting?

He brought his hand back up to my cheek. "Like I said," he smiled, as his eyes became bright again, "I'm very happy you woke me up."

Looking up into his drawn complexion and tired eyes I knew I had never felt worse in my life. The fact that my bullheaded stupidity had caused him so much worry and pain was more than I could take, not to mention the stress and trouble I'd undoubtedly brought to everyone else. *I'm so sorry*, I apologized, closing my eyes, ashamed, *I never should have left.*

He ran his thumb over my cheek. "It wasn't your fault. You were worried about Ryland, and Taron took advantage."

I knew he was trying to comfort me, but I still felt like an idiot. I opened my eyes, but didn't look at him. *If I would have stayed, none of this would have happened. I should have listened.*

"Yes, you should have. But in the end it wouldn't have mattered. Taron had everything planned down to the last detail. You can bet he would have found a way to get you out of the building, one way or another." I looked up as he finished and saw the flash of anger tense his face.

I'm sorry for that too, I said, my heart going out to him. *I know he was your friend.*

"I don't know if 'friend' is the word," he sighed, "but I did trust him. We all did."

Yeah, I laughed. *Everyone but me. Ironic. What's going to happen to him?*

"Jocelyn hasn't decided yet, bu–"

Oh! Cormac! I know where Cormac is! I interrupted, panicking at the thought of poor Cormac locked in a shed for almost a week.

"Shh," Alex soothed. "We found him, don't worry. He'd been drugged, but Min took care of him, he's fine. The last thing you need is to get worked up."

But he's OK?

"He's fine," he said, raising my fingers to his lips. "I promise."

What about Taron?

"He is under house arrest until we decided what to do with him. Jocelyn is still in the process of doing a full reading on him – thoughts, memories, everything – to find out the extent of the damage he has done to us over the years, as well as get any information he might have that could help us."

And?

"So far, all we have is a name, Ciaran Shea."

Who is that?

"We don't know."

And that's it? That's all he's found out? That can't be! He has to at least know what Darragh is planning, right?

"We'd hoped so, but Darragh is a smarter man than that. Think about it, why would he tell Taron his plans when he knew that there was always a chance that Taron would be caught and his mind read? He is not someone to take such a careless risk."

But you have a name?

"Yes," Alex said, "we have a name. And now I think it's time for you to go back to sleep. Your eyelids are sinking by the minute."

Damn. I'd hoped he hadn't noticed. *I'm fine*, I lied.

"You're exhausted and you're going to sleep. Besides, I have to send Anderson to tell Jocelyn that you woke up, so you're about to lose your microphone."

Spoilsport, I grumbled, already feeling the heavy arms of sleep start to pull me under.

He stood up, carefully placing my hand down on the bed and went over to the door.

No, wait, just a few more minutes! I called, only to see him chuckle as he stepped outside.

And sure enough, a few seconds later, Mr Anderson's ability began to fade as he left the hall, then the building, and I was forced to break our connection. Alex came back inside, trying not to look amused – and failing horribly.

"You see," he said grinning down at me, as I did my best to scowl at him, "we don't need Anderson after all, I know exactly what you'd say if you could." He came back over to the bed leaning over me once again, his hand holding the side of my face. "Now, go to sleep. I'll be here when you wake up."

He thought he was clever, but no way was I letting him win this, no matter how exhausted I was. I closed my eyes, grabbing hold of every ounce of strength I had left, throwing it all in to one final breath, just barely getting out, "I love you."

It was the faintest breath of a whisper, but even though I couldn't see him his gasp told me he'd heard. I felt a pair of lips press against my cheek, and a warm drop of moisture fall onto my forehead and roll down into my hair. And the last thing I heard, before surrendering to the inviting call of sleep, was Alex's voice echo softly, "*Is breá liom tú ró, mo lómhara. Tá tú gach rud a dom.*"

Hmm... Really should start going to class...

27

Over the next few days I made impressive progress in the strength department, if I do say so myself. The day after my first imparted conversation with Alex I was able to do most of my talking verbally – though we kept Mr Anderson around just in case – and by the evening after that I was actually sitting up. Granted I was still napping more than an infant, but hey, progress is progress.

During the time I'd been awake I had visitors galore. Min was always in and out, checking my *saol*, making sure nothing was wrong. Cormac was a little worse for wear from his ordeal, scratches and bruises on his face and arms, but he still came to see me, more than anxious to hear about my use of the Iris and what it was like. Chloe was with me whenever she could be, bringing me magazines, chatting away about this and that, and – bless her – brushing out and braiding my hair. Ryland was brought over to see me once I was strong enough not to scare him, and Mr Anderson and Mr Reid even moved their three o'clock game of the day from the Lorcan lounge to my infirmary room so I could play.

But even with all the care and attention I was getting from everyone around me, after ten days in the same room I was craving nothing more than fresh air and the sight of anything other than beige-gray infirmary room walls. Finally, after two days of begging, Alex agreed to take me with him to Lorcan when he went for a change of clothes.

The air outside was cold and blustery, and the sun was completely hidden behind the blanket of gray clouds. Most people would have considered it miserable, but to me it was heaven. I held his arm as we made our way over to Lorcan and up the front steps.

"I thought you needed clothes?" I asked, as Alex led me past the main stairs and down the hall.

"I do, but you're not ready for all those stairs yet. I need to drop you off somewhere first, and I'll pick you up after I change."

"Aw, you mean I don't get to watch?" I asked innocently.

His ears caught fire and he had to swallow before answering. "Um, no. Someone's expecting you. Maybe next time," he said with a wink, making it my turn to blush.

"Where are we going then?"

"Jocelyn's office."

"I should have known," I groaned.

"He wants to see you."

"Wants to yell at me, you mean."

"I'm sure he just wants to see that you're all right. He's been worried."

"Not worried enough to come and see me."

"That's not true; he was there a lot the first few days."

"Right, because that's better; he'll come to see me as long as I'm not awake."

As we arrived outside the door to Jocelyn's office, Alex turned to face me, placing his hands on either side of my neck. "Becca, listen to me. I know this isn't what you'd rather be doing, but please try and behave yourself in there. You're not strong enough to throw a temper tantrum, just yet." He smiled, though I could see the genuine worry hovering in his eyes.

Much as I wanted to argue, he had a point. My one-on-one times with Jocelyn didn't exactly have the best track record, and I could just imagine the scene he was envisioning: me throwing a fit, passing out, and having to live another week at death's door, all because I couldn't control my temper.

Yeah, I guess that sounded like me.

But not today. Today I had to keep it together, and take what was coming to me. I'd disobeyed a direct order and caused everyone loads of unnecessary worry and trouble because of it. I would be an adult about it and swallow my medicine like a woman.

In any event, Alex was right. Even if I wanted to try and fight back, I knew I couldn't. I was still too weak to get worked up, and I wasn't going to risk my safety. I needed to stay healthy for my own sake of course, but even more for the sake of the pale, worn, beaten-down man standing in front of me.

Alex had been through hell the past week and a half, that much was clear just by looking at him. Since the moment he found me almost dead in that old music room, he hadn't left my side once, not for anything. Even at night he stayed, flatly refusing to go back to his own room. Instead, he slept on the reclining rocking chair in my infirmary room, insisting it was comfortable. And I use the term "sleep" loosely, as I was sure that he was doing little more than catnapping, at best.

"OK, I'll make you a deal," I said, seeing an opportunity. "I'll go talk to Jocelyn, staying perfectly calm and collected – if you promise to do something for me."

"Which is?" he asked with a suspicious raise of his eyebrows.

"Tonight, you sleep in your own bed."

The wry amusement in his eyes vanished. "No."

"Alex, you need to sleep, you're a mess."

"No."

"You're not sleeping well in that chair, I know you're not. You can't keep this up, or you are going to hurt yourself."

"It's not going to happen, Becca."

"Fine," I huffed. "Then at least let Min give you something to help you sleep."

"No way, that stuff knocks you dead!"

"Have you seen a mirror lately? Trust me, you need it," I said, giggling.

"But what if…?" The worry in his eyes finished his sentence for him.

"Alex, I'm OK," I said softly, willing him to believe me. "The only thing wrong with me now is that I'm worried about you. Promise me you will let Min help you sleep tonight."

"Jocelyn is waiting for you," he said, trying to distract me.

"I haven't heard a promise yet."

"Fine," he sighed.

"Promise?"

"Yes."

"I'm going to watch you drink it," I warned, poking him in the chest.

"I said I will, now stop stalling and get in there," he said, nodding at the wooden doors behind me.

In one last ditch effort, I got up on my toes and kissed him, which was hard to do effectively, considering he was laughing.

"Nice try," he said, leaning back and spinning me by the shoulders to face the office. Before I could stop him, he reached around me and knocked loudly on the door.

"Come in," Jocelyn's voice said from inside.

"I'll be here to walk you back when you're done," he said softly, giving me a peck on the cheek. With that, he stepped over and pushed the door, holding it open for me. I shot him a scowl – which was intended to strike fear, but to my annoyance, only earned a chuckle – and walked past him into the office, my head held high.

As I stepped into the room, I looked up toward the desk to find Jocelyn with his back to me, staring out the window. As the door groaned to a close behind me, he turned taking a few steps toward me, hands behind his back, no expression on his face.

With a shaky breath, I walked forward, chin up, ready to get it over with.

I braced myself as he looked at me. "How are you feeling?" he asked, throwing me off.

"Good. Much better," I said, trying not to sound confused. I'd expected him to go right into my scolding. "Just tired," I added, in the interest of being honest.

"I'm sure," he said. Then, motioning me to one of the large brown armchairs, said, "Sit."

Normally I would have said no, but the walk over here had actually worn me out, and I figured sitting less a sign of weakness than passing out on the floor. Plus, it was probably a good idea to be seated for what was coming. Though, I had to admit, he didn't seem like a man who was about to deliver a first rate tongue-lashing. Even his suggestion to sit was just that – a suggestion. It wasn't a command or an order, but simply an offer made out of what seemed to be concern.

I sat, trying to hide my confusion. What was this? Why didn't he get on with it? Finally, I decided that if he wasn't going to bring it up, then I would.

"Look, I'm sorry. I know it was stupid." He didn't reply, but his eyebrows pulled together in confusion. "Leaving with Taron…" I said, though it sounded more like a question. Could he really not have known what I was talking about?

Realization flashed in his eyes and he nodded. "Yes it was," he said, "but I don't think you need me to tell you that. You can't be held to blame for that, in any event."

Now it was my turn to be confused. "Wait, so... you didn't bring me here to... you know... yell at me?"

He turned slightly away from me and looked down at the floor, his eyes closed. "No," he said quietly, turning and walking back toward the window. "I didn't bring you here to yell at you." The sadness in his voice made me feel suddenly guilty. "I brought you here to apologize," he continued without looking back at me. My eyes almost shot out of my head, but I kept my mouth shut. "I had no right to try and direct your personal relationships. The situation caught me off-guard, and I overreacted. Alex is a wonderful man, and the connection you share is exceedingly rare, if not unheard of. The two of you are very lucky."

"Thank you," I said after a moment. It seemed like the appropriate thing to say, but honestly I wasn't sure. At this point I was completely shocked.

"I reacted the way I did because I was trying to protect you. I didn't want you to have to suffer..." He trailed off, not finishing his thought, and was silent for so long that I started to think he wouldn't continue. Just as I opened my mouth to speak, he said, "I didn't think much about my reaction because I assumed that you would understand. You of all people have seen the damage..." Again he trailed off, and began to slowly pace back and forth behind his desk. "But I was wrong to think that. You had no reason to understand because I never gave you one, which was wrong of me."

He looked at the ground as he spoke, wringing his hands together behind his back. I'm not sure what it was

– the sudden tenseness of his shoulders, the slight furrow in his brow, the way he seemed to be struggling for words – but something began to make me feel awkward. My gut was warning me that whatever it was he was about to tell me, I didn't want to hear. I laced my hands together in my lap and waited for him to continue, uncomfortably on edge.

"There are things I'd like to tell you about me, and my past, but I will only do so if you wish to hear them." He looked up at me, and while I didn't look away I didn't quite meet his eyes. "All I ask is that you give me the next few minutes before you make a decision. There is only one thing I wish to tell you about today. After that, if you decide you would like to know more about me, I will be happy to tell you the rest over time. But as I said, I am only asking. I understand that you owe me nothing, and I won't force anything on you."

As he waited for my answer, I fought to keep my expression neutral. I had no idea what he wanted me to know, nor was I so sure I wanted to know it. But what could I say?

"OK," I agreed, my voice a little thinner than I would have liked.

Seeming pleased that I was willing to listen, his stance relaxed slightly as he walked slowly back toward the window. "I don't know if you are aware of it, but this past year was my two hundredth on this earth. A great deal has happened to me and to the Holder race in general in the last two centuries, but today I will give you only the information that is applicable to the story at hand."

He paused behind his desk, staring down at the floor, as if he were not sure where to start. After a long moment, he looked up – though not at me – and began. "When I was a boy, I attended school here at St Brigid's. Back in that time, it was a boy's boarding school, one of the finest anywhere in the world, in fact. I began my schooling here at age seven, and when I was sixteen my Awakening occurred. With no other Holders in my acquaintance at the time, I had no idea what was happening to me. Why I could suddenly hear everything that everyone around me was thinking. I began avoiding people, hiding. For a while I believed I was possessed. Nearly two years after my Awakening was when Darragh found me. He took me in, explained what had happened to me, what I was. He had a Sciath forged for me," he said. He held up his right hand, with the large ruby ring and said, "and even introduced me to other Holders, Taron being one of the first. I stayed with Darragh for many years, quickly becoming his second. Of course, he was very careful that I never found out who I truly was, and that it wasn't mere chance that he found me and took me under his wing. I never realized that he'd been looking for me – looking for the only one who could give him what he truly wanted."

"You mean the prophecies and all that? He never told you?"

"No. I only knew that he had something called the Black Iris, that it was somehow the key to ultimate power, and that Darragh had not yet discovered how to use it – that last bit being, of course, a lie. He knew how to use it; he simply didn't have the means, which is why he needed me. I had no idea what he was planning to do with it. I didn't know about all the horrible things he was doing, not only to the humans he despised so much, but to other Holders as well. He wanted me kept in the dark until he was certain that I was irrevocably behind him. When he discovered I wasn't nor would I ever be, I was forced to escape."

"How did he find out?"

"I refused to create Drones for him. The man that assisted Taron during your capture was a Drone."

"Yeah, I heard Taron say that, what does it mean?"

"A Drone is a human who has had their entire memory erased. Every thought, every sight, every feeling – gone. All they are capable of is existing and following orders. Mindless slaves." The censure in his voice was hard to miss. "When he tasked me with their creation, I refused, finally seeing Darragh for the monster that he was. A few days later I made my escape."

"But how? And if Darragh only wanted you so that you could give him someone who could use the Iris, why didn't he just make you have kids right away? And if he had the Iris back then why do we have it now?"

He smiled at my curiosity, shaking his head. "Those are all stories for another time. For now, suffice it to say I got away, but still had no knowledge of any of the prophecies regarding myself."

"When did you find out?"

He stiffened slightly at my question, and I got an uncomfortable feeling in the pit of my stomach.

"Not until it was too late," he said, with an echo of hopelessness in his voice. "I was on business in London when..." He hesitated, his jaw tight. "On second thought, there isn't time today for me to tell you how I met your mother, but I can tell you that after that moment – the moment she shook my hand – my life ceased to be my own." After a long pause, during which I focused my eyes on the leg of his desk, he continued. "I resigned my position as headmaster of St Brigid's, and told the Order – which was only just beginning at the time that I was leaving. I was ready to be done with it all and have a real life. Ready to be happy." He leaned back against the frame of the window, arms crossed, with a far off look in his eyes. "Judith and I left for the States, and were married. Moved into the house in Maine. Had you." He glanced over to me, then away again. "They were the happiest years of my life," he added softly. "We hadn't planned on having Ryland. He was what you might call a happy accident. And on that subject," he looked up at me, "you have been wonderful to him. Taking care and looking after him the way you have. He was very lucky to have had you growing up, as I'm sure he knows."

"You told me to," I whispered without looking up. The words were out before I could stop them. When he didn't respond, I glanced up to find him looking at me with something between surprise and pain.

"I didn't think you would remember that," he breathed.

But I did remember. I remembered it like it was yesterday, though I'd not let myself think about it in almost a decade.

As the memory of that final meeting reared in my mind, I stamped it back down, in no condition to go there, nor did I want him bringing it up. My emotional state was on shaky enough ground as it was, and honestly, he didn't seem to be faring much better.

Luckily, he cleared his throat and moved on. "A week after Ryland was born I received a letter in the mail. It had in it the prophecy regarding both me and my son, and a note that said Darragh was on his way to take us all. I panicked. I'd seen firsthand the sort of things Darragh did to those he captured. I knew Ryland would be used only to power the Iris, and you and your mother would be either droned or killed. There was no time to call for help, no time to do anything but run. But I didn't want that for you. I wanted you to live your lives, not to have to spend them constantly in fear. There was only one thing I could think of to do – hide you all away where no one could find you. Not even me.

That evening I did something I swore I would never do. I compelled your mother. I made her believe we'd planned to move. Put false memories in her mind about house-hunting and job-searching. Then I told her that I would have to stay behind to finish my semester at the university, but that…" He tapered off, then tried again. "But that I would follow." After another pause, he added quietly, "I want you to know that you were right the other day. What I did was selfish. I've always known that."

I looked up at him, only to see so much guilt etched on his face that I had to look back down.

"At the time I'd considered the alternative scenarios I could have left her with. I'd even considered making her believe I'd died. But, I couldn't. I... wanted her to remember me. I pretended the reason was Ryland. I knew one day I would have to bring Ryland here and that it would be easier to get Judith to agree if she knew who I was. But I've also always known that to only be an excuse. What I did, I did for me. I wanted to keep the hope that one day, when all this is over, that I could..."

He dwindled off again, and I wasn't sure how much more of this I could take. Just as I was going to excuse myself, offering to finish this another time, he continued. "The only person I entrusted any of this to was Taron, who I'd believed had long split with Darragh, as I had. I told him about the letter and that I would be returning to St Brigid's. I had him make all the arrangements for your move – the travel, the house, even getting the position at the hospital for your mother – so I wouldn't know where you were. I assumed that it was safer that way, not realizing it was all done in vain, as thanks to Taron, Darragh knew where you were all along." There was so much bitterness in his tone that I started to wonder if Taron was in fact still alive. "He also made all the arrangements for your new name."

"New name?"

"Changing your name to Ingle, I mean. I had Taron send new identification for you all, so there wouldn't be any trouble."

"No, that can't be right. My name has always been Ingle, even before all of that."

He shook his head. "You were born Rebecca Clavish. When I spoke to you in my office before you left," he paused for a moment before continuing, "when I told you to take care of Ryland, the last thing I did was change your name."

"You compelled me too?" I whispered, not doing much to mask the fact that I was upset by the idea.

"I had to."

"I don't remember that."

"You wouldn't," he said with a humorless smile.

I remembered Jocelyn calling me into his office the evening before we were set to move. He sat me up on his desk and told me that I was going to have to take care of Mommy and baby Ryland while he was away. I told him that I was a big girl now and promised that I would take care of everything. Yet, as the images of that meeting ran through my mind, they seemed oddly different. While I'd never let myself think about that night as a whole, I'd always remembered Jocelyn looking tired and distant. As a girl, I had assumed it was because he had spent all night packing with Mom and needed sleep. When I was older, after I knew he had left us, I assumed that he was simply tired of us. Tired of the family he didn't want, and anxious to be on his way.

But I'd been wrong. I could see through my hate and pride to the horrible clarity underneath, where tired distance can, in different lighting, look a lot like sadness.

My throat closed up on me and I doubted it was possible to feel more terrible than I did at that moment. Could it be true? Did I want it to be true?

Jocelyn was silent for a moment, letting me collect my thoughts, or possibly collecting his own, before he said, "You should get back to the infirmary, you still need your rest. It was probably wrong of me to put all this on you when you are still so weak, but you deserved to know. Will you be able to make it back?" He walked over to my chair and extended a hand, helping me up.

"Alex is waiting to walk with me."

He nodded then slowly walked back to the window. I turned to leave, but his voice stopped me.

"I know you think that I mistreated your mother terribly, and there is no one on this earth that agrees with you more than I do," he said quietly, with his back to me, once again staring out the window. "But I want you to know that no matter how long I live my last thought on this earth will be of her."

He didn't turn to look at me, and he said nothing else. I tried again to leave, worried that the tears I could feel burning my eyes were going to brim over before I was able to make it out the door. Yet I couldn't seem to make myself go. Something in me wouldn't let me leave – not like that. I could see how hard it was for him to tell me everything he had, and I wanted to let him know that – while I wasn't yet sure what to make of it – I appreciated it. I wasn't quite ready to ask for or offer forgiveness, but I had to somehow let him know that I understood.

I could have told myself that none of it was true, or that even if it was true it didn't matter. I could have said that it didn't change anything, or that I was past caring, or that I had gotten over everything, or any of the other claims I'd spent years making. But I couldn't.

As I stood there, looking at the father that I knew both so well and not at all, the man whom I'd both loved and hated, I realized that for the first time in almost ten years I didn't want to be the tough one, or the strong one, or the one who was always in control.

I realized that, just for this moment, I didn't want to pretend.

He didn't hear me approach. I didn't give him any kind of warning or apology; I simply leaned over… and hugged him.

At first he tensed – probably out of shock – but then slowly relaxed, bringing his arms up around me. His hug seemed wary at first, but soon became strong. Really strong. He was suddenly holding me so tight I could barely breathe.

"*Mo ghile beag*," he whispered raggedly into my hair.

After a few moments we released each other. I turned and walked toward the door without so much as a glance backward. I stepped out of the office and began to make my way down the hall in a fog, staring at the floor.

Mo ghile beag.

I walked right past Alex without even seeing him. He placed a hand on my arm and said something, though I didn't hear what it was. The next thing I knew, Alex had me in his arms, and I was sobbing into his shirt.

28

"The plural of cactus is 'cacti' not 'cactuses', you illiterate oaf!" Mr Reid snapped, kinetically lifting the u, s, e, and s off of the Scrabble board and hurling them into Mr Anderson's chest.

"No one says cacti! Never in my whole life have I heard anyone say cacti!"

"Of course not, you grew up in Scotland! You wouldn't know a cactus if you were sitting on one!"

"I do believe 'cacti' is correct," Cormac cut in timidly, holding his own tray of letters down against the table as though he thought they also might soon become projectiles.

As Mr Reid and Mr Anderson continued to argue, and Cormac tried in vain to keep the peace, I brought my legs up onto the ottoman I was seated on with an amused smile. I'd opted out of the evening's Scrabble tournament, but was more than content to sit with Chloe and watch the grammatical high jinks unfold.

It was the morning of my first official day out of the infirmary, and I was feeling much better. My strength had returned almost entirely, finally allowing me to climb a flight of stairs without becoming winded, and take a shower without having to sit down and rest on the edge of the tub halfway through.

However, despite the fact that my physical being was almost one hundred percent, my emotional state – while much improved – was still far from perfect. It had been two days since my meeting with Jocelyn, followed by, bar none, the worst night of my life. After Alex had gotten me back to the infirmary, I'd basically spent the night blubbering, stammering, and sobbing, until finally passing out sometime in the wee hours, only to wake up the next morning dehydrated and puffy. Since then I'd been better, though I still wasn't ready to actually see Jocelyn in person, which was why I was currently sitting in the lounge listening to this week's Scrabble war instead of with Alex and Min in Jocelyn's office hearing how the remainder of Taron's reading had gone. I knew I wouldn't be able to avoid him forever, but seeing him meant thinking about everything he'd told me, and right now that was all still too confusing. At some point I'd think about it and decide what I wanted to do with the information he'd given me, and, honestly, it would probably be someday soon.

Just not today.

But… soon.

"It's twelve points, not nine!" Mr Anderson yelled, trying to snatch the score sheet and pencil away from Mr Reid.

"I see, so you can count, you just can't spell?" snipped Mr Reid, holding the sheet behind him like a game of keep-away.

"For heaven's sake!" Chloe chimed in, looking up from her history assignment. "Is it so hard to behave like men and not prattling boys?"

"Yes, exactly," Reid agreed, waving at Anderson. "Stop acting like a child!"

"I'm a child?" Anderson retorted. "Perhaps you should take it like a man!"

"Bloody hell..." Chloe huffed, shoving away from the table and stomping across the lounge to the bookshelf.

"You'll get nine points, or you'll get none!" Reid said, pointing the tiny game pencil in Anderson's face.

"Perhaps we could make it ten and a half?" Cormac suggested meekly. "You know, split the difference?"

"No!" both Anderson and Reid yelled simultaneously, glaring at poor Cormac like he was out of his mind.

I felt the comforting pull in my chest before I heard his voice say, "You'll have to forgive them, Cormac. They're a couple of idiots when it comes to these things."

"Alex," said Mr Anderson, ignoring the jibes, "'Cacti' or 'cactuses'?"

He stepped up behind me and placed his hands on my shoulders, grazing his thumbs up and down the back of my neck. "I believe it–"

"Cacti," Chloe announced loudly, holding a large volume from one of the bookshelves. "C-A-C-T-I."

"Ha!" Mr Reid barked. "There, you damn fool, I told you so! And that's nine points," he said, making a bit of a show writing the number down on the sheet. "Thank you, lass," he said to Chloe.

"Pleasure," she said, not hiding her sarcasm as she closed the book with a slap and stuffed it back on the shelf.

"That's weird," Alex said as Chloe returned to her table, "I was sure both were correct."

"*Sst!*" Chloe hissed, shushing him quickly while glancing over to the game table to make sure no one else heard. "And have them fighting all day?" she whispered, giving Alex and I a sneaky smirk before returning to her work.

I felt Alex chuckle behind me. "You up for a walk?" he asked quietly, squeezing my shoulders.

I nodded still smiling, and we left the lounge hand in hand. "Where are we going?" I asked as we paused at the stairs.

"I wanted to go down to the lake, but it's a little cold for that, so balcony?"

"Great."

He waited until we got up to the second floor to ask, "How are you doing?"

"All right," I said, knowing he was referring to Jocelyn. "Better." I waited until the balcony door was closed behind us before continuing, "Still afraid to see him. Still have no idea what to do, or think, or how to feel. I have spent years hating him, and part of me still does. But now there is this other part of me that doesn't, and the sick thing is, I don't want that. I *want* to hate him, even though I know that's horrible, and yet, at the same time I *don't* want to hate him..." I squeezed my eyes shut with a frustrated huff. "I don't know."

Before I had a chance to open my eyes, I felt a pair of arms holding me securely.

"You're not sick," Alex said quietly, lightly kissing my forehead, "and you're not horrible. What you're feeling – all of it – is natural, and no matter which side you come out on, what really counts is that you're trying." He took my chin between his thumb and forefinger, lifting my eyes to meet his. "One step at a time."

"Yeah, I guess," I said, letting out a long breath. "And step one is getting over being weirded out by the whole name change thing."

"What do you mean?"

"Think about it: he actually changed my name and I had no idea! How creepy is that? It would be like someone telling you that up until yesterday the sky had been purple, even though all you can ever remember it being is blue. I can barely even wrap my mind around it, not to mention that the whole idea is scary as hell! He could do anything he wanted! He could change history, and no one would even know!" I sat down on the window seat with a deep breath, trying to quell my paranoia. "I guess I just figured that if someone messed with my mind like that I would know. Or at least know that something wasn't right, but there is nothing."

"It's a dangerous ability to have," Alex said sitting next to me, "which is why it is so important that we stop Darragh before he is able to do any real damage."

"Speaking of Darragh, how did it go? Did Jocelyn get anything useful out of Taron?"

"No." Alex shook his head, clearly disappointed.

"Nothing else. Just that same name, Ciaran Shea."

Well that was a little let down. "What do we do now?"

"Jocelyn looked into it, and it appears Ciaran is one of the Originals, or that's what they call themselves, anyway. They are a group of Holders who live in Dublin," he hesitated with a slight eye roll, "but they are not like us."

"What do you mean?"

"Let's just say, they don't like to get their hands dirty."

"And Ciaran is one of them?"

"Looks that way. Jocelyn is arranging for some of us to go and meet with them, and see if we can find this Ciaran for ourselves."

"But if he and Taron were working together, wouldn't Darragh know about him too?"

"We're not sure what Darragh knows at this point, which is why we have to move fast."

We sat in silence for a minute while I looked for a new topic, not liking at all how uncomfortable the Darragh subject was making me.

"I'm not sure I'll know what to do in my own bed tonight," I said, hoping my diversion tactic wasn't as plain to him as it seemed to me.

"I know," he laughed. "What will you do without the creaky, rock-hard mattress, and the constant running of the broken toilet in the bathroom?"

"And the nurses constantly coming in to check on me, and then there was this guy who would not go away..."

I peeked over at him with a grin, to find him shooting

me a wry glance. "Sounds awful."

"Oh, it was!" I bit back a giggle. "I swear he was with me twenty-four seven, poor guy must have no life at all."

"Must have been hell. You had to spend all that time staring at him, was he at least good looking?"

"Ah," I shrugged, no longer able to contain my smile, "he's all right."

"Just all right?" he growled through his grin, grabbing me around the waist and dragging me with a shriek up onto his lap.

The next moment his mouth took hold of mine as both of his hands wound into my hair. My eyes fluttered as his lips worked their way down, nipping at my chin before blazing a tingling trail to my collarbone, then climbed back up the side of my neck, ending at his favorite spot just under my ear. The noises coming out of my mouth as my head lolled back were entirely involuntary and not exactly graceful, but given Alex's reactions to them, they were exactly what he wanted to hear. I slid my hands down his back then slowly up his sides, relishing the moan that rumbled in his chest. Just as my fingers reached the buttons on his shirt, he let out a long breath and rested his forehead on my shoulder.

"We should stop," he said with a hoarseness that made me shiver.

"No, I don't think we should."

He looked up at me with a grin. "We are in public, after all."

"Then let's go somewhere private," I whispered,

bending forward and kissing his neck as he'd done mine. As my lips teased the hollow of his throat, his chest begin to heave under me and suddenly his hands were grabbing at my back, fisting my shirt, pulling me closer.

"Becca," he breathed after a too-short moment, "we have to stop." Reluctantly, he took hold of my shoulders and lifted me away from him. "You're not ready for this yet, you need more time."

"Fine," I sighed, with a frustrated grin.

"Don't worry," he said, kissing me lightly on the nose. "Soon."

We sat, both of us trying to get our pulses back down to where they should be, while I was again trying to find a topic of conversation. Wonderful as kissing Alex had been for – *ahem* – personal reasons, it had also kept my mind from the hard lump forming in my stomach that I was trying desperately to ignore. I felt the tension creep into my face, and hoped I could find a new distraction before Alex noti–

"Becca, what's wrong?"

Damn. "It's nothing," I said, standing. "Let's go back in."

"Becca," he said, reaching out and grabbing my hand before I could walk away. "Please tell me."

I looked down at the soft concern on his face, and felt the truth spill out of me before I could stop it. "I… I'm scared, Alex," I admitted, looking away. "Darragh… he knows about me, I know he does. Cail would have told him by now. This is getting so serious, and I'm supposed to be the one who fixes everything. I'm not supposed to want to hide in my room." I stopped, still looking down at the floor, both relieved to get the words out and ashamed at what they were. "What if I can't make everything better?"

"Come here," he said, pulling me back down onto his lap. He held the side of my face, and looked hard into my eyes. "Listen to me. It's OK to be scared, it would be foolish not to be. But I want you to understand that it is not up to you to make things better. It's up to all of us. You are never going to be alone, do you hear me? I will always – *always* – be there, right next to you. Even if I am just all right looking," he chided, trying to get me to smile.

I tried to grin, but I don't think it worked. "This is going to get really dangerous, isn't it?" I asked, already knowing the answer was yes.

I looked at Alex expecting just for a moment that he would tell me no, and not to worry, and that everything would be fine, and anything else that he thought might comfort or reassure me. But of course he didn't. He didn't, because Alex would never lie to me. He simply nodded and said, "Probably."

"Are you scared?"

"Yes. I'm scared for what may come, scared for what could happen if we fail, but more than anything, I'm terrified for you. You have no idea what it does to me to know that Darragh is after you. To not know what he's planning, or how you're going to be involved."

"So what do we do?"

"We trust," he said, brushing his fingers lovingly

through my hair. "I trust in you, you in me, and we in us. We trust the Order to have our backs and we trust that, together, we will all find a way to win. It will be hard, but the way I see it, as long as we have each other then we have everything we need to make it through."

As I looked into his stormy-gray eyes, a calming sensation rippled through me like a gentle gust of wind over a silk flag. He was right, and in that moment, deep down, I believed that everything would be OK. I may not have known what was coming, but I knew that Alex was my rock, and as long as I had him next to me I'd be OK. Maybe this was why we were bonded. Maybe some fate somewhere had destined us for each other because she knew that individually we weren't strong enough for what lay ahead of us, but together we could face anything.

"I love you," I sighed, turning my head into his hand.

"I love you too," he said, kissing my forehead.

"I wish I could be more like you."

"Like me?" he laughed.

"Hmm," I agreed, leaning over onto him and resting my head on his shoulder. "I've wanted to say that for a while now, actually. You're amazing."

"Now I *know* you're still under the weather," he chuckled, feeling my forehead. "Shall we go in?" he asked.

I knew he was avoiding my statement, but let it go. It was OK if he didn't yet see how wonderful he was, because one day he would. I would make sure of it.

Acknowledgements

If I may paraphrase Confucius, "Show me who your friends are, and I'll show you the book you'll write."

OK, that may not be *entirely* accurate, but I'm pretty sure that most authors would agree when I say that the people around us are just as responsible for our books as we are. Our friends and family give us ideas and inspiration, they tell us when we've done well and when we've totally screwed up, and they give us the kick in the pants we need when our steam has all but run out. Without the support I've gotten from all the people I am lucky enough to have in my life, I know that this book would never have found its way off of my laptop. So to everyone who has lifted, encouraged, nudged, poked, kicked, shoved, and just generally put up with me; this one's for you.

From the moment I sent my amazing agent, Carly Watters, the email telling her that I had a new book in the works, not only did she refrain from panicking at the fact that I had completely changed genres on her, but she immediately got behind *The Holders* and couldn't have been more supportive. I can't express how fortunate I feel to have her in my corner along with the rest of the PS Literary team who are nothing if not tireless advocates for each and every one of their authors.

There isn't much I can say that would do justice to the gratitude I feel for Strange Chemistry and my brilliant editor, Amanda Rutter. They believed in my work enough to take a chance on me, and their support and enthusiasm has been more than I could ever have hoped for. To be counted as a Strange Chemistry author – as one of Amanda's authors – is truly an honor.

Don't tell anyone, but I can't spell. I'm not all that great at typing either, as my fingers often have a mind of their own – a problem that auto-correct tends to only make worse. I bring this to your attention so that you can better understand what incredible, patient, and all round wonderful people my Beta Readers are. These are the people who generously give countless hours of their time to read though all the wonky, typo-ridden, early drafts of my work so that I can make it better. Mary Smith and Cathy Pleskovich: my proofreaders, Elizabeth Shaw: my resident go-to, Samantha Smith: my detail-oriented YA expert, Mary Arnold: a surprise fan and always my cheerleader (also my grandma), Patti, Beth F., Jocelyn, Beth L., Ondrew, Julie: my Chocolate Books support system, and Natori Walters: the first person to read my work who was actually a young adult.

A huge thank you to fellow author, Carol Oats, who was kind enough to call upon her Irish heritage to help me make some sense out of the beautiful but incredibly complicated pronunciations of Irish Gaelic. Big hugs are also due to one of my best virtual friends and queen of my online support system, Angela Cook, whose passion, drive, and positive attitude never fail to impress me.

Finally, to my amazing husband, without whom this book would still have huge plot holes, nameless characters, and a missing chapter. Your endless support is the only reason I am able to do this at all, and not a day goes by that I am not amazed by everything you have done to help my dreams come true. You've read, plotted, sacrificed, listened, re-read, listened some more, changed diapers, fed kids, and eaten cereal for dinner more nights than any grown man should ever have to. Anything I need, you find a way to get it for me, and anywhere I need to be, somehow you always get me there. Thank you for believing in me and making me the luckiest woman in the world.

STRANGE CHEMISTRY

"It's like the best kind of video game: full of fun, mind-bendy ideas with high stakes, relentless action, and shocking twists!" – *E C Myers, author of* Fair Coin

EXPERIMENTING WITH YOUR IMAGINATION